A FALCON'S TALE

WASHINGTON FISH & WILDLIFE DETECTIVE TODD A. VANDIVERT (RETIRED)

Printed by: **Create Space**
Distributed by: **www.amazon.com**

Copyright © May 2020, Todd A. Vandivert. All rights reserved. This book is protected under the copyright laws of the United States of America. Any reproduction or unauthorized use of the material herein is prohibited without the expressed written permission of the author.

ISBN- 979-8-6316-99854

THIS BOOK IS FICTION. The names, characters, locations, and events are either the products of the author's imagination or used in a fictitious manner. Any resemblance to actual persons, living or dead, or actual events is purely coincidental.

Cover created by- Bruce Weild, www.b-creative.ca/design

DEDICATION

To the first responders and medical professionals around the world, who bravely and unselfishly risked their own health and safety to protect the rest of us. You are true heroes. Thank you!

"EARTH PROVIDES ENOUGH TO SATISFY EVERY MAN'S NEEDS, BUT NOT EVERY MAN'S GREED."
MAHATMA GANDHI

CHAPTER 1

Finally, alone, Joe and Lisa sat quietly in the backseat of the Cadillac Escalade, until they saw their two new-found friends walk into the high-level drug dealer's home through the open garage door. This was the first time they had been left alone, and they needed to quickly iron out a few details before their criminal "friends" returned.

This was the second straight day WDFW (Washington Fish and Wildlife) Officers Joe Ramirez and Lisa Bennington had been working this UC (undercover) assignment, and yet Joe still couldn't shake the feeling they had been discovered. Joe had a nagging feeling the two drug traffickers, he and Lisa had been working, either knew or suspected Joe and Lisa were cops. Joe wondered if they would be tortured, killed, or both. Either way, Joe had a strong feeling this deal was going to go very badly.

"I've got a horrible feeling about this," Joe announced quietly as he watched the two men walk back to the Caddy.

"Come on, follow me. He wants to meet you two," said Karl (the man who had driven them to this location), "and bring the cash."

"Just stay calm, we're almost done," Lisa whispered to Joe as they walked towards the dealer's home carrying a grocery bag full of cash. "We will be out of here in under five minutes."

Lisa and Joe followed Karl as he entered the house, through the garage. Once inside, Lisa immediately noticed three things: what looked like a full kilo of cocaine on the kitchen counter, a multitude of firearms including a short-barrel shotgun, and three very mean-looking men.

Karl made introductions, followed by instructing Lisa to show the cash to the smaller of the three men, a man who Karl had identified as the organization's leader.

"It's all there. Twenty-two thousand just like we agreed. Count it if you want," Lisa said as she waited to be handed the coke.

"Why thanks for giving me permission to count my money, but there's no need. Nobody ever shortchanges me," said the smaller man.

"Then do we have a deal?" asked Joe.

"Just let me check on one thing first, then we will conclude our business," the dealer answered. "Karl, would you go grab my cell phone?"

As Karl hustled out the door, Joe and Lisa couldn't help but think something was very wrong. Now, the drug trafficker had their cash, the coke, and all the guns (Lisa and Joe were unarmed).

Soon Karl came running back in with a newer iPhone in-hand, which he immediately handed off to the smaller man. Joe noticed both of the dealer's "friends" had moved to within an arm's reach of the firearms, a maneuver which made Joe even more nervous.

"As soon as we all listen to a short audio clip, we will finish up here," announced the drug dealer as he prepared his phone for the audio replay. "You see, I'm not very trusting of people I've never done business with, so I told Karl to use my cell phone to record your conversation when nobody else was around. He left this phone recording under the seat in the Escalade, while he left you two sitting alone in my driveway. Let's listen together, shall we?"

Even before the audio began playing, both Lisa and Joe knew they were dead. It was just a matter of how they would die, but it would be very soon. Upon being told of the recording, both undercover officers instantly remembered breaking out of their undercover roles, to discuss the details of the undercover operation, while sitting in the backseat of the Caddy.

No more than forty seconds into the audio recording, the lead drug trafficker walked over and picked up a loaded Smith and Wesson M&P .40 caliber semi-automatic pistol.

"Well officers, do you want to give each other a little goodbye hug before we conclude our business?" asked the dealer with a wide grin.

"No?" continued the dealer, "Then I'm afraid it's time to say goodbye."

With his two newly armed assistants standing one on each side, the dealer aimed directly at Joe's heart from nearly point-blank range. Even though she had known the shots were coming, Lisa still jumped as each of the two shots were fired into her partner. A split-second later, the dealer turned the pistol on Lisa and repeated the same two-shot sequence to her heart.

"King's X everyone. Great job kids, except you're both dead," said Spokane Police Department's Officer Clark Hyde, "or you would be if this had been for real."

As the five role players emptied their training firearms of the Simunition Securi Blank training rounds, Officer Hyde continued, "Without a doubt, you two did the best of any of the students, until this little screwup today. In class, we told all of you to always stay in character until you are totally done with the undercover contact, and now you know why. The good news is, I am certain neither of you will ever make that mistake again."

"I know I will never forget this. As soon as the role player came walking in with the cell phone, I knew we had screwed up. I'm just glad we learned this lesson in a mock-scene rather than in a real undercover," said Lisa.

"Alright, can I get you two to give our role players a hand packing this stuff over to the storage room in the gym, then we will all meet up in the classroom for the final debrief," said Officer Hyde.

"Will we still graduate?" Joe asked.

"Joe, if we failed every student who made a mistake in mock scenes, we wouldn't graduate anyone," answered the officer. "These two weeks have been about learning, and I know you learned more from this last exercise than during any of the lectures. So yes, you will graduate today with all the other students. Now relax."

Two by two, the undercover academy students returned to the classroom, where they all compared stories with their fellow students.

It was then, Joe and Lisa learned that indeed, they were in fine company when it came to making serious mistakes.

As the last pair of students had returned from their mock scene, Lt. Mark Benson with the King County Sheriff's Office instructed everyone to take a seat and quiet down, "Before we go any further, I want you to join me in thanking our role players, each of whom came here on their days off just to help put on these mock scenes."

After the applause had died down, Lt. Benson continued, "As you recently learned, the mock scenes are the most valuable tool we use to get each of you prepared to work real-world undercover assignments. We can tell you over and over to answer slowly and carefully, think before you react, and always stay in character, but nothing drives the point home like that sinking feeling you get when you realize you just blew it. We all make mistakes, and it's a whole lot better to make them here than out there."

Officer Hyde then stepped up and said, "For one last time, we want to talk about always staying in character."

Lisa and Joe both felt their faces flush as they realized they were about to be called out in front of the other students.

Hyde continued, "At the conclusion of the mock scenes, all of the instructors and role players got together to compare notes. You will all be relieved to learn that 100% of the undercover teams fell for the hidden recorder trick. Not one of you stayed in character when you were left alone in the suspect's vehicle. In the past undercover academies, we found teaching you to always stay in character was the toughest challenge, but once we began using the hidden recorder trick, we are confident none of our students will ever make that mistake again."

The students, who all thought they had been the only ones to screwup and get caught out of character, breathed a collective sigh of relief.

Lt. Benson then addressed the students, "On the back table, you will find a sign-up sheet. If you are interested and willing to assist other agencies when they have a need for an undercover operative, please add your name and contact info to the list. We have put together a collective of undercover officers who are willing to work in other areas or even other states when an agency needs a fresh face who won't be recognized. We would greatly appreciate it if you would step up and volunteer. Speaking of volunteering, all of you who live within a four-hour drive of this location, just volunteered to help out in the mock scenes at next year's academy."

Benson continued, "Before we break for the afternoon, I have a couple of announcements. First, your certificates are in alphabetical order on the table by the door, next to the signup sheet. Next, we will start serving food at the barbeque starting around six-thirty. And most importantly, the keg will be tapped at five. See you all at the barbeque. Class dismissed!"

Six months earlier, Captain Cody Jacobsen, who headed up the WDFW SIU (Special Investigative Unit) had approached Lisa and Joe and had asked if they were ready to work a little undercover work. Both officers said they would gladly work undercover assignments if requested. After gaining approval from the officer's chain of command, Captain Jacobsen signed Joe and Lisa up for the undercover academy.

The undercover academy was an offshoot of the CJTC (Criminal Justice Training Center, just south of Seattle) and was conducted by current and former undercover operatives from a multitude of state, county, and city agencies (the feds have their separate undercover training). Lisa and Joe were the only attendees from WDFW, and to the surprise of some, excelled in all aspects of the training.

Captain Jacobsen recognized the value of Lisa, as not only a female but as a squared away officer who already had extensive experience in large-scale complex cases. Joe, being Hispanic, would certainly provide SIU with opportunities to work undercover operations in the Hispanic community. The fact that both officers spoke fluent Spanish was the icing on the cake.

Lisa, who at the time was thirty-four years old (although she could pass for mid-20's), was only 5'04" and 145 lbs. and was in top physical condition. Joe, who was only twenty-seven years old, was 5'10" and around 175 lbs. and was also in great physical condition.

Little did the two officers know, but their first undercover case was already awaiting them. They only needed to acquire their certification of completion from the undercover academy.

After picking up their certificates of completion, Joe and Lisa headed back to their motel, so they could drop off their materials, and change clothes for the barbeque.

Upon returning, and as Lisa and Joe rounded the corner to the outdoor kitchen area, they realized the instructors had already tapped the keg and were doing their best to make sure there wouldn't be any beer left-over when it was turned back in. As Lisa approached the keg, and the surrounding crowd, she noticed Captain Jacobsen, who was off to the side having a conversation with Lt. Benson.

"Good afternoon captain. What brings you here?" Lisa asked.

"Free beer, free ribs, and good friends," the captain replied, "couldn't pass up an offer like that."

"So, Lisa, what did you think of the training?" asked Lt. Benson.

"I thought it was outstanding, and I'm not just saying that for your benefit, I mean it. This was far better than I had even hoped," Lisa went on. "When I first heard about this class, I had my doubts it would prepare someone, with no undercover experience, for the real world, but I feel confident I could work UC right now."

Lisa noticed Lt. Benson had a wide grin on his face as he looked over at Captain Jacobsen.

"Well, I'm certainly glad you feel you are ready to go out there and work a real-world UC case because we already have one lined up for you and Joe. Before you leave the party tonight, I would like to have a word with both you and Joe at the same time, so don't head out without finding me first," said the WDFW captain. "We need to talk."

CHAPTER 2

Seated in his first-class seat on the Emirates Airlines flight, Mohammed Abdul Almaktoum did his best to look casual, as if this was routine and monotonous for him. Sitting in first-class was exciting enough for Mohammed, but to do so with a beautiful adult gyrfalcon on his arm was a dream come true.

The flight, from King Khalid International Airport in Riyadh, Saudi Arabia to Dubai International Airport in the United Arab Emirates would take only two hours, so Mohammed would likely allow the falcon to remain perched on the protective sleeve over his arm for the entire flight.

The bird Mohammed was transporting had recently been purchased by his employer from a Saudi raptor dealer for 2,200,000.00 dirhams (the currency of the UAE) or just over $600,000.00 in U.S. dollars.

In 2002, the government of the UAE (United Arab Emirates) began requiring "falcon passports" for all falcons entering the country. The passport ID number must correspond to the leg band all falcons are required to wear. Several Middle Eastern airlines allow falcons (or other birds of prey) to ride in the cabin, in either first or business class, but only with the proper documentation. Getting this particular bird on the plane and into the UAE proved to be a cakewalk, because of who his employer was. Upon arrival to the UAE, customs simply waved Mohammed and the falcon right through with nothing more than a cursory glance at his documentation.

Mohammed was born and raised in Pakistan, where he had remained until about five years prior, when his current employer Rashid Shaheen had hired Mohammed and twenty-nine others from his village, to work on the construction of Shaheen's palatial estate. The construction, landscaping, and decorating took thirty-one months from start to finish, during which time Shaheen had come to appreciate Mohammed's work ethic, intelligence, and values more than any other of the other employees. At the conclusion of the construction project, Mohammed was offered a permanent position as Shaheen's personal assistant and head of the household staff.

Despite the UAE government's official stance on the subject, the kafala system was still the law of the land. Under the kafala system, migrant workers are only allowed into the county if they first have an in-country sponsor (normally an employer). Once in the UAE, many employers collect the worker's passports, thus preventing them from leaving. Just as in many forced labor situations, workers are required to work long hours for very little pay. Additionally, many employers charge their workers for room and meals, thus leaving a small pittance of take-home wages. Abuses are widespread, with little chance of abusers being held accountable for their violations of basic human rights. Mohammed was one such worker until his employer had appointed him to the higher level position he now held. Because of Mohammed's new position, he was allowed to live in the main house right along with Shaheen's family and was able to send his parents a sizeable amount of money each month.

Rashid Shaheen, the son of Sheikh Khalid Al Shaheen, was UAE's minister of energy and oil, and at forty-three years of age, was already one of the top 100 richest men in the world and climbing.

Mohammed was happy to have the job he did and would do anything necessary to keep it. While he knew that at the whim of his employer he could be sent back to Pakistan, or worse, he pushed those thoughts out of his head. After all, for the entire five years of working for Shaheen, Mohammed had only seen Shaheen lose his temper once. Two years after the workers from his village had arrived, one of the workers, Ahmed Al Khmeri, was seen taking cell phone photos of one of Shaheen's wives without her knowledge. Upon hearing of this, Shaheen seized and searched Khmeri's phone finding several photos of women, including photos of two of Shaheen's wives. Despite the explanation from Khmeri's friends, that Khmeri was developmentally disabled, Shaheen personally decapitated Khmeri in front of the other workers, then instructed them to "bury him under the concrete".

Mohammed knew he was going to be picked up at the airport this day, but had assumed the vehicle would be driven by one of Shaheen's drivers/body-guards, but instead, he noticed the Mercedes GLS was driven by Shaheen himself.

"I trust the trip was comfortable and uneventful?" Shaheen asked.

"The dealer had the bird ready to go, and the flight was wonderful. I was treated like royalty the whole way. I greatly appreciate your generosity and trust in allowing me to bring this magnificent animal to you today while traveling in such luxury," said Mohammed.

"Think nothing of it. Had my Bombardier Global not needed maintenance, you would have experienced real luxury. Next time," answered Shaheen. "Now let's get this bird into his mews (a specially designed house for raptors)."

As Mohammed and Shaheen were leaving the air-conditioned mews building, Shaheen stopped, turned, and admired his collection of seven raptors.

"My beautiful birds give me strength," Shaheen announced, "and my collection has just begun."

Mohammed smiled as he knew this meant many more luxury flights ahead for him.

Falconry is simply defined as the hunting of wild animals, in their natural habitat, by way of well-trained birds of prey. Falconers spend countless hours training their birds to patrol the skies looking for prey (primarily game birds, and rabbits).

Falconry is believed to have first been practiced in the Al Rafidein Region (now called Iraq) in 3500 BC, and over time became an integral part of Middle Eastern culture, popular with kings, sheikhs, and men of wealth and power. Still to this day, owning birds of prey is a sign of power and strength in many Middle Eastern cultures.

In Muslim culture, falconry has one huge benefit over other hunting methods, in that falcons normally bring their captured quarry back to the handler alive. Muslims are only allowed to eat meat that has been killed according to Sharia law, which means the animal must be killed by an adult Muslim by cutting the throat with the single continuous motion of a sharp knife.

In Saudi Arabia, the falconry season is timed to coincide with the annual migration of falcons. The most valuable of birds are two to three-year-old wild falcons, as their hunting skills are already well-honed.

The value of these birds varies wildly and depends on a variety of conditions: species, age, physical condition, size and weight, and gender (female falcons are larger and stronger than their male counterparts) are all factors taken into consideration.

The vast majority of birds of prey owned by Middle Eastern falconers come from North America and can be worth up to a million U.S. dollars. Birds of prey offered for sale are eyas (raptors taken from the nest before fledgling), passage (raptors taken from the wild in the fall of its first year), haggards (wild raptors over one year of age), or raised from eggs (taken from a nest in the wild or from breeders). While many species of raptors will make fine hunters, most falconers prefer falcons over all others primarily because of its speed and sleek body shape. In fact, peregrine falcons are the fastest animal on earth, reaching speeds over 200 mph in a dive.

Middle Eastern falconers will often have collections of twenty or more birds of prey.

CHAPTER 3

At about 11 PM, Captain Cody Jacobsen waved Lisa and Joe over and pointed to an empty table in the corner of the cafeteria.

The captain started with, "I'm about ready to call it a night, but I wanted to brief you guys on what we have in store for you."

"Lay it on us Cody-man, let's hear your big plan," Joe said in a drunken slur.

Looking directly at Lisa with disgust, the captain asked, "Are you drunk too?"

"No, sir. I'm the designated driver," Lisa answered.

"Good, then drive his ass back to the motel," Captain Jacobsen instructed as he stood to leave.

"What about our briefing?" Lisa inquired.

"I'm heading out at 7 AM tomorrow, so if your partner sobers up by 6 AM, give me a call and we will discuss it over breakfast," he answered as he rose to leave. "Otherwise, forget it."

As the captain walked towards the parking lot, Lisa whispered, "Jesus Christ Joe, you couldn't stay sober on the one night we were meeting with Captain Jacobsen? What the hell man?"

"Ah screw him. I'm a big boy. I don't need someone telling me what to do all the time." Joe muttered.

CHAPTER 4

Frank's Firearms, in Pasco, WA, was nothing more than a one-man business run out of Frank Pierce's basement with nothing more than a filing cabinet, a laptop computer, a printer, and three large gun safes.

Despite the fact Frank's business far outsold all the other local gun shops, rarely had anybody seen the inside of Frank's "shop". Frank possesses an FFL (Federal Firearms License) which allows him to purchase and sell firearms from his home "shop". Federal law does not limit the number of firearms a dealer can sell to any one individual, however, licensed dealers must report to federal authorities if they sell more than one handgun to the same person within five consecutive business days. While Frank sells pistols, the bread and butter of his business is the AR-15 rifle. As a matter of fact, approximately 75% of his firearms sales are AR-15s, with the second most popular firearm being the .50 caliber sniper rifle.

While every American is familiar with the AR-15, very few know much about the .50 BMG rifles. The .50 BMG Frank sells the most of is the Barrett M107A1 long-range sniper rifle. The Barrett M107A1 fires a .50" 660-grain bullet accurately to well over 1,500 meters, with documented one-shot combat kills from over a mile away. The .50 BMG (Browning Machine Gun) round will penetrate concrete or cement-block walls, and virtually obliterates anything it strikes.

Frank sells AR-15s for anywhere from $800 to $2,500 depending on the manufacturer and accessories, with the average being in the neighborhood of $1,800. On the other hand, the Barrett retails for

$12,000 (Frank pays just under $10,000 each), but Frank sells them to his special customers for $15,000 because those sales put him at risk of arrest.

By federal law, dealers have no limitations on the number of rifles they can sell to one person in a single day. Four years back, Frank left California and moved to Washington to escape some very restrictive California gun laws, one being that firearms dealers in Arizona, California, New Mexico, and Texas are required to notify ATF if they make multiple sales of certain rifles during the same day.

Frank liked to keep sales to five of any one rifle per person, to avoid unwanted attention, thus he would sell five AR-15s to a single person in one day, with no additional paperwork required, nor any questions asked.

On this particular day, Frank was cross-checking the serial numbers on the firearms transfer forms, against the rifles he had laid out on a plastic folding table. Four Barrett M107A1 rifles, and six Ruger AR-556 rifles (Ruger AR rifles use 5.56 NATO ammunition, but can also fire the standard AR-15 .223 ammo). Included in the sale were fifty 30-round AR-15 magazines, and 10 5- round Barrett .50 BMG magazines, all for a grand total of $70,000 including tax. Frank had two receipts made out, splitting the guns between the two customers. Frank had never met either of the customers who he would transfer the firearms to, as these guns (and many others) were ordered and paid for by Frank's single largest customer- Antonio. Antonio was a man Frank had dealt with for years, but whose name did not appear on any firearms documentation.

Straw purchases are simply defined as those purchases made by one person on behalf of another. When it comes to firearms, straw purchases are very much illegal, and something ATF watches for. Because of the extra attention sales of multiple assault rifles will attract, Frank asked Antonio to try his best to not reuse the same buyers very often.

After Frank had completed the paperwork, he loaded everything, including the 58" long Barrett rifles, in his Chevy Tahoe, and headed out to meet his "buyers". While dealing with Antonio was very profitable, it also meant Frank was potentially facing prison time if caught conducting these straw purchases. When Antonio first proposed the gun buying plan to Frank, he was opposed, but after he gave it some thought, he realized as long as Frank was paid for the firearms up front the only real risk he had was the slight chance of getting arrested. Frank felt that since Antonio seemed to be a very careful man, their operation was fairly safe.

At exactly 10:47 AM, Frank pulled into the gravel truck parking lot next to the Burger King across from the King City Truck Stop and Restaurant. The gravel parking area had two idling semis, but no dark blue Toyota Tundra as the "customers" said they would be in. Five minutes later two men drove in and pulled alongside Frank's truck. It took only 4 minutes for Frank to finish completing the transfer of firearms forms and to get the men's signatures. Once the forms were completed, Frank handed the rifles to the men, one by one, which they loaded in the back seat of their truck. At 11:12, Frank was on his way home.

A $23,000 profit in one day. Not too bad, Frank thought on his way home.

CHAPTER 5

Freddie Shereford, his brother Wade, and another Yakama tribal member found themselves stuck in the snow again. This time the men had been up Wildcat Road north of the tiny community of Rimrock, WA in Yakima County. After loading up both of the cow elk they had killed, the three Indians had attempted to turn their 4-wheel drive Ford F-150 around in the narrow logging road and had sunk into the deep snow in the road's borrow ditch.

The Yakama tribal hunting regulations specified no taking of cow elk after January 1st, and this date was January 23rd. Despite the fact their elk were not legally taken, even by tribal regulations, the three men were unconcerned about being caught in the middle of the road with elk legs sticking out of the bed of their pickup. From experience, they knew WDFW officers were far more likely to catch them than the tribal game wardens. Because WDFW officers were unable to enforce most of the state's hunting laws on tribal members, the Sherefords weren't the least bit concerned with them. The brothers had both previously been caught poaching by WDFW officers, who simply turned the information over to the tribal police. After that, neither brother had ever heard a word from the tribal police, or anyone else, leading them to believe that when it came to hunting they could do whatever they wanted.

The Shereford brothers were prolific big game hunters, generally killing well over a dozen elk per year between the two of them. Since the Sherefords lived together, with nobody else, they could only consume one or two elk a year. The brothers sold the remainder of the elk to be able to afford the black tar heroin, and beer they both craved. So far, on this particular year, the Sherefords had already killed fourteen elk and were well on their way to beating their own record of seventeen elk in one season.

CHAPTER 6

"I first want to say, I'm very sorry about last night. I guess I just had the need to exceed, but I know my timing was bad. Again, I'm sorry captain," Joe said as soon as they sat down at the table with Captain Jacobsen.

The Denny's was fairly quiet, but for additional privacy, the captain had picked a booth in the back corner of the restaurant, with no other patrons within earshot.

"Joe, we all like to let loose once in a while, and I've certainly had a few too many multiple times in my life, but work must always come first. Working undercover you will be allowed to consume alcohol on duty, if necessary to maintain your cover, but getting drunk is totally out of the question," Captain Jacobsen added.

"Understood sir, and it will not be a problem," Joe replied.

Jacobsen said, "Good. Enough said. Now let's talk about an undercover assignment we would like you two to give a shot."

"Since both of you are fluent in Spanish, you are the perfect fit," Jacobsen said. "We received an anonymous tip, from a source we believe to be an employee, that the Buena Comida Mexican restaurants have been using poached deer and elk meat in their dishes for years, and that one of the managers, Antonio Vargas was a drug dealer. We have tried to get inside, but they seem to only deal with other Hispanics," the Captain said as he slid a copy of the anonymous tip across the table to Joe.

"Buena Comida translates to good food," Lisa said. "I have never eaten at one, but I hear they are good. Guess they figured out how to stretch their money a bit more, without changing the flavor enough that people would notice it."

"Can't you just buy a few meals there, keep meat samples, and have its DNA tested to identify the species of animal in the meat?" Joe asked.

"Yes, we have already done so but we then faced a couple of problems," Captain Jacobsen continued. "First, the DNA of cooked meat is often so badly degraded that positive species identification is not possible. The second problem is even when we find elk meat in the food, we don't know how it got there. What employees are in on what, we don't know. We need to find out if this is an isolated problem, or if the restaurant's owner and managers are aware of what's going on too. We also need to identify the people who are poaching the animals and selling the meat to the restaurants. As you both know, the sale or purchase of deer or elk meat is a felony-level crime, so we want to make sure our case is as solid as possible going forward."

"So, what would you like us to do?" Joe asked.

"We would like you two to simply drive up to the back door of the Buena Comida, with a fresh deer in the back of your truck, and strike up a conversation, and see where it goes," Jacobsen said.

"Where do we get a deer to sell? Do we just go shoot one ourselves?" Lisa asked.

"We will put out a request to all officers to notify us when they get a fresh deer or elk, most likely from a seizure or depredation hunt. Then we will get it to you ASAP, but in this cold, we shouldn't have to rush," answered Jacobsen.

"How many Buena Comida restaurants are there?" Joe asked.

Jacobsen replied, "Two, both in Kennewick. Feel free to try either of them. It's up to you. They aren't a franchise, they are all owned by one man. The details on the owner are in the files we will provide to you."

"Sounds good to me," Lisa answered.

"Count me in too," Joe added.

"Alright, I will put out the request for deer and elk and will be in touch. Meanwhile, you two work on your background stories, practice with the covert cameras, and get your truck outfitted the way you want," said Jacobsen.

"We don't have any covert cameras or an undercover truck," Joe said.

"You do now," the captain said as he slid a keychain to Lisa. "Those keys fit the older silver Dodge pickup, parked at the WDFW Mill Creek office, in the back parking lot. The cameras are in a case on the backseat, along with two copies of a file with everything we know about the Buena Comida restaurants and the people involved. You two can swing in and pick it up on your way home. I hope you two rode over here together, so one of you can drive the UC truck home."

"We took my truck, so Joe can drive the UC truck home," Lisa explained.

Jacobsen continued, "I've cleared this with your chain-of-command, so you're good to go. You will still answer to Sergeant Howard and will work your normal duties until it's time for you to head out on a UC, then you're mine. SIU will provide your backup and will handle the evidence. I know questions will come up, and I always have my cell phone with me 24/7, so call anytime. Any questions now?"

"Not from me," Joe answered.

"Me either, right now, but I'm sure I will be calling. Thanks for the opportunity," Lisa added.

"Look, you two have great potential for undercover assignments, but, as you found out in mock scenes, it's not as easy as it looks. You have to be on your toes, and constantly aware of your surroundings, all while looking relaxed," Captain Jacobsen continued. "As you two know, SIU is full of old white males, which limits our UC opportunities. I am hoping with you two, we will be able to shut down some of the large-scale commercial poaching operations which have gone untouched. We will start with the Buena Comida restaurants, then continue on with bigger cases until the snow melts in your patrol areas and your sergeant wants you back."

"Sounds good to me," Lisa said.

Looking straight at Joe, Captain Jacobsen said, "There are two things to always keep in mind; first, none of our cases are worth getting hurt or killed, and second, remember while you are undercover everything you say and do, will come out in court, so think before you speak, and remember you may have to explain why you did what you did every step of the way."

Joe simply answered, "Understood."

With that, the captain paid the check for breakfast, got up, and headed out the door.

"Let's get over to Mill Creek and grab our new truck," Lisa said. "Hopefully I will get to see Sergeant Greene and some of the guys from my old detachment."

The new truck was parked exactly where the captain had said it would be. The pickup had a matching canopy and overall looked to be in pretty good shape, without looking too nice.

"Hey kid, I thought that was you," said Sgt. Tim Greene as he walked towards Lisa.

"Hey, Tim, this is my partner, Joe Ramirez," Lisa told the sergeant.

As the sergeant shook Joe's hand, he said, "I've heard a lot about you, and heard you had a pretty tough couple of years. I hope things are going well for you now."

"Thanks. I'm all good. Looking forward to trying a little UC work," Joe replied.

"Well, when your partner here had been in our detachment a couple of weeks, we all knew we had a good one, but then she up and left us for cowboy country," Sgt. Greene said.

"Is anyone else here?" Lisa asked.

"Nope, they are all out in the field catching bad guys, but they will be disappointed they missed you," Greene went on. "Next time give us a little heads up so we can all meet up and do lunch or something."

"I will. This was a surprise to us, as we didn't know we were going home with an extra truck," Lisa answered.

"Take care Lisa, and don't forget where you came from," Sgt. Greene said as he headed back into the office.

Before they got into the respective vehicles, Lisa asked Joe, "You wanna meet up tomorrow and work on our cover story, and come up with a plan to take on the Buena Comida?"

"Sure. When and where?" Joe answered.

"Why don't you just come down to our house tomorrow. Emily is finally on days now, so she will be out the door by 7 AM, so anytime after that," answered Lisa.

"I will be there at seven if you promise to have coffee ready," said Joe.

"Alright, I will see you in the morning. The way you drive, you will be going through Omak before I even make it over the mountains. Try driving carefully Joe," said Lisa.

CHAPTER 7

Dressed in a long white kanduras (an ankle-length garment similar to a robe), Mohammed Abdul Almaktoum carefully removed the falcon's leather hood before passing the bird to his boss- Rashid Shaheen. Today, Rashid was racing his fastest bird in the final round of the UAE Falconry President's Cup race.

In 2014 Sheikh Khalifa bin Zayed Al Nahyan (the king of Abu Dhabi) started a falcon racing competition named The President's Cup. The President's Cup is held every year at the end of January and offers a grand prize in the equivalent of $11 million US dollars. Numerous other prizes are given out including seventy new vehicles, and lesser cash awards, but the most important prize is a gold engraved trophy presented by the royal family.

Racing falcons is a relatively new contest, one created because of the lack of game birds available to hunt in the UAE. The racing course is a straight flat 400-meter stretch with laser triggers at the start and finish lines, to time the races to the hundredth of a second. The falconer stands at one end of the field, while at the other end is the falconer's assistant swinging a feathered dummy on the end of a rope to entice the bird into staying on course and going as fast as possible.

The President's Cup is an event as steeped in pomp and ceremony as the Kentucky Derby, with all of the elite Emiratis in attendance. There are lavish spectator tents set up all along the course, offering porcelain bowls of fruit and pots full of Arabian coffee.

Unlike the Kentucky Derby, the UAE Falconry President's Cup is a 12-day, 75-round event, with around 2,000 falcons flown by close to 300 falconers.

As the contestants prepared their birds for the final round of the competition, Rashid Shaheen turned to catch a glimpse at the current rankings on the large reader board.

Rashid Shaheen brought Mohammed over to strategize. Rashid currently held 56th place, but if his falcon were to complete the final round in 17.500 seconds or less, he would likely move up in the rankings. Rashid had been scheduled near the end of the final round, so at least he knew the times he wanted to beat.

For this final race, Rashid went back to the fastest falcon he owned, a dark gray gyrfalcon. Rashid stood at the ready until he was given the signal, at which time he released the falcon. Immediately, as soon as Mohammed started swinging the feathered lure 400 meters down-course, the gyrfalcon took off like a guided missile streaking towards the feather dummy. By the time the bird had reached the halfway mark, Rashid knew this would be the bird's fastest run ever. Rashid had never placed in the top twenty of the President's Cup, and despite the bird's lightning-fast run still won't, but he was looking forward to at least landing in the top fifty.

All was going well until, with approximately 100 meters to go, the falcon veered off-course to the right. Something had caught the bird's attention for a few seconds, but that was all it took. Rashid needed a time of 17.360 seconds or faster, to get in the top fifty, but it was not to be. Once the falcon got back on the course, he had added about five seconds to his run, coming in at 22.84 seconds thus placing Rashid in 83rd place.

Even though Rashid was both angry and dejected, he had to mingle with the other contestants, and congratulate the winners, all with a forced smile on his face. Before Rashid began socializing, he approached Mohammed as he was busy crating the birds for the long drive home.

As Rashid pointed to the dark gray gyrfalcon, which had raced in the last round, he told Mohammed, "This one doesn't come back with you. Remove his leg band, then I never want to see this bird again, am I clear?"

"Understood, it will be taken care of," Mohammed replied.

As Rashid worked his way through the crowd, congratulating the winners, and showing his respect to the royalty, he was approached by Sheikh Saeed Damadaran.

"My friend, may I be so bold as to offer a few words of advice?" asked Sheikh Saeed.

"Of course. As you observed today, I could use some help," Rashid responded.

"I have watched you and your man-servant train and handle your birds, and you are doing nothing wrong," Sheikh Saeed explained. "It is my belief you have gotten all of the speed, out of your birds, as they are capable of. I believe the problem is not with the training, care, and handling, but rather with the birds themselves."

Sheikh Saeed continued, "Rashid, how many birds to you have?"

"Until today, seven. Now six," answered Rashid.

"As you know, most men bring their top six or seven birds to this event, but those birds brought to this event are the top birds out of collections generally in the range of fifty birds. You need to have more variety to choose from. Just like with people, your birds will have good days and not so good days," Sheikh Saeed said. "I also noticed your birds are all gyrfalcons except one kestrel falcon, am I correct?"

"Yes, what of it?" answered Rashid.

"Wikipedia will answer that for you. Look at this, the top speed ever recorded for a gyrfalcon was 209 km/h. The top speed for a peregrine was 389 km/h." Sheikh Saeed read from his cell phone, "The gyrfalcon is always my choice for hunting, but for racing, the peregrine is the only way to go. You have some of the best hunting birds in the world, but they are not racing birds, for that you need peregrines."

Rashid asked, "Might you be willing to share your source for peregrines?"

"Indeed, I can. I will text you the contact information for two of my sources. One is strictly a captive breeder, while the other will offer birds taken from the wild," Sheikh Saeed said. "In my opinion, wild birds are far superior to captive-bred birds. No bird is faster than a peregrine eyas (a raptor taken from the nest before fledgling). There is simply no comparison."

"Thank you, my friend, but do not be upset with me when I beat you next year because I followed your advice," Rashid said with a smile.

"It looks like the award ceremony is about to begin. Ma'a as-salamah (go with peace)," said Sheikh Saeed.

"Ma'a as-salamah."

Later that evening, Rashid received a text from Ma'a as-salamah, "For captive-bred- Ali El Amery +9665552674. Wild- Adam Getty +1-206-555-7984, I have sent both of them messages that you can be trusted. I wish you the best my friend and it would be my honor to lose to you in next year's President's Cup."

CHAPTER 8

Americans always laugh when they hear there is a state in Mexico named Chihuahua. All they can think of is that God-damned little shit dog, Jorge Bautista thought to himself. *Pretty soon everyone will know who we are.*

The city of Chihuahua is in the state of Chihuahua, Mexico, which is all controlled by the Juarez Drug Cartel. To the southwest, lies the Sinaloa Cartel (formerly headed by Joaquin "El Chappo" Guzman). If the Sinaloa Cartel wants to move product north to America, they must move through either the Sonora Cartel's ground or through Chihuahua, which is controlled by the Juarez Cartel. In recent times, battles between the rival Sinaloa Cartel and the Juarez Cartel had erupted all over the state of Chihuahua, and the Juarez Cartel wanted to end it quickly and decisively.

None of that was under Jorge's control, as his job (with the Juarez Cartel) was to modify trucks to haul smuggled products. Jorge had facilitated the smuggling of people, all of the various narcotics, identification, cash, gold, firearms, ammunition, grenades, live animals, and even human body parts, but he told himself at least he had never hurt anyone.

Starting in his father's failed automotive repair shop in Chihuahua, he learned all the skills necessary to successfully construct "almost" undetectable hidden compartments in commercial trucks and/or in their trailers. Jorge felt that where most mechanics went wrong was going with the same old thing over and over. In their trade, the saying of "If it ain't broke, don't fix it" doesn't apply. Keep filling tires with tightly wrapped kilos and eventually, even the dumbass Border Patrol guys are gonna figure it out, and when they do, only idiots would use that technique again.

He smiled as he thought about the American television series "Border Wars". In the series, produced by National Geographic, US Customs and Border Protection officers show the world how they detect, then recover hidden contraband. Jorge knew several other men, in his field of work, who also watched the show. When referring to the show everyone joked that if they (Customs) found it, the hidden compartment wasn't that well-hidden.

Despite what everyone thought, NAFTA (The North American Free Trade Agreement) was not dead but instead had been joined by CTPAT (Customs Trade Partnership Against Terrorism) and FAST (Free and Secure Trade for commercial vehicles). The cartel owned company Jorge worked for, as well as all of its drivers, were certified and approved under both CTPAT and FAST programs. These programs allow vetted companies, their vehicles, and drivers to easily cross the US/Mexico border, as long as they meet certain conditions. The CTPAT program advertises the benefits of joining including: "Reduced number of CBP (Customs and Border Protection) inspections, front of the line inspections, and even shorter wait times at the border."

Today, Jorge was told to create compartments no less than 60" wide, at least 10" deep, and a total length of 120". It would be acceptable to make any number of 60" x 10" compartments as long as they totaled at least 120". For this job, he picked a reefer (refrigerated) trailer number L-7874C. From his extensive research (watching

American police television shows) and from things the drivers had told him, Jorge held to the belief that cops don't look up very often. Because of this belief, Jorge favored compartments above one's normal line of sight.

After considering several options, Jorge decided to use the insulated ceiling. The ceiling of this reefer was made of a white plastic panel material, which he knew would be difficult to find replacements for. Jorge and his two assistants carefully went about the arduous task of drilling out and removing all the blind rivets (also called pop rivets) which held the 90-degree concave trim piece (which covered the junction between the wall and ceiling panels) in-place and attached the white ceiling panels to the sixteen aluminum cross-members which were spaced every 36" of the fifty-one feet of the trailer.

Once the panels were removed Jorge went to work on dropping the ceiling cross-members by 4". The gap between the roof of the trailer and the ceiling had been 6", which was filled with insulation. One-by-one Jorge cut, removed, and lengthened all sixteen cross-members by four inches. On the third day, Jorge and his crew riveted all but the forward four panels back in-place on the ceiling. The forward four sections of the ceiling provided his employers with four 94" x 10" x 36" compartments, far more room than he had been asked to provide. The last thing Jorge did before closing up the trailer, was to leave enough insulation material to fill the forward compartments, the rivet tool with instructions, and four times the number of rivets it should take to install the four panels.

Before Jorge left the shop, he took the burner phone from his desk and sent his cousin Gabriel a text, "L-7874C, forward 4 ceiling panels, drill rivets."

Almost instantly Jorge received a reply, "Got it. I will re-use same for return."

As he left for home that evening, Jorge couldn't help but wonder what that trailer would haul north. One thing Jorge knew for certain, was there would be another trailer coming in tomorrow, and this one had to be unloaded. Jorge was not looking forward to that task, as there were already too many guns in his city.

CHAPTER 9

On January 23rd, the day the Shereford brothers had killed the elk, they had taken them home, then skinned and cut up the elk in their garage. They had simply cut the four quarters, the tenderloins, and the backstraps off each elk and left all of the meat laying in the bed of their pickup. While the meat sat, "aging" in the filthy bed of the pickup, the brothers got going on some serious partying. With relatives and friends coming into and leaving the 24-hour party at all hours, the brothers finally shut down the festivities after four straight days of drinking and drugging. On the afternoon of the 27th, the Shorefords decided they better get the elk meat to Kennewick soon or it would all be wasted.

It was 11:25 on January 28th, when Wade and Freddie Shereford pulled their Ford pickup into the alley behind the Buena Comida Restaurant, on Clearwater Avenue in Kennewick, WA. They had been told to always come to the restaurant between 9 AM (when the kitchen crew began their day) and 11 AM (when the restaurant opened) to avoid being seen by customers.

"You're late, again," Felipe Vargas said. "You will get us in trouble being late."

"Traffic was a bitch," Wade Shereford said with a sneer.

"What do you have today?" Felipe asked.

"Two beautiful adult cow elk," answered Freddie, "$800 for both."

"When did you kill these animals?" Felipe asked as he sorted through the meat, "At least half of this is spoiled. See here, it looks like you left it laying on the ground because one side of each quarter is turning black. I will give you $100, and that's being generous."

"Shit, that won't even pay for our gas. How about we knock off a hundred bucks. Give us $700 for all of it, and you've got a deal. There is at least 350-pounds of meat here," answered Freddie.

"The meat that isn't rotten is filthy. It's all covered in dirt and hair," said Felipe. "$100 or go find someone else to buy it."

"$100 and a bottle of your best, for the road trip home," Freddie offered.

"You know where the cooler is, get it in there while I get the money and your whiskey," Felipe said.

"Cheap bastard. We need to find another buyer," Freddie told Wade as they carried the meat into the restaurant's walk-in cooler.

As Felipe handed the cash and a fifth of Seagram's 7 to Freddie, he said, "Don't come here after 10:30 in the morning again or we won't open the door, and if you don't take better care of the meat, we won't buy it. We can't have people getting sick from eating our food."

"I'm pretty sure people get sick from your food whether we had anything to do with it or not," said Wade as they turned to walk back to their truck.

"You really need to be more respectful, or someday you will be taught respect," Felipe answered.

"Oh yeah, and who's going to teach us respect?" Wade asked.

"You just never know who you are fucking with," Felipe said with a sinister grin.

It wasn't what was said, but how Felipe said it that made the hair stand up on the back of Wade's neck. For the first time, Wade saw Felipe in an entirely different light. At that moment, something about Felipe scared the living crap out of Wade, and he decided to keep his mouth shut.

"Gilipollas (asshole)," Felipe said in Spanish as he walked back into the restaurant.

CHAPTER 10

Joe pulled up Lisa's driveway just before 7 AM, and walked to the side-door, only to find Lisa holding a fresh cup of coffee for him.

"You look like you haven't slept in a month. Are you okay?" Lisa asked.

"Wow, and good morning to you too," Joe answered. "Just don't sleep very well anymore, but I'm good."

"If you insist, but I'm worried about you. I know you don't want my advice, but you need to slow down and get some sleep. You can't keep up the way you're going," Lisa explained.

"Thanks, Mom, now can we move on to figuring out our plans for this undercover?" Joe answered.

Joe sat at Lisa's dinner table and sipped his coffee, while she grabbed a notepad.

"I assume you read the case file on the Buena Comida restaurants?" Lisa asked.

"Not yet, I didn't get to it yet, but I will," Joe said quietly.

"What the hell Joe, it isn't that long. Read it now and I will check my emails while you do." Lisa said with frustration clearly showing.

Fifteen minutes later Joe announced he was done reading the report.

"Both restaurants are owned by a man named Angel Lopez. Mr. Lopez is apparently a very wealthy man, owning not only both of the Buena Comida restaurants but also LITE- Lopez International Transportation Enterprises, and the newly opened The Angel's Touch Winery and Event Center. According to the department of revenue, his restaurants have been raking in the money, with gross revenues of over $650,000 per month for the two or $325,000 per month per restaurant. That's almost eight million a year. Of course, that's gross, so with a net profit margin of say 10%, that would mean a net income, to Mr. Lopez, of over $800,000 per year, and that's just the restaurants." Lisa explained.

"Man, guess I should have opened a restaurant instead of taking this job," Joe said with a smile. "The only problem is I can't cook worth a damn, but for that kind of money, I could learn."

As Lisa entered a question on Google on her laptop, she said, "I want to see what an average restaurant grosses in Washington per year."

"Well?" asked Joe.

"Looks like somewhere between $120,000 and $200,000 per month, with most restaurants in the same size-range bringing in sales of around $155,000 per month gross," answered Lisa. "Even if he is not spending as much money on meat, I can't believe Mr. Lopez is doing that much better than the state average."

"No kidding," Je answered.

"Did you read the newspaper articles in the file?" Lisa asked.

"I skimmed them, why?"

"It sounds like Mr. Lopez is not only a great businessman but also a hero of the community. This article talks about the donations he has made to the communities his restaurants serve. He's a very generous man and seems to do a lot of good for the people. He gives out over $500,000 a year in scholarships for Hispanic students, and has a ton of other charities too," Lisa said. "If he ends up being dirty, we will likely be in for a very well-funded criminal defense for a guy the community loves."

"I think we might be getting a bit ahead of ourselves since we have absolutely nothing but rumor on any of the employees of the Buena Comida restaurants, but I guess it doesn't hurt to plan ahead," answered Joe.

"Do you have a preference on which restaurant we start with?" Lisa asked.

"I guess it's just a coin toss really, so let's go with the Clearwater Avenue restaurant," Joe said.

"We will have time to hit both of them in Kennewick, so let's try the Clearwater Avenue on first," Lisa responded. "So, what's our story?"

"I don't know if we really need much of a back-story for this. I can't imagine there will be much need for long conversations," Joe added. "Don't you think this will be a matter of do they buy it or not?"

"Ideally you are correct, but I would rather be ready for every possibility just-in-case, so let's come up with something," Lisa replied.

"Alright, if you insist," Joe answered. "Let's start with where we are from, and what we do, besides selling deer and elk meat."

"I would say we go with Pasco as our hometown. Out of the three cities (Pasco, Kennewick, and Richland), which make up the Tri-Cities, Pasco has the highest percentage of Hispanics (55%) and is large enough for us to be hard to find if anyone looks. As they said in the UC course, we need to spend a full day just poking around Pasco and the Tri-Cities so we know the landmarks, the roads, and the larger businesses," said Lisa.

Lisa went on, "Now, how about jobs, and our relationship?"

Joe said, "How about this; we just moved up here, six months ago from California, so I could work in residential construction with my dad's friend, but things are slow in the winter so I'm not working right now. How's that sound?"

"That will work, and I will be an unemployed veterinary assistant," Lisa answered.

"How about our relationship? You wanna go with mother and son?" Joe said with a laugh.

"Real funny punk. Since I look extremely young for my age, I don't think anyone will realize I'm a couple of years older than you," Lisa responded.

"Seven, you are seven years older than me, not just a couple of years," Joe said with a smirk.

"That's no way to talk to your girlfriend," Lisa responded.

"Alright, your dream can come true, you can be my girlfriend, as long as Emily is okay with it. I don't need my butt kicked by a woman," Joe said.

Emily, a detective with the Okanogan County Sheriff's Office, and Lisa had been married for seven years at that point.

"Since we have that all ironed out, the next thing will be to check out Pasco, figure out where we are going to claim we live, then get our UC identification for that address," Lisa went on. "It will take us about four hours to get to Pasco, so we can be there by 11:30. You want to head down there now?"

"Sure, why not. Let's go check out our new home," Joe answered.

"I've got to text Emily and tell her what's up, then we can head south," Lisa said before heading out the door.

"I'll drive," Joe announced.

"Great, if we aren't killed, we will get there in record time," Lisa said.

CHAPTER 11

It was 7 PM, and Gabriel Cardenas and his most-trusted employee were alone in the Pasco, WA shop. On this day, Gabriel's job was to create a hidden compartment, in a 24' Ford box truck (truck number D555), capable of transporting over $500,000 in cash.

Gabriel knew from experience, the five-thousand $100 bills would take up around 350 cubic inches and would weigh 11 pounds, so he didn't need a large compartment. Additionally, empty trucks going south are very rarely searched at the border, so this should be an easy one.

The first thing Gabriel did was to remove the passenger seat from the eight-year-old truck. Next, Gabriel and Diego carefully separated the seat's back from the bottom. Gabriel then removed the vinyl seat cover, then the seat's foam cushioning. Gabriel then cut a piece of 1" foam cushion to the exact dimensions and shape as the original foam. Using duct tape, Gabriel secured the 1" foam to the seat skeleton. He then carefully and evenly spread the individual bundles of cash to the foam from the top of the seatback to the bottom. Then came a layer of 1" foam, which had been doubled around the edges, so on the outer edges there would be a double layer of this foam, while the entire inner part was bundles of cash rather than foam. After Gabriel put the cover back on and reassembled the seat, nobody would be able to tell it had been altered. Gabriel sat in the seat and bounced around to see if he could feel the cash, but he detected nothing.

After watching Diego try out the seat, Gabriel asked, "Well, what do you think?"

"It's perfect. You can't see any unusual bulges and I can't feel it even bouncing up and down on it. You are a master," Diego answered.

Before locking up, Gabriel sent his cousin a text, "555 box, right seat back".

Jorge replied, "Suena bien (Sounds good)."

CHAPTER 12

The drive from Lisa's home in Tonasket to Pasco took just under four hours with Joe driving. Four hours of looking out the window at sand, sagebrush, and vineyards. Lisa realized a lot of land, in that area of the state, was just plain ugly.

As Lisa looked out the window, she said, "It's no wonder why they used this area for nuclear waste. Damn it's ugly here. Except for fruit orchards, there isn't a tree in sight."

"That's because you are from Western Washington, where you are used to being surrounded by forest. I'm from Arizona, and this area feels great to me. I like it," Joe said.

"Well, you can have it. Just don't move away on me, until I retire," Lisa said with a grin.

Joe and Lisa arrived in Pasco right before noon. "You want to head to one of the restaurants for lunch?" Joe asked.

"You mean do I want to go eat some mystery meat from a restaurant we are here to investigate for selling uninspected game meat, taken by God knows who?" Lisa asked, "I think I'll pass."

"Alright, how about we just stay with the seafood dishes?" Joe asked.

"Sure, why not? Improperly handled seafood is probably way safer than improperly handled elk meat," Lisa answered. "But, you're right, we need to go to one of them. I will find something to eat from their menu."

"How about the Buena Comida Restaurant on Clearwater Avenue?" Joe asked.

"Works for me. Let's hit it," Lisa answered.

The Buena Comida Restaurant was tastefully decorated in traditional Mexican décor. With a quick table count, Lisa estimated the restaurant could seat forty-eight patrons.

The sign next to the cashier's counter told customers to "Seat Yourself", so Lisa chose a small four-seat booth. Within thirty seconds, a server came out from the kitchen, grabbed a pitcher of ice-water, two menus, some tortilla chips, and salsa, and made her way to their table. Joe simply couldn't take his eyes off of the young woman. Joe guessed her to be 23 to 25 years old, about 5'05", and she was breathtakingly beautiful.

After checking the name on her server's name tag, and her bare ring finger, Joe said, "Lucia es un hermoso nombre (Lucia is a beautiful name)."

With a wide smile, Lucia answered in English, "Thank you, it was my grandmother's name."

Lucia filled their water glasses, handed over the menus, chips, and salsa and left Joe and Lisa to themselves.

As Lucia walked away from the table, Joe took one look at Lisa and asked, "What? If you have something to say, just say it? It looks like you are about ready to explode."

"Nope and I agree with your assessment," said Lisa.

Joe replied, "What assessment?"

"I saw the way you looked at her. You think she's hot, and you're right. If I was still single, I would be all over that. Did you notice the way she looked at me?" Lisa asked before breaking into laughter.

"Knock it off. I'm not having a conversation with a woman about how hot another woman is, plus I saw her first," Joe said with a smile.

"You two really would make a great couple, and your babies would be gorgeous," Lisa replied.

After they had been given ample opportunity to make their choices, Lucia returned to take their order. After Lisa had ordered, Joe said, "Me gustaría empezar con una cerveza (I would like to start with a beer)."

Before Joe could continue with his order, Lisa interrupted and said, "No creo que sea una buena idea (I don't think that's a good idea). You are supposed to work this afternoon."

"Wow, I got told huh? I guess I will change that to a Pepsi," Joe said before completing his order.

Lisa had ordered the Pollo Asado (a char-broiled chicken breast), while Joe ordered Chile Colorado (chunks of "beef" in a red chile sauce).

After Lucia had walked back to the kitchen, Joe asked, "What was that about? You're supposed to be my girlfriend, not my mommy."

"Let's talk about this in the truck, okay?" Lisa said in a soft calm voice.

"Sure, whatever," Joe said with a sulky pout.

At the end of a lunch that had no conversation, Joe stealthily retained a piece of the meat, in his napkin, which then went into his coat pocket.

"How's your Chile Colorado?" Lisa asked.

"Great. Tastes like beef," answered Joe.

Once out in the truck, Lisa turned to Joe and said, "Look, Joe, they said we can consume alcohol on-duty, to maintain our cover, not just because we want to. It was an exception, not an expectation. We need to save the beer for after work, or when necessary to maintain our cover. Do you disagree?"

"Hey, no problem. I just didn't know you had joined the policy police," Joe replied. "I will try to behave myself, boss."

Even though Joe and Lisa were both the same rank, technically Lisa was in-charge if it were just the two of them, because she had significantly more seniority.

"Well, I didn't know you couldn't go a couple of hours without a drink," Lisa regretted making the statement as soon as it left her mouth.

"Because you are my partner and friend, I won't respond to that bullshit," Joe responded.

"I'm sorry Joe. That was out of line. I wish I could take that stupid comment back. I'm only trying to look out for you, and I went too far," Lisa replied.

"Do you have concerns about working with me?" Joe asked.

"No, not at all. You know me, I am pretty fanatic about following the rules and policies, and sometimes I just worry too much," Lisa said.

"Let's just forget it, and go find a place to live," Joe said with a grin.

"Just one more thing. I hope you know you can talk to me anytime about anything. You are not just my partner, but one of my best friends. I have seen a lot of changes in you lately, and you seem to be under a great deal of stress. Just know if there is anything I can do to help, just say the word," Lisa offered.

"I'm sorry for being a little difficult, I just have some stuff to work out in my mind, but I will be alright. You are the only person in the world I can talk to about some of my issues. Thanks, partner!" Joe said before hugging Lisa. "Sometimes you are the only reason I keep going."

Joe and Lisa had decided to look for a mobile home community to claim as their home. After looking through the choices on the internet, they had tentatively settled on the River Rapids Mobile Home Park.

River Rapids was a community of 250 mobile homes. All surrounded in chain-link fencing. After getting the lay of the River Rapids community, from the outside looking in, they became confident in their choice.

"I like it. Nobody will be able to find out anything about us in there, but what do we do about people who look up the property records on the county website, and find we don't own a house in River Rapids at all?" Joe asked.

"Simple, we don't own our place, we lease it from the owner, who moved to Arizona permanently," Lisa answered.

"That should do it. We just need to pick an address from one of the 250 choices of homes, for our ID. I like the Vantage Road, and we can pick any house number we want," Joe replied.

"Alright, with that decided, let's go explore the Tri-Cities," Lisa said.

For the next four hours, Lisa and Joe drove around the three cities, getting to know the lay of the land and where the various businesses were located. By 5 PM, the two felt they had enough knowledge about the area, to at least bluff their way through a conversation regarding their new hometown.

"You ready to head home?" Lisa asked Joe.

"Whenever you are. Just say the word," answered Joe.

"Let's hit it," Lisa replied.

"I'm sorry for being so grumpy lately. I don't mean to take it out on you. You and the sarge are both super supportive, and I do appreciate it. You know most of what haunts me. I have been under a lot of stress lately, and I guess I'm not handling it too well," Joe said. "I will try my best to get my act together, and I'm sorry if I offended you in any way."

"Is there anything you want to talk about?" Lisa asked.

"Not right now, but thanks. It's just stuff I need to work out for myself."

Lisa replied, "Well, my offer always stands, and I know both Logan (Sergeant Logan Howard) and Clay (retired Game Warden Clay Newberry) would be more than willing to talk if you prefer to talk to men."

"Thanks, Lisa, I will be okay," said Joe.

"On a different note, I am going to text Captain Jacobsen and tell him we are ready to go, and just need to finalize our UC identification, and get some game meat if you think we are ready," Lisa said.

"Yep, let's go for it. You will still need to show me again how to run the cameras, but otherwise, I'm ready."

Lisa then sent Captain Jacobsen a text, "Got all lined up to take a run at the one on Clearwater Avenue in Kennewick. We need to get our driver's licenses and vehicle registration, and the game meat. The address we want to use is 6842 Vantage Road, Pasco, WA 99301."

"Great. I will get the IDs finished and mailed to you ASAP, you should have it by the end of the week. I will work on getting you a couple of deer or preferably an elk by Sunday. Lisa, give me a call first thing in the morning," Captain Jacobsen responded.

"Will do. Have a good evening," Lisa said.

"And you too," was the captain's reply.

CHAPTER 13

Two months ago, and immediately upon arrival in the Patagonia Region of Argentina, Adam Getty had purchased the materials necessary to build two new bal-chatri raptor traps. The bal-chatri was invented and first used in East India, to catch raptors for the purpose of falconry, and is still in use across the world today.

The bal-chatri is a simple device made of 3/8" mesh galvanized screen, J-clips (to assemble the pieces of the screen), a J-clip crimping tool, a couple of wire ties, and a spool of Stren 20 lb. green colored monofilament fishing line.

The galvanized screen is cut into four separate pieces, one for the floor, one for the top, and one for each end. The goal is to produce a half-cylinder (as if a cylinder had been cut in half lengthwise) with a flat bottom panel, and two ends made with a straight line on the bottom and an arch on top which matches the arch of the half-cylinder. The trap is 18" long 12" tall (at the top of the arch), and 16" wide. One end panel is permanently put in place with J-clips, while the other end is attached with plastic wire ties, so it is easier to open and close.

Once the trap is completed, a live bait animal (normally an ensnared live pigeon or rat) is placed in the trap, then the loose end panel is wire-tied in place. The top of the trap has dozens of monofilament loops sticking up. When a raptor sees the bait animal it will swoop down, land on the top of the bal-chatri, and its talons and legs will become entangled in the monofilament. This is one trap where the targeted animal is caught on the outside of the trap.

Bal-chatri are not passive traps, but rather must be continuously monitored to avoid the raptors harming themselves. Falconers who use the bal-chatri will drive the roads looking for the desired bird hunting from a perch. Upon seeing a raptor up on a perch (i.e.- power pole), the falconer will drop the trap as quickly as possible (often from a moving vehicle), move away a couple of hundred yards, and wait. More often than not, the raptor will swoop down to get the prey bird and will become entangled in the fishing line.

Using traps to capture adult birds was far safer than climbing the steep cliffs where peregrines can be found nesting, but robbing nests can be far more productive.

Peregrine falcons generally lay 3 or 4 mottled brown eggs, one every 48-hours, in nests high up on cliffs. The birds do not bring in any materials to build their nests, but rather simply rearrange existing materials on the flat cliff shelf they selected to lay their eggs. After the eggs are laid the female does the majority of the incubation, only giving way to the male when she needs to find food.

After 30 days of incubation, the nestlings (called eyases in the falconry world) stay in the nest for another 35 to 40 days, and dependent on their parents for an additional 4 to 6 weeks.

The time for peregrine breeding, in North America, was coming soon (in mid-March through the end of April), so Adam knew he would need to head north in three days. So far, during the two-plus months, he had been at it in Patagonia, Adam had successfully captured two peregrines (one male and one female), an extremely rare aplomado falcon, four cinereous harriers, and an endangered chaco eagle (also called the crowned solitary eagle).

Adam already had a buyer lined up for the aplomado falcon ($200,000 US dollars), the chaco eagle ($375,000 US dollars), and two of the harriers (at $1,800 each). Adam was only willing to sell the peregrines as a pair, which brought in another $100,000 US dollars. So far this trip had brought in commitments in total of $678,600 US dollars.

Just as with all his other trips to Argentina, Adam was staying the entire trip at "El Lugar Salvaje", which translates to "The wild place". Long ago, Adam had become good friends with Joaquin Alvarez (the owner of El Lugar Salvaje) who took great care of his favored guest. To assure he was not disturbed, Adam always paid very generously for the entire facility, during his stay. For the $7,000 US dollars cash per week, Adam had the four-bedroom lodge to himself, with Joaquin and his wife Sofia bringing his meals to him from their beautiful home on the grounds.

Adam had chosen El Lugar Salvaje because the lodge was situated right in the middle of some of the best raptor populations in the world. Before Adam's first visit, the Alvarez's had run the lodge and the surrounding acreage primarily for nature lovers who came from all around the world to watch and photograph the unique and plentiful animals of Patagonia. When Adam realized the value of this place for a man in his profession, he sat and shared a bottle of Fernet (a dark, syrupy liquor, similar in taste to Jagermeister) with Joaquin to try to work out an arrangement.

Joaquin had inherited the ranch from his father, who had raised cattle on the ground for fifty-two years. When Joaquin and Sofia became the ranch's new owners, they immediately started construction of the lodge. Joaquin saw how high the demand for eco-tourism destinations was, and his 64,000-hectare ranch was perfect. He could run a reduced herd of cattle while making more money from housing, feeding, and showing tourists around.

Over the years, several people had approached Joaquin about hunting the plentiful big game on the ranch, but Sofia insisted the red deer be left alone. She correctly said a trophy red stag is worth way more alive, than dead.

But what Adam proposed to Joaquin involved no killing. As a matter of fact, Adam had pointed out that because of their over-abundance of raptors, the populations of other birds and small mammals were being decimated. Adam explained how managing raptor populations is as responsible as managing a herd of cattle. Too many in a confined space is bad. Adam also assured Joaquin that all of the raptors would be well cared for and would eventually be released to the wild in places they were needed for a natural balance.

After convincing Joaquin, Adam went to work on Sofia. Adam proposed to Sofia that he would visit them twice a year, for a month or two each time. Once would be in their spring season (when he could get eggs and eyases, and the second visit in fall or winter for adult birds. Since he agreed to $7,000 per week, this meant the Alvarez's would bring in between $56,000 and $112,000 per year from this one guest. Adam had only two uncommon requests; he insisted absolutely nobody know what he was doing, and he asked for Joaquin to build him two mews (housing for raptors) and one incubation box, according to the plans Adam had provided. The mews, which Joaquin told other guests was for parrots he no longer had, were built to last and were far better than Adam had ever hoped. In the end, it turned out Sofia was easier to convince than Joaquin, as her primary concern was maximizing income. Thus, a business relationship that had already lasted five years had begun.

After getting off the phone with Delta Airlines, to firm up his return flight from Buenos Aires to Seattle, Adam placed a call to Saudi Arabia. The phone in Saudi Arabia went straight to voicemail, so Adam left a message, "Bariloche Airport, 10 AM on Wednesday the 12th local time and date. Let's round it off to 678, for the six. See you on Wednesday."

Adam smiled as he thought about the process. By this afternoon, his bank account would show a deposit of $678,000.00 from Arabian Petrochemical Industries, which would be reflected on his US federal income taxes as foreign income from his job as a "petrochemical consultant". Adam knew having large amounts of untaxed cash would make it pretty easy for the feds to pick you off. Although Adam certainly didn't like giving the US government a large chunk of his income, it relieved him of one substantial risk. Nobody could ever go after him for tax evasion, as he certainly paid his fair share.

Bariloche Airport was the perfect spot to conduct these transactions. The airport was small, quiet, and with almost no security. The 7,700' runway was adequate for the seventy-two million-dollar Gulfstream G650 company jet, which would take the birds to their new home.

Long ago, Adam had narrowed his airport choices to one each in Mexico and Argentina; Bariloche Airport in Argentina and the General Roberto Fierro Villalobos International Airport in Chihuahua, Mexico. Adam had made certain all of the appropriate people had received their substantial "bonus payments" to look the other way during these deliveries and pickups, but for security reasons, Adam had never even been to Mexico and intended to keep it that way.

On Wednesday morning Adam would release the two unsold harriers, pack the remaining birds for travel, and hit the road. After transferring the birds to the Saudi courier, Adam would turn in his rental car, get on the 2 ½ hour Latam Airlines flight from Bariloche to Buenos Aires. Next, Getty would transfer to Delta Airlines where he would relax in his first-class seat all the way home. By Friday afternoon, Adam would be enjoying a Dalmore 18-year old single malt scotch, and a couple of lines of cocaine in his North Bend, WA home.

CHAPTER 14

At 9 AM the temperature in Chihuahua, Mexico was already 91 degrees, a very warm day, especially for the middle of February. Since it was a Sunday, Jorge Bautista was working alone in the shop.

With the shop's steel doors locked and the reinforcement bars put in place, Jorge Bautista first went to work on the 24' Ford box truck. Jorge started by removing the entire passenger seat and placing it on the shop floor. Sitting on his adjustable shop stool, Jorge carefully removed the seat cover, then the foam cushioning, the tape, and finally the bundles of cash. Jorge gathered the cash up in a black plastic bag and carried it to the office. In the office stood two very large safes, both bolted not only to the floor and wall but to each other, making it virtually impossible to remove the safes from the office. One safe was for inbound cargo, and one was for outbound.

Jorge locked the half-million dollars of cash in the safe on the right, before removing six kilo bundles of meth. Once the money was tucked away, Jorge went through the process of concealing the thirteen plus pounds of meth in the seatback. After getting the foam cushioning back in place, and the cover put back on, the seat was ready to reinstall back in the truck. Once the seat was back where it belonged, Jorge opened the rear doors of the truck and left them open. He then fired up the propane-powered Hyster forklift, which Jorge used to load twelve pallets of watermelon, two pallets across by six rows deep.

When the box truck was done, Jorge moved on to refrigerated trailer number L-7874C. Upon opening the trailer door, he realized this was a trailer he had worked on a few weeks back. Jorge immediately began drilling the pop-rivets out, first from the 90-degree trim piece (where the ceiling meets the wall). Once that piece was free enough to pull the ceiling panels down, Jorge began drilling the ceiling panel rivets out too. Jorge had removed half of the ceiling panel rivets when he realized the panels had been holding up a great deal of weight. With the panels removed, and the cargo sitting on a workbench, he assessed the situation.

"Holy shit," Jorge said as he took a step back to take in the haul; Four Barrett M107A1 rifles, six Ruger AR-556 rifles, fifty 30-round AR-15 magazines, and ten 5- round Barrett .50 mags. The Barretts weighed just under 30 pounds each, compared to the 6 ½ pounds each for the AR rifles.

This was the part of his job he hated the most. In Jorge's view, the drugs were only hurting the rich Americans who have enough money to buy them, but the guns were killing thousands of his people in Mexico, and he very much wanted it to stop. Jorge had four immediate family members who had been killed in the cartel wars, and an endless number of friends and associates. It sickened him to know he had a role, no matter how minor, in all the violence. He wished there was a way he could stop it, or at least to refuse to handle the guns, but he knew better than to even try.

Once the guns were recovered and locked away in the inbound safe, Jorge removed the sixty single-kilo packages (132+ pounds) of cocaine from the outbound safe and went about the task of hiding the precious cargo back in the ceiling.

Jorge then sent his cousin a text, "L-7874C, forward two ceiling panels. 555 box, right seatback."

Two minutes later, Jorge received a reply from his cousin Gabriel, "JCX, 17F-250, 2nd bed, 2M".

Jorge right away knew he would be receiving a 2017 Ford F-250 pickup, with JCX in its license number, and it would be carrying two-million dollars in cash under the false bed of the truck. Jorge and Gabriel learned, a long time ago, how to weld a second pickup bed over the top of the original bed of the truck, leaving a 2 ½" gap between the two truck beds for the entire area of a pickup's bed. Because removing the second bed from the truck will leave obvious signs of having had that second bed, the smugglers would not reuse these trucks but rather would give them to their most valued employees to use as family vehicles.

Jorge looked at the date on his watch and realized tomorrow it would be time for him and Gabriel to destroy their phones and activate their new phones, as they did every Monday.

CHAPTER 15

The two men pulled their Chevy Silverado pickup behind the Clearwater Avenue Buena Comida Restaurant, in Kennewick, WA at 9:15 AM on a Monday. Both men were Hispanic and in their mid-fifties. After repeatedly banging on the rear steel door, Felipe Vargas finally answered the door, with one of his cooks standing next to him.

Felipe spoke first, "¿Qué tienes para nosotros? (What do you have for us?)."

The taller of the two men answered first, "tres venados de cola blanca (three whitetail deer)."

Felipe followed the men to their truck, where he saw three skinned and properly cleaned deer carcasses covered with a blue tarp.

"Ponlos en la nevera y obtendré tu dinero (Put them in the cooler and I will get your money)," Felipe instructed the men.

Five minutes later, Felipe handed the men $300 total for the three deer and said, "Gracias mis amigos. ¿Quieres algo para comer? (Thank you, my friends. Do you want something to eat?)."

The shorter Hispanic man answered, "Gracias, pero acabamos de comer. quizás la próxima vez. (Thank you, but we just ate. Maybe next time)."

"Hasta la próxima, amigos míos. (Until next time my friends.)," Felipe said as he shook hands with the two men.

CHAPTER 16

Frank poured the last of the coffee into his S&W logo cup, then moved down to his basement to unwrap the packages UPS had delivered the previous day. On this order, Antonio had added a couple of pistols, which Frank theorized were destined for the bosses of the organization. The pistols were nickel-plated Colt Government Model .45 ACP 1911A1 with mahogany grips, inlaid with gold spiders on each grip.

The guy who gets these guns must be something like El Spidero, or some other such horseshit, Frank thought to himself, *they all seem to have stupid street names.*

Besides the two .45 auto pistols, Antonio's order also included four Smith and Wesson M&P (military and police) AR-15s, a single Barrett M107A1 long-range sniper rifle, 100 AR-15 magazines, and 1,000 rounds of .223 ammunition for the AR-15s.

After completing the required ATF firearms transfer forms, Frank sent a text to the husband and wife team Antonio was sending him for this order, "Your firearms arrived. Would you be available to meet up in the gravel truck parking area next to the Burger King at the King City truck stop, at 4 PM?"

"We will be there at 4. See you then," was the answer Frank received.

CHAPTER 17

On the morning after Lisa and Joe had returned from their scouting trip to Tri-Cities, Lisa remembered Captain Jacobsen had wanted her to call. Looking at her watch, Lisa wondered if 7:10 AM was too early but decided the captain seemed like the kind of guy who wakes up at 5 AM every day.

"Morning captain, hope I didn't wake you," Lisa led with.

"Actually, you did. We just finally all fell asleep around 4:30 this morning. My wife and both of our little ones are home sick and have been up all night. It's no big deal, I'm sure they will sleep better tonight because of this early wakeup," answered Captain Jacobsen.

"Oh crap, I'm really sorry. I thought you would be up and at 'em by 5. Please tell your wife and kids, I'm very sorry," Lisa said with her head hung low. "How old are your kids?"

"Twenty-seven and thirty-one, and my wife is at the gym right now and has been since six. Damn you're a sucker. Are you sure about doing this UC stuff?" the captain joked.

"Very funny. I will remember this, and don't complain when I get you back," Lisa replied.

"So, tell me about Tri-Cities," Captain Jacobsen.

"We only went to the one on Clearwater Avenue, came down the alley, and checked out the back first. Then we went around to the front, parked, and had lunch there," Lisa explained.

"You're braver than I am, to eat there," said Captain Jacobsen.

"I went with the chicken," Lisa answered.

"Nothing out of the ordinary. A nice place, and relatively clean, but not very many customers for lunchtime," she continued.

"After lunch, we found our house, which is in a mobile home community," Lisa explained. "Then we went for a scenic tour of Tri-Cities. Nothing but sagebrush and sand as far as you can see. Not my kind of place, but Joe felt right at home there."

"Speaking of Joe, how is your partner doing?" Captain Jacobsen asked.

"Fine, why?"

"There are just some rumors going around that he is currently a little distracted and maybe even a bit unstable," Captain Jacobsen responded. "I also heard he may be hitting the bottle a little too much lately."

"First of all captain, you will never hear me say a bad word about my partner. Joe is a good man and a loyal and trustworthy partner. I trust him with my life, as it must be in our line of work. Joe has been under a great deal of stress lately, and I hope someday he will open up and talk to me about all of it, but in the meantime, rest assured it is not interfering with his work," Lisa replied with frustration. "I don't know who is giving you this kind of garbage information, but it is just ugly unfounded rumor. It's total bullshit. If I see any problems arise with Joe, I will handle them myself, one on one between me and Joe, and if and only if that doesn't work, I will talk to you or Sergeant Howard about it."

"That's good enough for me. I had to ask. I hope you understand," the captain replied.

"No problem. I fully understand, it's just that I feel like I'm betraying Joe just having this discussion without him present," Lisa said.

"Consider that discussion closed. Now, are you about ready for a couple of critters?" asked the captain.

"Whenever you can get us some, we are ready to go, at least once we get our undercover ID"

"Region 1, in Spokane, has an elk depredation hunt, to reduce the damage to agricultural crops, going on right now down in the Blue Mountains. We put in a request for the first elk killed, so I'm guessing it will be any day now. I told them just to call you directly. It will likely be Officer Kevin Webber from Dayton who calls you."

Lisa replied, "As soon as we get our hands on an elk or deer, we will head down and see what we can make happen."

"I will double-check today, and make sure your undercover IDs and registration are on the way, but otherwise you are good to go. Make sure and give us enough lead time to get your backup in place before you go in for the sale," said the captain.

"Will it be detectives or officers who are doing the backup for us?" Lisa asked.

"I have a couple of Region 3 officers who have volunteered and of course my detectives. It will largely depend on how much advanced notice we get. If the deal has to be made quickly, we will go with the officers, but if we can get the detectives over there on time, it will be my people," answered Jacobsen.

"Sounds like a plan. I can't wait to try our first UC contact," Lisa said.

"Just don't get your hopes up. I sent two of our detectives to the Ely Street Buena Comida, and they struck out. The manager even threatened to call the police and turn them in if they didn't leave immediately," answered the captain.

"Talk to you soon, and thanks for giving us a chance," Lisa said.

"Knock 'em dead young lady," replied the captain.

CHAPTER 18

Rashid Shaheen was sitting at the desk of his home office when his cell phone buzzed indicating a new text had arrived. Upon opening his text messages, he saw it was from his friend Sheikh Saeed Damadaran. The text included a photo of Sheikh Saeed with a bird on each of his outstretched arms.

Unfamiliar with either bird, Rashid was pleased to see Sheikh Saeed had included information about them, "The larger bird on my left arm is an endangered chaco eagle, and the bird on my right is an aplomado falcon. Both from Argentina. Beautiful, aren't they?"

Rashid picked up the phone and called Sheikh Saeed, "When and how did you acquire these magnificent creatures?"

"Adam, the man from the United States I referred you to sent them to me. Have you spoken with him yet?" asked Saeed.

Rashid replied, "I have not, but this photo points out the foolishness of my not making that call yet. Did he have any peregrines available?"

Sheikh Saeed answered, "Not to rub salt in your wounds, but he did capture a beautiful young pair of peregrines, which were purchased by a Saudi friend of mine- Sheikh Ahmed Jha Nishad. You will see him at all of the big events."

Sheikh Saeed went on, "Adam will soon be hunting all over North America for peregrines eggs and eyas, so you should give him a call soon."

"Thank you for the reminder. I have been so focused on my work, I had forgotten about this. I will call him today," Rashid responded.

"Ila al-liqaa (until we meet)," Sheikh Saeed answered.

After ending his conversation with Sheikh Saeed, Rashid summoned Mohammed Almaktoum to his office.

"I need you to call this man and ask about placing an order for some peregrines. I want four adults and six eggs or eyas. See if he can assure us delivery, what the cost is, when I can get them, how he wants payment, and how we take possession of the birds," Rashid said. "And, most of all, I want a white gyrfalcon

"I will do as you asked, right away. Thank you for entrusting me with this important task," Mohammed.

Mohammed then went to his small office where he readied himself with a notepad and pen before dialing the number.

Forty-minutes later, Mohammed returned to Rashid's office and was ushered in.

Reading from his notes, Mohammed said, "Mr. Adam was very informative and accommodating. He first wanted to make sure we understood that he currently has no birds available at all, and there is no way of knowing how many birds and eggs he may be able to gather in the next couple of months, but if it's a normal year, he should be able to fill your order without any problems."

Mohammed continued, "He stated he normally sells the adult peregrines in a range between $35,000 to $50,000 depending on the bird's size, age, appearance, and demeanor, which he judges himself. The peregrine eggs or eyas sell for a flat $6,000 per. As for the white gyrfalcon, he said the odds of him coming up with one is very low, but he will do his best. If he can find the gyrfalcon, he wants $600,000 for it. All prices are in US dollars. Within the first ninety days, if you aren't satisfied with the adult birds, he will give a full refund in exchange for getting the live birds back. He offers no guarantees on the eggs, other than they are from wild peregrine nests. He does not deal in captive-bred birds at all and considers them to be inferior. Mr. Adam said his prime hunting time is now through the next eight weeks, so we may hear back soon."

"And what of the payment and delivery?" asked Rashid.

"He does not require any deposit but has put you down on his list. When he gets everything you wanted he will contact us, and then you will have 48-hours to deposit the payment in his account. He needs the income to be reported, as payment for petrochemical consulting work. After that, we will need to have someone fly to Roberto Fierro Villalobos International Airport in Chihuahua, Mexico to pick up the birds," said Mohammed.

Rashid asked, "If he is collecting the birds in North America, why do we have to fly to Mexico to get them? I understand that place is about as safe as Iraq."

"He uses an established and reliable smuggling operation, which exists to move merchandise from the western US to Chihuahua,

Mexico and back, and he has never lost a shipment. He said US Customs is much more difficult to deal with than the Mexicans, so this is a far more reliable way to get the birds here. I had asked about the potential hazards of travel to Mexico, and he assured me that nobody will even approach our jet unless invited by us. He is required to make generous payments to the local drug cartel for use of the airport which is under their control, but is then totally protected by all involved."

"Very well. Call him back and tell him to proceed with my order," Rashid said.

"It will be done. Is there anything else?" asked Mohammed.

"That will be all for now."

CHAPTER 19

On the very morning Lisa and Joe received their undercover identifications in the mail, Lisa received a call from Officer Kevin Webber from Dayton, WA.

Webber advised Lisa, "One of my depredation hunters called, and it looks like they have a very large cow elk down. I'm on my way up to help gut it and pack it out, but I was told to call you immediately if we had one ready for you."

"Awesome. Do you have someplace you can hang it overnight, while I get everyone lined up?" Lisa asked.

"Sure, I will just hang it in my garage tonight. Then what's the plan?" Webber asked, "I assume you would like me to skin and quarter the elk?"

"I hate to ask, but yeah, that would sure save us a bunch of time and work. Thanks in advance for that," Lisa responded.

"My neighbor and I help each other out all the time. I will get him to help me and it should only take an hour or two," answered Webber.

"Alright, I need to line up our backup and surveillance assistance, and as soon as I know when they will be available, I will let you know. How far is Dayton from Tri-Cities?" Lisa asked.

"Too damned close. It's just a little over an hour's drive," Webber replied.

Is there a discreet place about halfway between them?" she asked.

"Yep. As you are coming towards Dayton on Hwy. 124 right as you get to the Lyon's Ferry Road intersection, you will see a grain elevator on your right. Take the exit, turn right on the Harvey Shaw Road, then an immediate right, and I can meet you behind the elevator. Nobody will be there this time of year," Webber replied.

Lisa replied, "Thanks, Kevin. I will be back in touch this afternoon."

"I've gotta warn you, I am not a fan of these depredation hunts, especially when the cow elk are pregnant, so I wouldn't count on getting too many more of these, at least out of my area," Webber said.

"Understood, but if this works, we will be saving way more animals than the few it will take to make the case," responded Lisa. "Thanks for taking care of this for us Kevin. We owe ya."

After ending her conversation with Kevin, Lisa shot Joe a quick text, "Are you available to head to Tri-Cities tomorrow? We will have an elk ready for us."

Joe responded almost immediately, "Sure. What time do you want me to pick you up?"

"I need to call Captain Jacobsen and check with him about our backup, then I will let you know, but I assume we will need to leave really early in the morning. The restaurant opens at 11 AM and we want to get there well before they open," Lisa answered.

Lisa started working out the timeline in her head. They needed to be at the restaurant by 10:30 AM at the latest. It would take them a little less than an hour to drive from the grain elevator, where they would meet Kevin, to the restaurant. So, in order to meet Kevin at 9:00 AM, Joe would need to leave Oroville no later than 4 AM. Maybe it would be better if they drove down tonight.

Once Lisa had the schedule worked out in her head, she called Captain Jacobsen, "Morning captain. Kevin Webber just called and it looks like we will have an elk available for us tomorrow morning. I think Joe and I will head down tonight, just so we aren't dragging in the morning," Lisa said.

"Do you know where you are staying tonight?" asked the Captain.

"I saw a Red Lion over by the Columbia Center Mall, so I'm going to try them first, but I haven't called yet," Lisa answered.

"Alright, I will send Detectives Amy Higgins and Dave Briggs over today. Why don't you call the Red Lion and make sure they have rooms available, then," Captain Jacobsen continued. "You four can get together this afternoon and work out the times and details."

After the conversation was completed, Lisa received a text from Captain Jacobsen with the cell phone numbers for the two detectives.

Lisa decided she better call Joe to tell him they were going to leave that day.

"Hey, it looks like we will need to leave this afternoon, and spend the night in Tri-cities. Will that work for you?" Lisa asked.

"Yeah, no problem. When do you want me to grab you?" Joe replied.

"How about 2 o'clock?" Lisa continued, "That way we will be there just in time to find a good place to eat and not the Buena Comida. Detectives Higgins and Briggs are coming over tonight too. I'm going to call them next, to see what time they plan on getting there."

"Alright, I will see you at two," Joe answered.

Lisa's next call was to Detective Amy Higgins, "Hi Amy, this is Lisa Bennington. I don't know if you remember me, but we met at the last in-service training."

"Kinda hard to forget you, Lisa, after that case you and Clay put together a few years back," Amy continued, "So, what's the plan on this?"

"Joe and I are heading down this afternoon, leaving at 2, we should be at the Red Lion in Kennewick by 6. We were just wondering what time you two would be over?"

"Sounds like it will take us the same amount of time to get over there, so we will plan on 6 also. How about we all eat dinner together somewhere, and work out the plans for tomorrow," Amy continued. "Do you have everything you need?"

"Yep, we have the undercover truck, three covert cameras, and we are picking up the elk in the morning, so I think we are set."

"Alright, I will be back in touch when we get there. See you soon," Amy responded.

The last call Lisa had to make was to Kevin Webber again, "Hey Kevin, would 8:30 work for tomorrow morning?"

"Perfect, see you then," Kevin replied.

Lisa answered, "See ya in the morning."

Lisa spent the remainder of the morning packing and catching up with her wife Emily. Emily had been working nights up until last week, so they hadn't seen much of each other.

At 1:50 PM Joe pulled up their driveway, then walked to their backdoor.

"I hear you're going all secret squirrel tomorrow," Emily said to Joe.

"Yep, me and my dear girlfriend here," Joe said as he put his arm around Lisa's shoulders.

"Well just remember, you are only borrowing her, she belongs to me," Emily replied with a wide smile.

"I will bring her back in one piece. If you want me to?" Joe replied.

"I guess if you have to. I will take her back," Emily went on. "In all seriousness, you two be careful. UC work can be really tricky."

"Hey, you too Em. Your job isn't exactly risk-free," Joe replied.

"He's got you there Em," Lisa said.

"Alright you two, get going. Some of us have to shovel snow today," Emily replied.

After the goodbyes, all the way around, Lisa jumped in the passenger seat of the UC truck and threw her bag on the backseat.

"The roads are really slick, so would it be possible for you to keep it under the speed of sound on the way there," Lisa asked Joe.

"Hate my driving?" Joe asked.

"No. I'm just asking to not be terrified the whole way down there. Please."

"You have a deal on one condition, I get to pick the tunes," Joe answered.

"Deal," Lisa responded as she began checking the emails on her phone.

A few seconds later the truck was filled with the sounds of trumpets and accordions, on a local Latino radio station.

"Real funny," Lisa said.

"Just getting us into our roles," Joe said as he broke into laughter.

Lisa and Joe pulled into the Red Lion at 6:11 PM, checked into their rooms, then Lisa gave Amy a call, "We are here, how about you guys?"

"We are in the bar. Come on down," Amy answered.

"Alright, we will go throw our stuff in our rooms and will be right down," Lisa said.

As Lisa conveyed the message to Joe, she thought about asking Joe to keep the alcohol consumption to a reasonable level but thought better of it. Joe was a big boy and had to make his own decisions. She just hoped he didn't embarrass himself again.

As Joe and Lisa walked into the bar together, they wondered if they would recognize Amy and Dave. Lisa did a quick scan of the uncrowded bar and noticed an attractive brunette sitting at a corner table with a muscular average-sized man with a Van Dyke beard. As they walked over to the table, both Amy and Dave rose to shake hands.

After introductions and drink orders, Dave started the conversation in a quiet voice, "You already know a couple of our detectives tried this restaurant last year and got shut down. So this is certainly not a guaranteed deal at all, but you two should have a much greater chance of success since the guys who tried it last couldn't speak Spanish, and the employees they talked to could barely understand English at all."

Next, Amy jumped in, "As the captain told you two, he has an anonymous source who the captain believes to be an employee of the restaurants here in Kennewick, but the source appeared to not be willing to get directly involved, and only provided limited information."

"Do you have any idea who the source is?" Joe asked.

"We don't. Only Captain Jacobsen has dealt with the source and even he doesn't know his or her identity. I guess he or she must be pretty terrified of being outed as an informant. I'm not sure why the fear, but we have to respect the source's requests for confidentiality," Dave answered.

"You know those Mexicans. They are all in the cartels," Joe said jokingly.

Dave apparently didn't get that Joe was joking, as he replied, "I guess that is remotely possible, but I don't think that's something we necessarily need to worry about here but be prepared for anything."

"Any words of advice on this contact tomorrow?" Lisa asked the pair.

"One of the things so many officers are worried about on their first couple UC contacts is appearing nervous," Amy said.

"I can identify with that," Lisa said.

"The funny thing is, that in a real bad guy to bad guy contact, they are nervous too. You don't know who you are dealing with, and scared of getting ripped off or hurt or getting arrested, of course people are going to be nervous. So, don't worry about being nervous, it's perfectly normal even for the real bad guys." Amy said.

"Let them do most of the talking. The more you talk, the greater the chance of getting caught in a lie or screwing up. Let the bad guys do the talking. Most of them like to brag anyway," Dave added.

"And don't be disappointed if they turn you down. As I'm sure they told you in the UC training, cold contacts like this, with no introduction by someone on the inside, have a very low success rate. Just don't get discouraged." Amy added.

Next, Joe asked, "How much should we get for an entire elk like this?"

"Two to five-hundred bucks is about normal." Amy answered, "Don't go too low, nothing under three-hundred bucks, and don't be afraid to walk out on them. If they want it, they will stop you and offer more every time."

"Unless you two object, I will take Joe with me in the morning, to scout out a good position for me and Amy to keep an eye on you from a distance, while Amy and Lisa go to pick up the elk," Dave said.

Lisa and Joe exchanged glances before Lisa answered, "Works for us."

"Should we all meet in the lobby at eight tomorrow morning?" Lisa asked.

"Sounds like a plan," Dave answered.

"Alright, if that covers it all, let's eat," Amy said as she waved the server over to their table.

After they had finished their meals, the group ordered another round of drinks and began sharing the "war stories" of their past cases.

By eleven PM Lisa was ready to hit the sack and said goodnight to the others.

"Me too. I am throwing in the towel too. See you guys in the morning," Amy announced.

"See you tomorrow, buddy, but I'm crapping out on you too," Dave Briggs told Joe.

CHAPTER 20

By 7:45 AM, Lisa was in the lobby packed up and ready to go. Within minutes both Amy and Dave had arrived, but no sign yet of Joe.

"Lisa, before you take off, you will probably want to put your suitcase in my truck, as it might be a little tough to explain why you both have suitcases packed when you are supposed to be living in Pasco," Dave said.

"Good idea, thanks," Lisa answered before borrowing the truck keys from Dave to put her suitcase away.

By 8:00 AM there was still no sign of Joe, so Lisa called his cell phone.

"Oh shit. I never heard the alarm go off. I will be down in a couple of minutes," Joe muttered.

Lisa was seething as she spoke with Joe, "I will be at your door in two-minutes. I need the keys to the UC truck, so Amy and I can take off to get the elk."

"Yeah, yeah, just come to the door and I will hand them out before I jump in the shower," Joe said.

"Screw the shower, Joe. Everyone is waiting for you. You have got to get going," Lisa said before heading to his room.

As Lisa returned to the lobby with the truck keys, she motioned to Amy to follow her. As they were heading for the door, Dave asked, "What about Joe. Where's he?"

"Sorry, but I don't know when he will be down. I wouldn't wait too long," Lisa said as she walked out the hotel doors.

"Is this a regular issue with Joe," Amy asked Lisa as they pulled out of the parking lot.

After a long pause for thought, Lisa answered, "I hope you will keep this conversation between us, but no it's not a regular problem with him yet, but I worry that it might get to be. He hasn't been himself for a long time now. I love him like a brother, and it hurts me to even say anything negative about him, but I'm really worried. He won't talk to me about whatever is going on, so I just sit and watch him spin out of control. He has moments where he is the old Joe, but then he slides right back downhill."

"Is he safe to work with when he's like this?" Amy asked.

"I know this for certain, no matter what is going on with Joe, I have zero doubt, none, that without a thought he would give his life to protect me at any time and anywhere, so yes he's safe to work with."

"Do you think he has a drinking problem?" asked Amy.

"Not yet, but I think it might be heading that way. Do you mind if we switch the subject now?" Lisa asked.

"I'm sorry Lisa, I wasn't trying to pry. It's none of my business," Amy said.

"No, you weren't prying at all. It's good to have someone to talk to about it. My wife is in law enforcement, so she understands, but you know the department and the dynamics of it," Lisa replied.

After a few minutes of silence, Amy asked, "So how did you end up signing up for the UC work?"

"Shortly after I was hired, and newly in the academy, I got a visitor one day after class. I was called to the reception counter, where I came to find a six-foot-five, 225-pound grey-haired guy who looked like a retired mafia hitman. The guy led me into a small office where he introduced himself as SIU Captain Aaron Hamlin. When I asked what I could do for him, Captain Hamlin said something that at the time didn't make much sense to me. He simply said, don't let the department make you into one of their poster children. Don't pose for photos, don't agree to television interviews, and stay the hell off social media. Then he just stood to leave."

Amy just grinned as Lisa went on, "As he got up to leave, I asked him why not and his response was simple, he said because you are not a white male who looks like a SWAT team recruiting poster. You will have a great deal of value for future undercover work if you can stay the hell out of the media."

By the time Lisa was done telling Amy the story, Amy was laughing hysterically, and said, "That's pretty much word-for-word what he told me too."

"Yeah, I kinda figured that since he told Joe the very same thing a few years later," Lisa responded.

Amy then said, "Captain Hamlin was right. Just like every other governmental agency, WDFW likes to show everyone how diverse our workforce is, by having female and minority officers featured in everything from television interviews to recruiting posters to the fishing pamphlets. It's become predictable. That's all great unless that same officer later wants to work UC. The guys can grow a beard, and long hair and look totally different, but there's not that much we can do to change our appearance to the point we wouldn't be recognized."

"I know, it's just the way Captain Hamlin presented it that cracked me up," Lisa answered.

"Yeah, he wasn't much for long conversations, but he was a great guy to work for, and very supportive. I hated to see him retire, but Captain Jacobsen is a super great guy too, and he has our backs one-hundred percent," said Amy.

"That's good to know," answered Lisa.

Soon the two officers saw the sign for the Lyon's Ferry/Harvey Shaw Road ahead, then the tops of the grain elevators Kevin Webber had talked about.

As they pulled in behind the grain elevators, they noticed Kevin was already there waiting for them.

"Good morning ladies, would you like to buy an elk?" Kevin said to the two UC officers.

"Morning Kevin. Thanks for doing this for us. I know it was a lot of work to get this taken care of for us," Lisa said before realizing Kevin may not know Amy. "I'm sorry, do you know Amy Higgins?"

Kevin's response about floored Lisa, "No, not really but I have no desire to get to know her either. You can keep her the hell away from me, or you might get to see me kick the living shit out of a woman."

Amy rushed past Lisa before Lisa could stop her and grabbed Kevin's uniform shirt right below his throat and told him, "Bring it on asshole. Anytime."

"Amy! Stop!," Lisa yelled as loudly as possible. But then Lisa went from shock and disbelief to bewilderment as she saw Amy give Kevin a big hug.

"You look good kid. How have you been?" Kevin said to Amy as they stood face to face.

"I'm doing well, except my buddy doesn't call me much anymore," Amy replied.

"No excuses. I promise to do better," Kevin said with a grin. "But I seem to remember that phone calls can go both ways nowadays."

"Wow, that was really amusing you two. If I had been in uniform and had my pepper-spray you both would be rolling around on the ground crying like babies right about now," Lisa continued. "Okay, so how do you know each other?"

"We attended the academy together forever ago and have remained good friends ever since. Every year Kevin and his wife go on a vacation with me and my husband Will. It's a tradition we have kept up on for over a decade now," Amy explained.

Looking directly at Amy, Lisa asked, "So why didn't you tell me you knew Kevin so well?"

Amy answered simply, "You never asked."

"Kev, we are on a bit of a tight schedule, so I guess we better get the elk and get out of here," Amy told Kevin.

"Okay Lisa, I will drop the tailgates, then just back your truck right up to mine, and we will just slide the elk quarters in. No lifting required," Kevin said.

After transferring the elk meat to Lisa's truck, Lisa took out her cell phone and took several photos of the elk meat. Next, Lisa retrieved a zip-lock sandwich bag, which contained a pair of latex gloves and a razor blade in a sheath, from the truck's console box. After donning the gloves, and removing the cardboard sheath from the razor blade, Lisa removed a tissue sample from the elk meat, bagged it, and returned the bag to the console box.

Seven minutes later, with the elk loaded, they were on their way back to Tri-Cities.

As Lisa drove, Amy fired off a text to Dave asking where they wanted to meet to switch passengers. Almost immediately, Lisa received a response, "How about Hood Park, right at the intersection of Hwy. 124 and Hwy. 12, just before you cross the Snake River. We will be there in twenty minutes or so. And, I have sleeping beauty, and he's raring to go."

"Good, see you there," Amy replied.

"Your partner made the bus. He's with Dave now," Amy told Lisa.

"Well, that's a start," Lisa said.

Thirty minutes later, Lisa and Joe were on their way to the Buena Comida on Clearwater Avenue in Kennewick.

"Don't even start on me. I just overslept, it's not the end of the world," Joe said.

Lisa ignored what Joe had said, and acted as if nothing had happened, "Are we all ready for this?"

"Yep, let's give it a try," Joe answered.

"Let's start the cameras," Lisa said as she started the cameras mounted in the back of their truck as well as the camera hidden in the truck's visor which pointed forward. She looked at Joe who had started the camera hidden in his watch.

"This is James Bond kinda stuff. It's cool," Joe said.

When Lisa arrived at the Buena Comida she first did a full circle of the restaurant before pulling up to the back door.

"Alright, let's do it," Joe said.

Previously, Joe and Lisa had agreed the best approach would be to get right to the point, without spending the time to try to establish some kind of connection with the restaurant manager, at least at this point.

Before approaching the back door, Lisa had noticed the parking lot had four vehicles parked in back, so she made sure Joe captured each of the vehicles and their license plates on his "James Bond" camera.

Joe and Lisa stood side-by-side as Lisa rapped on the metal security door. After over two-minutes with no response, Lisa pounded harder.

Soon the door opened to reveal Lucia, the same beautiful server who Joe had been so stricken by when he and Lisa had eaten lunch on their scouting trip.

"Lucia isn't it?" Joe asked.

"Yes, do I know you?" Lucia answered in English.

"No, we came in for lunch a while back, and I remembered you. My name is Jose, and this is my friend Anna," Joe answered.

"For some reason, he always remembers the beautiful women," Lisa said with a chuckle.

"Well, what can I do for you, Jose?" Lucia asked while ignoring Lisa.

"We have some meat to sell and have heard your restaurant will buy it," Joe answered.

"What kind of meat?" asked Lucia.

"Fresh elk. It's in great condition. Well cared for," Joe answered.

"My Uncle Felipe makes all of the purchasing decisions. Let me find him for you," answered Lucia.

As soon as Lucia disappeared back into the kitchen, Lisa leaned over to Joe and said, "She likes you."

"I sure as hell hope so. Sorry, but she has me considering trading up," Joe answered.

"Wow, that fast. Well good thing I have a backup waiting at home," said Lisa with a smile.

Soon Lucia returned with an older Hispanic man, who was wearing a long white apron.

"Uncle, this is Jose," Lucia said in Spanish, followed by addressing Lisa, "I'm sorry, I forgot your friend's name."

This is my girlfriend Anna," Joe said.

"Nice to meet you, Anna. Let's take a look at what you brought me," said Felipe.

Once Joe had opened the truck's canopy and dropped the tailgate Felipe hopped in and began turning over the meat, so he could see all of it.

"Well cared for and very clean. Just the way we need it. How much are you asking?" asked Felipe.

Lisa answered before Joe could speak, "Five-hundred."

"Aren't you the feisty one?" Felipe said in Spanish, "I will offer you four-hundred dollars and no more."

"You have a deal," answered Joe.

"Well, I better get back to work, I have classes this afternoon," Lucia said. "It was nice meeting you Anna and it was good to see you again Jose. I hope we meet again."

Once Lucia had vanished, Felipe showed Lisa and Joe where he wanted the elk, while he retrieved the cash.

As Lisa and Joe were just bringing in the last of the elk meat, Felipe returned and counted out four-hundred dollars to Joe's hand.

"I will take all of that I can get if you take care of it this well. Deer too, as long as it's not that shitty tasting mule deer," Felipe said in Spanish.

"We will do our best. I am sure we will be back," Joe answered. "On a different subject, what's up with that thing?" Joe said as he pointed at a huge commercial dishwasher, which was partly disassembled and spread over the kitchen floor.

"It's our only dishwasher. It's very important to us and it quit working," answered Felipe.

"Do you want me to take a look at it? I'm a pretty decent mechanic," asked Joe.

"You know how to fix dishwashers?" Felipe asked.

"Nope, but I'm damned sure I can figure it out," Joe answered.

"If you can get it to work, there's another hundred in it for you."

Lisa looked at Joe as if he were nuts, and he knelt down in front of the disabled dishwasher and started digging into it.

After only ten minutes, Joe stood holding a metal piece shaped like a strange nail.

"This shaft pin keeps this large wheel in place on the shaft and keeps it from coming off the motor. The pin is broken, which is allowing the shaft to spin without turning the belt wheel. That wheel is what makes the drive belt go around, and that's the whole problem," stated Joe.

"Can you fix it?" Felipe asked.

"If you can find a pin or even a bolt this diameter and length, I will have it running in five minutes," Joe answered.

Felipe left, then a couple of minutes later came back with an empty one-gallon mayonnaise jug filled with a wide assortment of screws, nuts, and bolts.

Joe immediately took the jug and poured its contents on one of the nearby stainless countertops. After sorting through the hardware, Joe held up a bolt topped with a lock washer and nut.

"This should do the trick," Joe announced as he started reassembling the dishwasher.

"Okay, give it a shot," Joe said as he stood back and admired his work.

Felipe stepped forward, locked the dishwasher's doors down, and pushed the start button. Immediately, the dishwasher jumped to life, purring away.

"I am very impressed Jose. We could use someone with your mechanical skills. Let me get your extra money," said Felipe.

"No charge, that was too easy," Joe replied.

"Alright, then thank you," Felipe said as he shook hands with Joe and Lisa. "I hope we see you again. You eat here for free from now on. Just promise to keep the elk meat between us. No police."

"Thank you, sir, you can count on me being back, and don't worry, we won't say a word to anyone," Joe said as he and Lisa walked back to their truck.

Lisa and Joe made it about a half of a mile down the road when Lisa got a call from Amy, "You guys did it. Way to go guys!"

"It was all Mr. Goodwrench here. I don't think they even knew I was there. His girlfriend even pretended she didn't remember my name. She was blatantly hitting on my fake boyfriend right in front of me," Lisa said.

"Well, that bitch," Amy said following by a roaring laugh.

"Let's meet up back at the motel, in the parking lot to transfer the evidence, and do a short little debrief," added Amy.

Twenty minutes later, Lisa and Joe handed off the meat sample, the cash from the sale, and downloaded the covert videos to Dave's laptop.

"Thanks for doing this guys, you got into a group that nobody else could. Drive home carefully, and don't forget to call Captain Jacobsen to fill him in," Amy said.

"Until next time. Thanks," Lisa said.

As Lisa and Joe were on their way home, Felipe and his niece were chopping vegetables together when Felipe said, "Very nice people and they took very good care of the meat."

"Yes they were, and Jose is really cute," Lucia added.

"I noticed you paid extra attention to him, but I think that Anna is his girlfriend, so you are out of luck my darling," responded Felipe.

"I don't think so. A woman can tell, and I'm telling you there is nothing between them. They are just friends," said Lucia.

Felipe grinned from ear to ear as he said, "Well good luck in your pursuit of him. He did do one thing I just don't understand."

"What's that?" asked Lucia.

"He is so poor he took the risk of killing an elk illegally, but then he turned down one-hundred dollars when I offered it to him for repairing our dishwasher. I find that very strange," said Felipe.

"I think he fixed the dishwasher to impress me, not to make more money. He is a proud man," Lucia said.

"Perhaps you are right."

"Good afternoon captain. We are on our way home from Tri-Cities, have you heard from Amy or Dave yet?" Lisa asked.

"Nope, but I see by their GPS tracker they are on their way back," said the captain. "How'd it go?"

Lisa then remembered Captain Jacobsen said they would always be able to track the UC truck because it had a tracker built in permanently.

"Well, we have four-hundred dollars in evidence and the back of our truck is empty now."

"Outstanding. Tell me about it?" said Captain Jacobsen.

"It was pretty straight forward. We first dealt with a young woman, who by the way has the hots for Joe, and then ended up dealing with her Uncle Felipe," Lisa answered.

"Felipe Vargas, the manager," the captain said.

"Right. Anyway, we showed him the elk, and asked for five-hundred bucks, he immediately came back with an offer of four-hundred, and it was done," Lisa continued. "We carried the elk in, he paid us, then Joe repaired their dishwasher, and we were out of there."

"Joe did what?"

Lisa answered, "He repaired their dishwasher. When we carried the elk into the kitchen, we noticed their commercial dishwasher was torn apart. There were pieces all over the floor, so Joe offered to fix it. About fifteen minutes later their dishwasher was running like a top. Felipe even offered to pay Joe a hundred bucks, but Joe said the job was so easy he couldn't take his money for the repair."

"How in the hell did Joe know how to repair a commercial dishwasher?" asked Jacobsen.

"According to Joe, his dad is the kind of guy who can build anything and fix anything, and he taught it all to Joe," Lisa said.

"Impressive, but I would warn you guys about turning down money. Remember you are supposed to be a couple of low-lifes, looking to get cash any way you can. It doesn't make a lot of sense to turn down free cash."

"True, but I also think it endeared Joe to Felipe a bit more," answered Lisa. "Both Felipe and Lucia pretty much ignored me the whole time and were focused on Joe. I think he could easily do this on his own."

"We might want to consider sending him alone next time. You could switch to providing the back-up. Give it some thought. You two are now the ones who have to decide what the best way to work this will be," the captain went on. "Well congratulations on your success, and tell Joe awesome job. I will get ahold of Kevin's captain again and request another elk or at least a couple of deer. We will be back in touch."

"Oh yeah, I almost forgot. Felipe said no mule deer, he hates their taste," Lisa added.

"Picky, picky," Captain Jacobsen said before hanging up.

Once off the phone, Lisa asked Joe, "Seriously, what's the deal on your dishwasher repair trick? Where did you learn to repair dishwashers?"

"When I was growing up, my dad was trying to get his residential construction company going, but things were very slow, so he also did odd home repair jobs. I liked spending time with the old man, so I went on as many calls with him as I could. Over time he showed me how to work on just about anything you could think of. I built houses, repaired appliances, fixed plumbing problems, installed security systems, you name it," Joe answered.

"That's awesome you have that kind of relationship with your dad," Lisa said.

"I got pretty lucky in the parent department. I have no complaints. They are about as good as they come," replied Joe.

"Your dad still has his construction business, doesn't he?" Lisa asked.

Joe answered, "I don't see him ever giving that up or retiring. He now has around fifteen full-time employees and is booked months out for new home construction. He's finally really doing well. He has asked me no less than fifty times to come home to work the business with him."

Lisa silently wondered if Joe had been seriously contemplating the offer, which might explain some of the stress he seemed to be under.

"Is that something you are considering?" Lisa asked.

"Not really," was all Joe answered.

CHAPTER 21

It was 9:00 PM when Diego finally made it home. For eleven straight days, Diego Martinez and Gabriel Cardenas had been loading and unloading hidden cargo, and building hidden compartments, averaging twelve-hour days, and Diego was beat. The 12-pack of Budweiser, Diego had purchased on his way home was nearly gone.

As Diego pulled in the driveway of his Pasco, Washington home, he cringed at the sight of the 1995 Chevy Impala in the driveway. The car belonged to his stepson, a 20-year old doper with a big mouth.

"That's all I fucking need," Diego muttered to himself as he walked towards the front door of his house.

"What the hell is this piece of shit doing here?" Diego asked his wife.

"Diego, please be nice to Victor. He just came by to visit," Diego's wife Bonita pleaded.

"Yeah, and how much money did you give him?" Diego asked.

"Diego, that's not why he came," pleaded Bonita.

"How much?" Diego said in a very serious tone.

"Five-hundred dollars, but he is going to pay us back every penny," answered Bonita.

"He sure as hell is. Right now. Give me my money you fucking little prick," Diego commanded.

"Fuck you old man. You can kiss my ass. This money is from my mom," Victor answered.

Without hesitation, Diego attacked, punching his stepson in the face as hard as he could swing, resulting in Victor's nose virtually exploding. Even though Victor had already collapsed, Diego continued his attack by holding Victor's hair with one hand and continuously beating his face with his other.

"Diego, stop! You are going to kill him. Stop," screamed Bonita, as she ran to interfere.

When Bonita reached the men, she grabbed Diego by this left-shoulder and tried to pull him off her son, but for her efforts Diego planted a solid right-cross to her mouth, knocking a bloody tooth onto the floor.

With Bonita back out of the way, Diego returned to Victor, where he began kicking him in the head and face and stomping down on his head with his boots.

Once Bonita's vision began to clear, she crawled to the phone, where she immediately called 911 and begged for help to save her and her son from her husband.

As Diego realized what Bonita had just done, he ran to his wife and pulled the phone cord out of the wall. With the phone in his hand, Diego swung at his wife smashing the phone against the side of her face. Diego next grabbed his wife by the hair on the back of her head and slammed her face into the wall so hard it knocked a hole in the drywall.

As Bonita collapsed to the floor, Diego realized the police would be there at any minute, so he opted to leave in a hurry, but as soon as he stepped outside he could already hear the sirens coming his way.

Diego almost made it to the main road, from his driveway, when the first cop car arrived and blocked his exit.

Six minutes later Diego was sitting in the back of a patrol car, recovering from being tased twice. Diego watched as the first responders carried his wife out to the waiting ambulance, followed by Victor on a gurney. Diego realized just how much damage he had done to this stepson when he saw one of the paramedics administering chest compressions on Victor as he was being wheeled to the ambulance.

"Sir. Sir, I need you to answer. Do you understand your rights as I have read them to you?" a cop was asking Diego.

Diego had zoned out and hadn't heard a word of his rights, but he had heard them before, "Yeah, whatever."

"Having those rights in mind, would you be willing to answer some questions?" asked the same officer.

Diego answered with only one word, "Lawyer."

"Fine, that's your right. Right now, you will be booked on two counts of assault, but from the looks of your stepson, I think you can expect it to be upgraded to murder pretty soon. Do you have any questions?" asked the officer.

"Yeah, what's for dinner tonight?" Diego asked with a smile.

The following morning, Gabriel was watching the news while he ate his breakfast, when the story of a man beating his own stepson to death with his bare hands, and nearly killing his wife, caught Gabriel's attention.

"How can a man do that? What kind of a monster does it take to do these things to his own family?" Gabriel asked his wife.

"A horrible monster, not a man. No man would do that to his family," said his wife in response.

Scrambled eggs tumbled from Gabriel's gaping mouth, as Diego's photo and name appeared on the television screen.

"Oh my dear God, how could he do such a thing. I'm going to be sick," Gabriel said as he cupped his face between his hands.

"What is it, my love? What did you see?" Gabriel's wife asked as she consoled him.

"The monster who killed his family is Diego. Diego Martinez, the man I work with every day. I need to call the boss. This is terrible. I knew Diego was not a man of God, but I never saw any sign of this violence in him," explained Gabriel. "I worked with a monster."

Gabriel wanted to call the boss before he heard it on the news, so he went out to the garage and dialed Antonio's cell phone.

"Boss, we have a problem," Gabriel said as a start. "Last night my helper Diego got arrested for killing his stepson and nearly killing his wife. It was horrible. He beat them with his hands and feet."

"I have no use for a man who will beat his wife. Normally I only have to worry about someone cooperating with the police if they get arrested, but with this Diego man, I will feel good about removing him," Antonio went on. "Do you know what jail he is in?"

"It must be the Franklin County Jail since he was arrested at his home in Pasco," Gabriel responded.

"Excellent, we have several people inside who can remind him to keep his mouth shut and take his punishment like a man," Antonio answered. "I will see to it he gets the punishment he deserves."

Gabriel, "I do not mean to complain, but I was already down one helper, and now it's just me. Can you maybe have a couple of helpers brought up from Chihuahua?"

"Not while we have this war with the Sinaloas going on. We will need to find our own people here, and we will need to do it quickly. The bosses will hold us accountable for missed or delayed shipments. I will talk to Felipe and we will find you some help. Your work is too important to let this slow you down," Antonio said. "Until we get you some help, you will need to work more hours so you will receive your pay plus Diego's."

"Thank you, boss," Gabriel said, "because some things I can't do by myself."

CHAPTER 22

Mid-March had finally arrived, which signaled the start of the peregrine falcon breeding season in North America. Adam had his routine down to a science. Due to the snow in Eastern Washington, Idaho, Montana, and North Dakota this early in spring. Adam always concentrated his efforts in Western Washington for the first couple of weeks.

Adam had been at this game for decades and knew where the pitfalls to avoid were. For instance, one of the best places to find nesting peregrine falcons is on the cliffs of the San Juan Islands. Unfortunately, there are very few places not visible from houses, in the islands, and what can't be seen from homes, can be seen by the tens of thousands of pleasure boats. As tough as it was to pass up on, Adam had decided the risk was too high in the islands.

The second-best place, for nesting falcons in Western Washington, was the Pacific coast islands and cliffs from Neah Bay to Hoh Head (near the mouth of the Hoh River), on the far north-western portion of the Olympic Peninsula. Although not ideal, in part because of the land's ownership, the area was remote, unwatched, and very difficult to access, but full of nesting peregrines.

The properties Adam had traditionally hunted for falcon nests was owned and controlled by the Makah Indian Tribe and the Bureau of Indian Affairs (on the northern portion) and the National Park Service, the US Fish and Wildlife Service's Flattery Rocks National Wildlife Refuge, and the Quileute Indian Tribe (on the southern portion). Flattery Rocks consists of over 800 islands and rock pillars just offshore in the Pacific Ocean. Adam knew the greatest risk with hunting this area, was not the threat of getting caught but rather the sea conditions. In the northern portion of the Olympic Peninsula, the sea conditions can be anything from flat calm to twenty-foot seas in spring and can change rapidly.

Over twenty-five years back Adam had met an older well-respected Quileute tribal member by the name of Ricky Williams. Adam had originally met Ricky on one of his early falcon hunting excursions when Adam was looking for a place to stay in the LaPush area. Way before Airbnb or VRBO, Adam had found Ricky by simply asking around in the small village of 370 people. After randomly asking ten or so people about a place to stay, he finally ran into Ricky Williams. Ricky had told Adam that his son, who had lived in a single-wide trailer on Ricky's property, had been killed in a car accident, and that Ricky would be willing to rent his son's trailer out for fifty dollars a day. Adam had counteroffered with five-hundred dollars a day with a few conditions.

Similar to Adam's deal with Joaquin and Sofia in Argentina, Ricky had to first agree to keep Adam's activities totally confidential. Adam also demanded he be able to leave an egg incubation box and a mews for the birds on the property year-round. A few years later, Adam added an additional condition, that Ricky had to store Adam's new 18'8" Stryker rigid hull inflatable boat and trailer in a covered shed on his property (Adam paid for the shed to be built).

Since Ricky had been born and raised in the same village his entire life, he knew the area like the back of his hand, so when he agreed to drive the boat to take Adam out to the islands and cliffs,

Adam was ecstatic. Having Ricky drop him on an island, then return at a specified time to pick him up significantly reduced the odds of being caught because someone noticed a boat tied up to one of the islands (which are a closed to public access).

Over the two decades Adam had been hunting the area, he had never had a problem. Nobody in the village had ever questioned his activities (Adam and Ricky had told everyone that Adam was a researcher), nor had anyone with law enforcement ever contacted either Ricky or Adam. Because of Ricky's status in the tribe, everyone pretty much left him alone. Despite Adam's good fortune of never having been contacted by any government officials while hunting falcons, he still always carried his "special permits" with him every trip.

Long ago, through experience, research, and conversations with other falconers, Adam had learned of several weak spots wildlife officers, state and federal, had when it came to enforcing falconry laws. Adam had learned that most wildlife enforcement officers knew little about the practice of falconry, the associated laws, and even species identification. Most importantly, Adam found one huge benefit from the fact that at any given time, a dozen or more different entities might be permitted to work, outside of the legal parameters, in the name of research.

Raptors in the northwest corner of the Olympic Peninsula have been studied by three different state universities, the US Geological Survey, the US Fish and Wildlife Service, the Washington Department of Fish and Wildlife, the US Forest Service, the National Park Service, the Makah Tribe, the Quileute Tribe, the Washington State Department of Ecology, the Bureau of Indian Affairs, and the Environmental Protection Agency.

Because of the lack of communication between federal and state agencies, as well as poor communication within the federal and state agencies themselves, one entity never seemed to know when a different group might be conducting a study. Because of this flaw, about twenty years ago, Adam began the annual process of creating three separate letters of authorization to capture falcons for a wildlife study. Adam simply copied the agencies' logos, from their websites, then used those logos to create research authorization letters, all in his fabricated alias name. He made one letter from the Quileute Tribe, one from the US Geological Survey, and one from the Washington Department of Fish and Wildlife. Adam carried the three letters in waterproof zip-lock bags in three different compartments of his Patagonia Ascensionist climbing pack.

Adam always knew that the three governmental agencies whose personnel were most likely to contact him in the field were the Quileute Tribe, the US Fish and Wildlife Service, and the Washington Department of Fish and Wildlife. If someone with the tribe contacted him, he would produce the USFWS letter, if it were the USFWS which contacted him, he would produce the WDFW letter, and if it was the WDFW who contacted him he would provide them with the USGS letter. Adam's finishing touch was the placards he had made to hang on each side of his boat, which simply read "RESEARCH." It was Adam's belief these various agencies had never seen an authentic research authorization letter from the other agencies, and he was correct.

Over periods of trial and error, Ricky and Adam had found the best way to work on recovering eggs and eyas from their nests is to hunt the mainland on rough sea days and hunt the islands of calm days. The mainland and the islands required exact opposite approaches. When hunting nests on the mainland, Adam would need to rappel down the cliff face to the nests, then climb back up. With the islands (which were like giant rock pillars rising straight up from the sea) Adam had to climb up first, get the eggs, then rappel down. On the mainland, Adam could get Ricky to belay him (a skill which Adam had taught Ricky twenty years prior) for safety, but on the islands, mostly Adam was on his own. Because of the fact, Ricky rarely had room to belay him on the islands, Adam had eliminated over half of them as being too unsafe to climb solo.

But before Adam got ahead of himself in his planning, he first had to pack for the extended stay on the Olympic Peninsula. To assure he didn't leave any necessary items home, Adam had long ago made a list which he had laminated. First on his list, was his climbing gear.

Adam did not consider himself to be a rock climber, but he did know enough about it to get the job done safely. Despite the fact he had never had a climbing accident, he had never gotten used to the heights, which still terrified him.

The ropes Adam had chosen for his rock-climbing were the Sterling Evolution VR9 9.8mm x 60m Dry-Core Rope. Since LaPush averages right around 100" of rain per year, having a rope that resists water saturation was vital. In addition to the ropes, Adam packed his harnesses (one for him and one for Ricky), six locking carabiners, ten Black Diamond straight-gate carabiners, two Petzl Verso Lightweight belay/rappel devices, a Petzl STOP assisted-braking descender, a Petzl Sirocco Climbing Helmet with a face shield and handmade leather neck guards (for protection from bird attacks) on the sides and rear, two pairs of gloves, two rolls of 1" tubular webbing, an assortment of pitons and chocks, a climbing hammer, gear sling, and boots.

Next, Adam packed his clothing, raingear, a heavy Carhart coat, egg transport boxes, spotting scope and tripod, stabilized binoculars, six bottles of scotch, about four grams of cocaine, and Joshua Hammer's book THE FALCON THIEF. As Adam packed, he realized how tired he was getting with old age. At fifty-seven, Adam was starting to slow down, and was feeling aches and pains in places he had never had them before. He had already decided this might be his last year before retiring, but he was keeping open the option of going one more year. He had been at the business, of providing birds to Middle Eastern falconers, for almost thirty-seven years and estimated he had netted will over seven-million dollars during that time. The risks of an arrest, a fall, or drowning were very real, and Adam figured he better quit while he was ahead. He had decided not to tell Ricky of his retirement plans, as he knew Ricky's motivation to work hard for him would diminish if he were to know Adam wasn't coming back next year.

After getting everything packed and loaded into his silver 2020 Ford Expedition, Adam was ready to hit the road first thing the next morning.

The evening before his departure found Adam sitting by the fire, in his spacious living room, enjoying a scotch and reflecting back on his career. Thirty-seven years ago, when Adam had been hired by Craig Kretchen (of Masonville, Colorado) to recover eggs and capture adult birds, the market was flooded with people making decent money providing birds of prey to wealthy Middle Easterners. Kretchen was one of the dozens of men who ran around stealing eggs, fledglings, and adult birds from around the world, and smuggling them to the Middle East.

Kretchen's world got turned upside down on June 29th, 1984 when agents from the US Fish and Wildlife Service and state game wardens from Colorado raided his home. Kretchen had been caught up in Operation Falcon, a three-year undercover operation conducted by the US Fish and Wildlife Service and the Canadian Wildlife Services, and he had ended up as one of the sixty-three people arrested in the case.

Operation Falcon was aimed directly at the people who steal and sell illegal raptors, as well as the suspects who purchase and transport the birds and their eggs. In total, the operation netted 5 acquittals, 5 felony convictions, 44 misdemeanor convictions, and 1 civil conviction. Kretchen was sentenced to five years, with all but six months suspended. In the end, Kretchen followed the majority of others in "the business" and permanently suspended his operations, thus leaving a huge demand with a very limited supply. High demand and low supply mean big bucks, and that's when Adam made his move.

Since 1984, Adam had steadily increased his client list, to the point that he rapidly became one of the most prolific raptor dealers in the world. His reputation for providing top-quality birds, with the utmost discretion put him at the top of the list for wealthy Arabian falconers. Interestingly enough, Adam had never even become a blip on the feds radar screen, in-fact no law enforcement investigators, of any kind, had ever even heard of Adam Getty.

After Operation Falcon in the mid-'80s, Adam had seen no real effort to curb raptor smuggling, from any wildlife enforcement organization. Adam believed this was because both the Canadian and U.S. authorities thought they had put an end to the practice.

It was twenty-six years later when Adam's single largest competitor was arrested. In May of 2010, at England's Birmingham International Airport, an astute former security guard (at that time acting as a janitor in the Emirates Airlines first-class lounge), noticed some odd behavior from one of the Emirates passengers (later identified as Jeffrey Lendrum) and alerted airport authorities. Lendrum, a mid-50' former British SAS soldier, was found to be carrying nineteen raptor eggs strapped to his body, reportedly valued at $127,000 (or an average of over $6,600 per egg). In January of 2019 Lendrum, once described as the "The Pablo Escobar of eggs", was sentenced to three years and one month in jail. Lendrum became so famous, for his exploits, that in February of 2020, Author Joshua Hammer released a book about Lendrum's egg theft and smuggling activities, titled THE FALCON THIEF. Almost immediately after Lendrum's arrest, Adam Getty picked up several of Lendrum's former clients and referred several others to trusted acquaintances of his.

Adam was reading THE FALCON THIEF, solely to help him avoid the pitfalls which had led to Lendrum's demise. After what he had heard about Lendrum, and what he had read in the book so far, Adam realized Lendrum committed two major mistakes, which Adam had avoided for decades.

Lendrum's first mistake was smuggling the falcon eggs himself. Adam had never attempted to smuggle anything to the Middle East and believed such actions to be careless and foolhardy. One advantage of his taste for cocaine were the friends he had met who had drug smuggling connections. Over the last seven years, Adam had used these drug smuggling connections to get his birds out of the country and into Mexico where they could easily be picked up by anyone he authorized to take them. This system was much safer and thus far had gone without a hitch.

The second thing Adam thought was a huge mistake of Lendrum's, were the countries he smuggled through. Adam had five countries that he would never try to smuggle into or even through; the United States, Canada, England, Israel, and Germany. All of these countries had very proactive customs agencies whose employees seemed to be beyond reproach.

Adam thought his system for getting the birds and eggs to his customers, was about as perfect as one could get. His drug smuggling connections could get the birds to Mexico without breaking a sweat, then it was up to the customers to get their birds to their homes. Wealthy Emiratis (citizens of the UAE) were not subject to customs searches or inquiries in their homeland, and thus the only risk they faced was during the brief time they were in Mexico. Due to that slight amount of risk, Adam always instructed his customers to send an expendable employee to pick up the birds, rather than coming to Mexico themselves, but because of the Arab pride, many did not heed his advice, but that was on them.

Over the years several of his customers had complained about having to go to Mexico to pick up their orders and had told Adam it didn't make any sense. Adam would always answer the same, telling them it was either that, or they could find their birds elsewhere.

Getty smiled as he realized that by the time he was to retire next year, he would have sold thousands of raptors for millions of dollars over almost forty years, and had never even been questioned by law enforcement. He was way more successful than Lendrum had ever hoped to be, and had never come even close to being caught. Maybe when he retired, he would anonymously write a book detailing his exploits. Hell, with his record of success, they might even make his story into a movie.

I wonder who will play me in the movie? Maybe Harrison Ford, if he doesn't kill himself flying first, thought Adam.

CHAPTER 23

It was just after noon when Dean "Tiny" Reese stopped by the Shereford's house. Tiny tried the door but found it to be locked, so he began pounding until he finally awakened the brothers.

It was Wade Shereford who reached the door first, "Who the fuck is it?" Wade yelled.

"Tiny. Dude open the door," Tiny yelled.

When the door opened, Tiny realized the downside of waking Wade up, as a 300-plus pound Wade Shereford stood before him in nothing but his tighty whities.

"What's up, bro?" Freddie Shereford asked as he came out of one of the back bedrooms.

"I'm putting together an order for a half-pound of black tar (Mexican heroin) and wanted to see if you two dipshits wanted in?" asked Tiny.

"How much for an OZ?" Wade asked.

"Two-grand. It's a damn good deal," Tiny said.

"Only problem is we are about two-grand short of two-grand," answered Freddie.

"I'm getting the order together now, but I won't need the cash until the twenty-sixth. So, are you in?" asked Tiny.

"Nah, put us down for a half-ounce," Freddie said. "We can come up with that, then if we can come up with another thousand we will buy the whole ounce."

"Right on. I will save you a full OZ, and if you can swing it, that's good, if not, I can get rid of it easy," said Tiny. "Take it easy ladies."

Once Tiny was out the door Wade asked Freddie, "How are we gonna come up with a thousand bucks in two weeks?"

"That's only three elk. Get your fat-ass dressed and let's go kill some elk." Freddie told his brother.

Twenty minutes later the Sherefords were on their way out of White Swan, Washington on the way to the Selah, WA area. An hour and a half later the Sherefords were creeping their pickup up the Durr Road, looking for some elk to kill close to the road.

After driving only eight miles up the road, the men came across a small group of eleven elk, all cows, and calves. The elk were not only uphill from the road (a huge advantage for bringing the carcasses out) but were actually standing in the middle of a two-track dirt side road. Since both men had loaded their rifles when they first started up the Durr Road, all they had to do was get a steady rest and start firing. Freddie, who was seated on the passenger side, began firing out the window, while Wade exited the driver's side and laid his rifle across the truck's hood to fire.

Freddie's rifle was a .300 Winchester Magnum capable of holding only four cartridges, while Wade shot a 30-.06 which held five rounds.

When the shooting ended, the men had four elk down and had wounded an additional two, which they didn't bother to pursue any further.

The men then drove past the side road, then backed up it, stopping when the first dead elk was right behind their truck. The two brothers took only seventeen minutes to gut and load the first elk, before backing up to the second elk to repeat the process. One-hour and forty-six minutes after they had fired their first round, the men were on their way home with four dead elk, leaving two elk they had wounded for the coyotes to eat.

"We are gonna be skinning elk all night," Wade complained.

"Yeah, but tomorrow we will come home with sixteen-hundred bucks. If we have to, we can go kill another elk or two next week, and we can buy a full OZ," said Freddie.

Once at home, Wade backed the truck past his boat, a broken down car, and the gill nets spread over the yard full of weeds, and into the dilapidated detached two-car garage. The garage was cluttered with old car parts, a stripped-down Honda ATV, bags of empty Budweiser cans, and old antlers from elk and deer shot by the Sherefords.

A come-along hoist, hanging from the rafters, allowed the men to lift each elk out of the truck by the rear legs, hanging them vertically for the ease of skinning. Properly skinning an elk can be a time-consuming task, even for experienced hunters, but the extra time and attention pays off by producing cleaner and healthier meat. This time the men swore to take extra care of the meat, so they could get top dollar in Tri-Cities.

The next morning, the brothers first laid down a clean plastic tarp in the bed of the truck before backing their truck back into the garage. As Wade backed the truck up to each hanging elk, Freddie dropped each elk into the truck by simply cutting the rope which held them hanging. With all four elk loaded up, Wade put another clean tarp over the top of the elk, then held it down by draping a tow-chain over the tarp and topping it off with four old worn-out tires from his yard.

It was 10:15 when the Shereford brothers pulled up to the back door of the Buena Comida Restaurant on Clearwater Avenue in Kennewick. Freddie jumped out of the truck and began pounding on the backdoor of the kitchen.

When Lucia opened the backdoor, even Freddie could read the disappointment on her face.

"What's wrong honey? Not who you were expecting?" Freddie asked Lucia.

"I will get my uncle," Lucia said before closing the door and disappearing into the kitchen.

When the backdoor opened again, Felipe immediately asked, "Did you take better care of the meat this time?"

"Take a look for yourself," Wade answered as he threw back the tarp.

Felipe climbed in the back of the truck and closely examined all four elk before speaking, "This is more like it. If you bring animals like this, everyone will be happy."

"Two-thousand dollars for the lot and we are out of here," Wade responded.

"Sixteen-hundred, and you will bring two of them in here, and deliver the other two to my brother at the South Ely Street restaurant," Felipe replied.

Wade could see Freddie was coming in to argue, so he cut him off before he could answer Felipe, "You have a deal. Thank you."

"Move the elk. I will get your money," Felipe said.

Ten minutes later, Felipe returned with sixteen-hundred dollars, which he handed to Wade.

"I told my brother to expect you soon," Felipe told the men. "He will be waiting by the door. With that, Felipe turned and shut the door behind himself.

"What the hell happened to you dude. What was that about? You just bent over for him, and now we gotta drive all over hell delivering his elk," Freddie told his brother. "You didn't even get us a bottle. What the hell man. Why did you go all pussy on me?"

"Are you kidding?" Wade asked, "That dude doesn't scare you?"

"No man. I could take him out with one punch," said Freddie.

"I'm telling you man, don't fuck with that guy. There's something about him. He scares the shit out of me, and I don't even know why," Wade said.

"You're losing it man," Freddie said as they drove to the South Ely Street Buena Comida.

"Right in there. On the tarp on the floor," Antonio Vargas told the two brothers, while he pointed to a spot on the floor of his kitchen.

As Antonio inspected the elk meat, he turned to Wade Shereford and said, "This is the way meat should be processed. This is clean, fresh, and ready to cut up. You bring us this quality, and we will take all you can bring us. Just remember to keep your mouths shut and we will have a long and healthy relationship, but talk too much and there will be nothing long or healthy in your futures. Understood?"

It was Freddie who answered, "You've got it. You can trust us to keep our mouths shut. We don't want no problems with you guys. We're cool."

Once back in the truck and pointed towards home, Wade turned to Freddie and mocked him with a whiny voice, "Oh please Mr. Antonio, you can trust us, please. Let me kiss your ass to prove I am loyal to you. Oh please."

"Bite me asshole. You said it, these guys are scary," answered Freddie.

"Hey, in all seriousness, we can make some real money here, if we just do it the same way each time. Whack a few elk, gut them, skin them, and keep them clean and we get top dollar. I mean really. We just made $1,600 in two days, that's $400 a day for each of us. How else can you make that kind of money?" Wade said, "But we gotta be careful with these guys."

"I'm with ya. Maybe every other week or so, we can do a hunt," Freddie answered.

CHAPTER 24

It was March 23rd when Rashid Shaheen's phone indicated an incoming call from Sheikh Saeed Damadaran, the man Rashid obtained Adam Getty's contact information from.

"Hello, my friend. How are you on this day? Well, I hope?" said Rashid.

"Never better. God has indeed blessed me, my friend," Saeed replied.

"What may I do for you, Saeed?"

"No, it is I who can do something for you. I was just speaking with Sheikh Abdullah Amjad and he invited me to his home to look over the bird he had just acquired," Saeed said.

"And what bird did Sheikh Amjad recently acquire?" asked Rashid.

"An absolutely beautiful and endangered chaco eagle, which is also called the crowned solitary eagle. The bird is huge, powerful, and only two or three years of age. Abdullah paid $375,000 US dollars for the bird. I would have gladly paid $500,000 for that magnificent creature, but it was God's will that Abdullah receives the eagle," said Saeed.

"That is indeed good news, and not to be selfish, but you said you had something for me?" asked Rashid.

"I only have information," Saeed responded. "Abdullah told me he had just contacted Mr. Getty to place an order for four peregrine falcon eggs but was told his order might not be filled until next year because he had several pending orders including the next one which was for six eggs. Since I know you ordered six falcon eggs, it sounds like you are next up."

"That is excellent news indeed. I look forward to adding to my collection, and building an unbeatable racing team," said Rashid.

"I too look forward to that day, my friend," Saeed answered. "Although I do have one word of advice for you, in regards to picking up your order."

"And what advice might that be?" asked Rashid.

"When it comes time to pick up your order in Mexico, send an assistant of yours in your jet, and don't go with him on that flight. Mr. Getty has made arrangements with the local and federal authorities in Mexico, but there is still no reason for you to expose yourself to any risk at all. You can replace your plane and an assistant, but you only get one life," Saeed said.

"As you know, I just purchased my Bombardier Global 8000, for sixty-five million US dollars, should I charter a jet for the trip to Mexico instead?" asked Rashid.

"I see no need my friend. I have sent my plane there four times and have never had a problem. They may be animals there, but they know better than to steal from us." Saeed responded.

"Thank you, my friend, I will certainly heed your advice," answered Rashid.

CHAPTER 25

At 7:30 AM Lisa's cell phone rang.

"Who is it this early?" Emily asked as she was just starting on her second cup of coffee for the morning.

Lisa looked at the phone, and replied, "Kevin Webber from Dayton."

"Morning Kevin. I'm guessing you have something for me?" Lisa inquired.

"I sure do. I am standing over a big fat cow elk, lying dead in a wheat field. Do you want it?"

"Absolutely. Same place at 8:30 tomorrow morning?" Lisa asked.

"Works for me, but I want to warn you we are getting to the end of this depredation hunt, so there probably won't be any more elk available for a long time, at least from me," Kevin replied.

"At that grain elevator where we meet, if a full bottle fell from my truck onto the ground, and I just left it, would you pick it up or just leave it too?" Lisa asked.

"That's a weird question, but I'll bite. I would pick it up," Kevin said.

"What kind of bottle would you like it to be?" Lisa asked.

"Oh, gotcha. Well, I see a lot of Jameson whiskey bottles lying around, and I pick every one of them up. I hate litter," Kevin answered.

"Very good. You better keep an eye out, because I think you might find more litter behind that elevator," said Lisa. "See you in the morning."

Lisa didn't know if Kevin had help skinning these elk, but she knew he was putting in a lot of extra effort to get them high-quality clean elk meat, and a little thank you gift goes a long way.

After hanging up with Kevin, Lisa called Joe, "Morning sunshine. Are you up and at 'em yet?"

"Jesus Christ Lisa, it's too early to be so cheery. What's up?" asked Joe.

Lisa asked, "Wanna go see your Tri-Cities girlfriend tomorrow?"

"Do we have another elk I take it?" Joe asked.

"Yep, same plan, same place and same time," Lisa answered. "I would like to get out of here by 2:00 this afternoon if that works for you."

"You want me to check on the motel, and make some reservations?" Joe asked.

"Let me give Amy Higgins a call first and see if they can make it. I will call you right back after I talk to Amy. In the meantime, can you please make sure all of the covert cameras are fully charged?"

"Will do. Talk to you soon."

Next, Lisa called Amy Higgins, but the call went straight to voicemail. Lisa then tried Dave Briggs but had the same results. Desperate to find a detective, Lisa called Captain Jacobsen.

"Good morning captain. I won't bother asking if you were already up and going," Lisa said.

"You're learning. That's a good sign," said the Captain. "What can I do for you, Lisa?"

"I got a call from Kevin Webber this morning, and he has another elk for us, so I agreed to meet him tomorrow morning," Lisa explained. "I tried Amy and Dave first, but their phones went straight to voicemail, so you're it."

"Amy and Dave are on a case, and won't be back until the day after tomorrow, so I will be your backup. What time do you want me over there, and where?"

"We will probably get to the Kennewick Red Lion around six this evening and will have dinner there if you would like to join us," said Lisa.

"You've got it. See you at six. You need anything from me?" asked Jacobsen.

"Nothing I can think of. See you later," Lisa said.

After getting off the phone with the captain, Lisa sent Joe a text, "We will need three rooms if you can make the reservations. Then just pick me up at my house at 2:00. Also, Amy and Dave were not available so Captain Jacobsen will be the one coming over."

"Oh boy. Lucky us. See you at 2," was Joe's response.

What a grump, Lisa thought.

After her calls, Lisa returned to the family room and joined Emily on the couch. As soon as Lisa sat down right against Emily, their golden retriever Mayhem shoved her way between them, pushing them apart, and made sure both women understood she was to be the center of attention and was the only one worthy of that attention.

"I wish I could take you with me May, but I just can't," Lisa explained to Mayhem who sat patiently staring at Lisa, "Sorry girl."

"What about me Mayhem. I'm not good enough for you now?" Emily asked Mayhem as she went back and forth between her and Lisa.

"I take it this is the same place you dealt with on the last trip?" Emily asked.

"Yep, same place. We are trying to determine who everyone involved is. This will probably be my last or second to last trip. After this SIU will go in and serve warrants on the restaurant, and conduct interviews. Then back to uniform," Lisa replied.

"Just be careful," said Emily as she headed off for work.

"You too. See you tomorrow evening," Lisa answered.

Lisa spent the remainder of the morning packing, catching up on emails, and considering how to approach the Buena Comida restaurants. Originally, Captain Jacobsen had allowed Lisa and Joe to pick which one of the Buena Comida restaurants they wanted to work first, but without knowing how much information the restaurants share back and forth, Lisa figured there might be a good chance the other restaurant had already heard about her and Joe. If that were the case, how could they explain why they would try to sell to the other Buena Comida when they had an established relationship with the Clearwater Avenue restaurant. Without getting truly inside with one of the Buena Comida restaurants, Lisa saw no way to learn of any potentially illegal activities at the other Buena Comida restaurant.

By 12:10 PM Lisa was packed and ready to go. The more she had thought about the situation with the Buena Comida restaurants, the more she began to think the whole operation would work better with Joe doing the UC work alone. Clearly, both Joe's favorite waitress and her uncle had preferred dealing with Joe. With the attention Joe had received from Lucia he would potentially be able to gain far more information without his fake girlfriend by his side.

Lisa looked at the clock and remembered she needed to go buy Kevin a little gift, so she quickly jumped in her personal truck and rushed to the store to pick up a fifth of Jameson whiskey. Immediately upon arriving home, Lisa wrapped the bottle in bubble-wrap, put it in a box and gift wrapped it with birthday wrapping paper. Lisa figured with the captain there, she needed to be a little more discreet. Additionally, if it was decided Joe would do the UC solo, there would be no reason for Lisa to be the one to meet up with Kevin, so Joe would have to present the gift, and Lisa didn't want Joe knowing there was a fifth of whiskey in the truck during this detail.

At 2:08 PM Joe pulled into Lisa's driveway and walked to the door.

"Ready to go," Joe asked.

"Yep, let's hit it," Lisa replied.

On the drive south, Lisa continued to mull over the idea of Joe doing the UC contacts alone. On one hand, Lisa knew the restaurant employees only dealt with Joe when they sold the elk, and she supposed it may be because she is a caucasian American or it could have been because they liked dealing with a man better. Either way, Lisa grinned while she realized that the restaurant crew would probably not even notice if she weren't there with Joe.

On the other hand, Joe hadn't exactly been totally reliable or stable of late, but he had gotten the job done, and she still had faith in his honesty and integrity. Then there was the matter of safety, two officers are better than one when it came to safety, but in this case, she wasn't certain that was necessarily the case. As they had been told in the undercover class, when an undercover contact goes bad, it normally goes bad very quickly. If the bad guys were going to cause you harm, it would essentially be an ambush, as they would have time to set the stage for your arrival.

Since it was Joe's butt on the line, Lisa decided she better discuss it with him before they seriously considered it.

"Joe, what are your thoughts on doing the UC contacts alone, while I help with surveillance and backup?"

"Tired of me already?" Joe asked.

"Yeah, but that's beside the point," Lisa joked. "It's just that I think they might be more open and forthcoming without me there. On the last contact, I'm not sure anyone at the restaurant even knew I was there, so it's not like they are going to miss me."

"I'm cool with it. It's not like we are dealing with drug cartels or anything. This is a pretty small-time criminal organization, so far made up of an old man and his niece. I think I can handle them, plus I have the covert cameras, and we both have the Life360 tracking app on our phones. I will be fine, even if you abandon me," Joe replied.

Life360 is a free phone app the instructors told everyone about in the UC class. The app allows people to track the movements of their friends and family in real-time on Google Maps. Lisa and Joe both had installed and had activated the app so they could tell where the other one is with an accuracy of a few feet.

"So, seriously, what do you think?" Lisa asked.

"I think you're probably right. I may be able to make more progress without you there. For one thing, I think I can probably pick Lucia's brain a lot easier without you there," Joe responded.

"I'm not sure it's her brain you are interested in," Lisa said with a smile.

"Why do you have to always take everything to the gutter," Joe said while smiling for the first time that afternoon.

For the remainder of the trip, Joe and Lisa made small talk about the agency, and some of the officers in it. At one point in their conversation, Lisa asked Joe if he was still entertaining the idea of moving, which he had previously expressed to Lisa.

"I don't know. Somedays I love this job and where I live, but on the majority of days, I want to get the hell out of the Okanogan Valley and this job, and then I would never look back. I'm pretty sure I will never fit in the community and have pretty much given up on trying. So yeah, I still think about leaving," Joe answered.

"Where would you go? What would you do?"

"I don't know. About once a week my dad bugs me about coming home to take over the construction company, but I just don't know what to do. I like Mesa, Arizona a whole better than Oroville, WA especially when I'm shoveling the four feet of snow out of my driveway," Joe responded.

"Well, just know that no matter what your decision, I will always support you, but that doesn't mean I have to be happy about it. I don't want you to go anywhere. You are my partner and one of my best friends, even though you can be a bonehead at times," Lisa said.

"Me a bonehead? Boy, that's the pot calling the kettle black, whatever the hell that means," answered Joe.

Changing the subject, Joe said, "I agree the UC might be more productive with me going solo, so let's run it by the captain when we see him."

"Sounds good," Lisa agreed.

"What's with the gift-wrapped box. Brown-nosing the captain?" Joe asked.

"Nah, it's a thank you gift from us to Kevin Webber for all of the hard work he has done for us on this," Lisa replied.

"So, what did "we" get him?" Joe asked.

Lisa answered, "A fifth of Jameson, and let's keep that between us."

"Wow, when do I get a gift like that?" Joe asked.

"As soon as you gut and pack out two elk, then skin and quarter them," Lisa said.

"Guess no Jameson for me," Joe said.

"Certainly not today," Lisa said.

"Funny," said Joe.

By 5:47 PM Joe and Lisa were in Kennewick just coming across the Yakima River when Lisa sent Captain Jacobsen a text, "Should be there in ten minutes. You want to meet in the bar at 6:15?"

"I'm already there. See you when you get here," the captain replied.

Lisa and Joe once again checked into their rooms at the Red Lion and headed down to meet up with Captain Jacobsen in the bar.

After handshakes and greetings all the way around, the three returned to their corner table, where the captain ordered the first round.

"Well, are you two all set to sell another one tomorrow?" asked the captain.

"We are, but we also have something to kick around with you," answered Lisa.

"Okay, let's hear it, but if it's a request for a raise, you're out of luck," said Jacobsen.

"What's your thought on sending Joe in solo tomorrow? We both think he would have better success without me there," Lisa asked.

"Better success? You two are 100% on your UC work. You went in once and they bought the only game meat you had to offer. I would say that's pretty good success," answered Jacobsen.

"We realize that. It's just that we both think the employees are more open to speaking to just me. Last time we were there both Lucia and her Uncle Felipe barely spoke a word to Lisa. Lisa and I both agree the contacts should be more productive without her there," Joe added.

Captain Jacobsen kept spinning a cardboard beer glass coaster between his fingers, while he was mulling over their proposal.

"Are you positive you are good with this Joe?", asked the captain.

"Yeah, I think it will be more productive and no less safe," Joe replied.

"What about you Lisa? Do you agree this is the better approach to this UC?"

"I do. We will be right there, and clearly, they liked dealing with him better anyway, and in all seriousness, Joe can probably get a lot of information out of Lucia without me there," Lisa added.

"Alright, it looks like we have a plan. I want to make damn sure you have as many covert cameras going as you possibly can and keep your phone on in case we need to talk to Jose," said the captain.

After dinner was done, Lisa decided to head to her room so she could call Emily before too late, leaving Joe and Captain Jacobsen alone at the table.

"I will see you guys in the morning. Eight o'clock in the lobby?" Lisa asked.

"See you at eight," Joe answered. "And I won't be late."

Once in her room, Lisa first sent Kevin Webber a text, "It will be Joe Ramirez by himself meeting you tomorrow. Same plan except your gift will be in a gift-wrapped box instead of on the ground. Thanks again!"

"I have that effect on women. Meet me once and they never come back. Thanks for the gift, and I will take good care of Joe. Take care," Kevin wrote back.

At 07:55 AM Lisa came down to the lobby to find Joe sitting on a couch talking with the captain.

While tapping on the face of his watch, Joe said, "Good afternoon. Glad you could join us. We were worried you weren't going to make it."

"Very funny. What, did you sleep on that couch last night to make sure you were on time?" Lisa asked.

"Whatever it takes to get the job done," Joe said with a grin. "Are you ready?"

"Yep, just have to put our suitcases in the captain's truck, and we can hit it," Lisa answered.

"Mine and the captain's are already in there. I know I'm supposed to meet Kevin at a grain elevator, but I have no idea where it is," Joe stated.

"I put it in the truck's GPS under "Elevator". It should take you about thirty minutes to get there, so if you leave now, you will be right on time." Lisa answered, "Good luck Joe. Don't forget to take a photo and a DNA sample from the elk, and turn the cameras on."

"Got it," Joe answered.

As Joe took off, Lisa loaded into the captain's truck with him.

"We have time to check out the South Ely Street Buena Comida and pull some license numbers from the cars there," said Jacobsen. "Since Joe has all of the cameras, we will have to use our cell phones to take photos of the cars and their license plates, but if you see anyone at all, pretend to be speaking into your phone."

"Got it," Lisa replied.

By 8:20 AM Lisa was snapping photos of the only two cars parked at the South Ely Street Buena Comida.

"Pretty dead this early, but one of these cars must belong to the manager," Lisa said as she typed the license numbers into her computer and hit send.

"Yep, the 2020 Ford F-250 is registered to Antonio Garcia Vargas from West Richland, WA. He has to be brothers with Felipe Vargas from the Clearwater restaurant," Lisa said.

Twenty minutes later, Jacobsen pulled his truck alongside the rear of a closed Sears store, with a straight shot view of the Clearwater Buena Comida.

"Is this good for you too? Can you see the back door okay?" asked Jacobsen.

"Perfect," Lisa said as she viewed the restaurant with her Leupold binoculars.

At about 9:10, Lisa received a text from Joe, "Ten minutes out. Kevin said thanks for the gift."

Lisa had left her phone sitting on the console box, on the seat between Lisa and the captain. She turned beet red as she realized the captain was also reading the text Joe had just sent.

"What gift?" the captain asked.

"I just got him a thank you gift for all the extra work he did to get these elk ready for us."

"Scotch, whiskey, or bourbon, and what brand?" the captain asked with a wide smile on his face,

"A fifth of Jameson Irish whiskey, and yes I know it's a policy violation to carry alcohol in a state vehicle, but it's at least in an undercover vehicle and it's wrapped," Lisa answered.

"I don't have a problem with it. It's a good way to reward someone for hard work," answered Jacobsen.

"Here's our boy," the captain added pointing to Joe's truck as it backed up to the kitchen door of the restaurant.

While Joe was approaching the rear kitchen door he noticed three of the same four vehicles they had seen parked there before. He wondered if Lucia would be there.

Joe pounded on the door then waited. Soon the door opened and Uncle Felipe stepped out.

"Jose, you are back so soon. You are a very effective hunter. Let me take a look at what you have," Felipe said as he climbed into the back of the truck.

Joe watched as Felipe carefully inspected the elk carcass, before he addressed Joe, "I will give you four-hundred dollars, but then we won't need any more meat for a long time. We had other hunters bring in several elk, and we are getting pretty full up."

"That's too bad. I just found a great spot to hunt elk. It's very productive," Joe answered. "How about the other Buena Comida restaurant? Would they want some?"

"I don't have any say in how the other restaurant is operated. The restaurants run independently, so I have no idea if they would want it or not, but I would guess they would not. It is highly illegal you know."

"Yes, I am aware," Joe answered.

"If you will please carry the meat into the same spot in the kitchen, I will get your money," said Felipe.

After Joe had carried in the first hindquarter, he turned to find Lucia standing behind him.

"Good morning Jose. Where's your girlfriend?" Lucia asked.

"She is not my girlfriend; she is just a friend. As a matter of fact, she's gay. She's married to a woman," Joe said.

"That's very good to hear," Lucia said.

"What's good to hear, that she is just a friend or that she is gay?" Joe asked with a sheepish grin.

"Both," Lucia answered with a smile. "Everyone has a right to be happy."

"Do you live close by?" Lucia asked.

Joe immediately experienced a wave of panic, as he realized he couldn't remember where he and Lisa had decided to call home.

After drawing a blank, it finally came to Joe, "River Rapids in Pasco for right now. I am staying with my friend Anna and her wife until I can find something more permanent. I'm a builder by trade and am working on getting settled here for good."

"Can I make a lunch for you, before we open?" asked Lucia.

"Only if you will join me," Joe answered as Felipe walked back to the kitchen.

"I'm sorry. I have to work," Lucia answered.

"You are entitled to a break, take an hour and keep this man company," Felipe said from behind Lucia.

"Thank you, uncle, I will get started on our lunch. Is there anything, in particular, you would like?" she asked Joe.

"Absolutely anything. I am sure it's all excellent, thank you," Joe responded.

After Lucia had left to process their lunch, Felipe handed him the $400 and said, "Lucia has been waiting for your return. She likes you much. She is my sister's little girl, and she is like a daughter to me, so do not hurt her in any way or we will have a big problem. Do you understand me?"

"That is not something you need to worry about. I am an honorable man," Joe answered.

"Which is just what a bad man would say," answered Felipe.

"I guess that's true," Joe answered.

"Jose, would you be interested in a permanent job?" asked Felipe.

"Sure, what kind of job?" Joe asked.

"A job which pays very well, but one which requires complete confidentiality," Felipe said.

"Sure, what do I need to do?" Joe asked.

"My brother Antonio is the man you will need to talk to. He manages the South Ely Street Buena Comida. If you would like, I will call him and tell him you will be over after lunch. Do you have time to meet with him today?" asked Felipe.

"Absolutely. I look forward to meeting him," Joe said. "With this job would I be working in his restaurant?"

"No, he has another business, working on large trucks, and he needs someone who has mechanical skills. I have already told him about how you fixed our dishwasher, and he is interested," Felipe said.

"Excellent. I look forward to it. Thank you for giving me a chance," Joe replied.

As Joe walked through the kitchen to the dining area, he passed Lucia, and three older Hispanic women, all busy cooking away.

Joe asked the three women, "¿Hay algo que pueda hacer para ayudar? (Is there anything I can do to help?)"

The woman who appeared to be the oldest answered, "Gracias pero estamos bien. (Thank you, but we are fine)."

As Joe was leaving the kitchen for the dining area, he heard one of the older women say, "Es lindo y educado. Mejor no lo dejes ir. (He's cute and polite. You better not let him go.)" This comment led to giggling and laughter from all three of the older women.

Joe then heard Lucia's voice, softly say, "Para, me estás avergonzando (Stop it. You are embarrassing me)," which brought a smile to Joe's face.

Joe chose a table, in the empty dining area, by the large front window. As he sat waiting for Lucia to join him, Joe realized he better update Lisa on his status, so he got up and walked to the bathroom.

Once in a bathroom stall, Joe typed out a quick text to Lisa, "All is good. Got the $400. Eating lunch here now, then I'm heading over to the South Ely restaurant to have an interview with Antonio for a job that "requires complete confidentiality". Felipe said it will be working on a truck. I will keep you posted when I can. Do not reply right now."

After sending the message, Joe erased it from his phone, washed his hands, then returned to the table, only to find Lucia had brought out two plates of food, two glasses of water, and a Dos Equis beer (which she had put in front of Joe).

"It looks delicious. What is it?"

Lucia answered, "Ensalada Fajita. It is made from marinated and grilled meat, sautéed onions, green peppers, guacamole, pico de gallo, and sour cream on a bed of fresh lettuce. The meat is elk meat, but we don't tell the customers that. I hope you like it."

"I am sure I will, and thank you," Joe said.

After taking a few bites Joe said, "Oh my God this is delicious. It's the best I have ever had."

"Thank you. I'm glad you like it," answered Lucia.

"Lucia, tell me a little about yourself," Joe asked.

"I'm twenty-eight years old, single and I was born and raised right here in Tri-Cities. I went to high school at Pasco High, which I hated, and now I am just about finished with my master's degree in family nursing at the Tri-Cities campus of W.S.U. At the end of May, I will graduate, and will receive certification as a DNP Family Nurse Practitioner," Lucia said with pride.

"A nurse practitioner? Wow, that's just like one step under a doctor, right?" Joe asked.

"Well not quite, but close yes," answered Lucia. "I was the first in my family to graduate from college."

"What about your parents? Are they around here?" Joe asked.

"My father died of cancer when I was twelve, and you just spoke to my mother. She's the one who said you are cute," Lucia said. "I will properly introduce you after we eat."

"I'm so sorry to hear about your father," Joe answered.

"It was a very long time ago but thank you."

"And no husband, or boyfriend for you?" Joe asked.

"Nope, just me. I'm unattached," Lucia said.

"It amazes me a woman so smart and beautiful hasn't been scooped up by someone by now," Joe answered, which brought a blush from Lucia.

"Thank you, now how about you?" Lucia asked.

"I'm from Fresno, California, which is where I went to high school and college. I graduated with a degree in chemistry, which I have never used. My father owns a residential construction company, which I worked at for years. I've never been married and have only had one serious girlfriend ever. I too am unattached."

"What brought you to Tri-Cities?" Lucia asked.

"A job, or at least what I was told was going to be a job," Joe went on. "My father had a friend who was also in the construction business, and he worked up here. One thing led to another and my father's friend offered me my own crew and said I would be his construction manager, but right after I got here, he went bankrupt. I liked the area and decided to stick around and find work here."

"I just realized I don't even know your last name," Lucia said.

"Mendez. Jose Ricardo Mendez at your pleasure, and your full name?" Joe replied.

"Lucia Maria Bailey," said as she extended her hand for a handshake. "Glad to meet you, Mr. Mendez."

When Jose took Lucia's hand to shake, she turned his palm up and started running her fingers over the palm side of his hand.

"Your hands do not feel like the hands of a construction worker," Lucia said.

"I moisturize," Joe said which brought a good laugh out of both of them.

"I manage construction. I am normally the boss, so I don't drive nails and carry lumber anymore." Joe said hoping she bought it.

"That is much safer," Lucia said with a smile, "for your hands."

"Bailey doesn't sound like a traditional Mexican name. Are the Bailey's from southern Mexico, or the north?"

"From the far north. My father was from North Dakota, and came to Tri-Cities to work on the Hanford project," Lucia said.

"Do you like to dance Mr. Mendez?" Lucia asked.

"I'm not very good at it, and have only tried it a couple of times in high school, but yes, I like it," Joe answered.

"I also like to dance," Lucia said with a smile.

"Would you like to go dancing with me, Ms. Bailey?" Joe said with a smile.

"I would love to go dancing with you Mr. Mendez," Lucia said. "This is my last week of night classes, and I will be done the day after tomorrow. I work days at the restaurant on weekends, but I'm free on weekend evenings."

"Well then, how would you like to go dancing with me on Saturday evening?" Joe asked.

"That would be great. I would like that," Lucia continued. "What is your phone number?"

Once again, Joe could feel the anxiety rising, as he struggled to remember his undercover phone number, "509-555-8375" Joe said, hoping he was correct.

Lucia then put Joe's number in her phone and hit the dial icon. Immediately Joe's phone began ringing.

"There, now you have my number too. Give me a call to work out the details, but I really look forward to our dance night," said Lucia.

"As do I," Joe responded. "I guess I better get going. I am supposed to go over to the Ely Street restaurant and talk to your Uncle Antonio about a job."

Suddenly Joe noticed Lucia tense up and become very quiet.

"Is something wrong. You look like you have seen a ghost?" Joe asked.

"Be very careful with Antonio. He is not a good man, in fact, I think he is into some very bad things," Lucia whispered to Joe.

"Like what?" Joe asked.

Lucia looked around nervously, and said, "I don't know of anything in particular, it's mostly a hunch on my part. Now, before you go, you must meet my mother."

Joe followed Lucia back into the kitchen, where the same three women were still working away.

"Momma, I would like you to meet Jose Mendez," Lucia said to her mother.

"I am very glad to meet you, ma'am," Joe said. "You have a wonderful daughter."

"Most of the time you are right Jose, but she can be a handful sometimes," said Mrs. Bailey. "Watch yourself with her."

Joe then heard one of the women behind Mrs. Bailey say, "Sus bebés serán hermosas (Their babies will be beautiful)" followed by schoolgirl giggling.

Lucia ignored the comment and told her mother about their plans to go dancing this coming weekend, which made her mother smile.

"You be careful with this one Jose, and if she gives you any trouble, just let me know," said Lucia's mother.

"Thanks for the offer, and I may be calling," Joe said.

Before he turned to leave, Lucia's mother hugged Joe, and said, "You seem like a very nice young man."

"Thank you, and so do you," Joe answered before realizing how it came out. "I don't mean you seem like a nice young man. I just mean you seem very nice too. I guess I better quit while I'm ahead. It was very nice to meet you."

"I look forward to your call Jose, and I will see you soon. Remember what I said about your next stop," Lucia warned.

"I will be careful," Joe said as he walked away. "I will talk to you soon."

It was 11 AM when Joe started his truck and pulled out of the parking lot. Almost immediately his phone rang, and the caller ID said, Anna.

"You're on speaker. So, what's the deal on this job interview with Antonio?" Lisa asked.

"You pretty much know what I know, which isn't much. After we were done with the elk transaction, Felipe asked me if I wanted a job. Of course, I said yes since I am supposed to be a struggling unemployed builder," Joe went on. "Felipe said he had talked to his brother about my mechanical skills, and his brother would like to talk to me about a job working on trucks and said the work is highly confidential."

"A highly confidential job working on trucks. Now that otta make for an interesting story for the trip home," added Lisa.

"Joe, do you have your personal info memorized? I mean your address, phone, email, social security number, the works?" asked the captain.

"Yep, I've got it covered," Joe answered.

"Alright, we are going to pass you up here ahead, so we can be set up when you get there. Just be careful," Captain Jacobsen warned.

CHAPTER 26

At 11:38 AM Joe pulled into the front parking lot of the Ely Street restaurant. Upon entering the building, Joe provided his UC name to the woman at the counter and asked if Antonio was available. The woman disappeared into the back and came back out with a larger version of Felipe.

"Jose, I'm Antonio Vargas. I have heard all about your skills, and I think we may have a place for you. Would you follow me back to my office?" Antonio said, before turning and walking towards the back without waiting for a response from Joe.

Once in the tiny cramped office, Antonio shut the door and sat behind his desk, facing Joe who was seated in the only other chair in the room.

First, I must see some identification; a driver's license and social security card. We have to make sure we do everything legal here.

Joe dug through his wallet and produced both documents, which Antonio slapped on his printer/copier to copy. After scanning the cards, Antonio returned them to Joe.

"Jose, would you join me in a Don Julio?" Antonio asked as he poured two glasses of the tequila.

"Sure, but only one. I have to drive," Joe replied.

"Responsible and careful. Two qualities I respect," said Antonio.

As Joe sipped his tequila, Antonio explained, "We were already down one employee, and then we recently lost another employee and we need a replacement right away. We are falling way behind on our work there. Whether you take the job or not, you will need to keep this conversation strictly between the two of us, nobody else. Not Felipe and not Lucia. Agreed?"

"Of course. Not a problem," Joe answered.

"I also operate another business where we do specialty work on trucks, and I think a man who has your mechanical abilities would be perfect, as long as you can keep your mouth shut. The position will start at $7,000 a month, but we work long hours. With this job, if you were to talk too much, outside of work, it could mean very severe ramifications to you and your family. Are you still interested?" Antonio asked.

"For $7,000 a month, I will do just about anything," Joe answered.

"Do you have family nearby Jose?" Antonio asked.

"No, they are all in California," Joe answered.

"Alright, I think the best way to explain what this job is all about it to take you there and let Gabriel explain it to you," Antonio explained. "This is the point of no return, right here. If I take you to my shop and introduce you to Gabriel, and you ever say a word to anyone about our work, it will mean the end of your life. This is very serious business. Now, do you want to go see it?"

"Count me in," Joe answered.

"One more thing before we go. Do you use any drugs at all?" asked Antonio.

"No, why?" asked Joe.

"Because we do not allow it for our employees. We are very strict about it," Antonio answered before reaching in a desk drawer and coming out with a DTK 6-panel 5-minute drug test cup. "Take this into the bathroom, fill it up, and come back here."

Seven minutes after Joe had returned with his urine sample, Antonio looked at it and said, "All clean. Let's go."

"Why don't you hop in my truck with me and we will head over there," said Antonio as he rose to leave.

"Sounds good."

As Joe followed Antonio out to his Ford F-250 pickup, Lisa turned to the captain and asked, "Where in the hell are they going?"

"I'm guessing Antonio is taking him to wherever they do the top-secret shit, whatever that is," Jacobsen answered. "Now we can't follow him on the GPS tracker since it's in Joe's truck not on his person."

"Or we can just hang back and watch him on the Life360 app. It will live track him wherever his phone goes," Lisa said as she held up her phone to the captain.

"Damn, I forgot you two had that. Pretty slick for a couple of uniforms," said Jacobsen.

As Joe headed towards Pasco, Lisa and the captain followed from about a half a mile back. Antonio headed east on Hwy. 182 toward Walla Walla, before turning north on Hwy. 395 towards the King City Truck Stop. After a short distance, Antonio turned east on East Hillsboro Street and headed about a mile further before turning into a fenced and gated gravel-covered lot, with a metal building large enough to fit two full-length semis at once. After Antonio unlocked the gate, pulled through it, and locked it again, they drove to the building and parked next to a truck almost identical to Antonio's. The building had no marking on it, other than the address and the word LITE.

"Here we are. Gabriel knows we are coming, so there will be no surprises, but please don't touch anything without asking Gabriel," said Antonio.

"Understood," was Joe's one-word answer.

The heavy steel door had a lock like no other Joe had ever seen. The lock, a Strattec Advanced Logic RTS required both a PIN to be entered as well as a biometric fingerprint ID. As Antonio was entering his PIN, Joe looked at the face of the shop, and noticed security cameras on each of the shop's exterior corners, with an additional camera high above the doors.

Once Antonio opened the door, Joe could see the entire shop, which looked just like every mechanical shop he had ever been in. There were engine hoists, an overhead electric wench on a heavy I-beam, a two-stage 15HP 120 Gallon air compressor, two large Husky tool chests, a wall of hand tools with racks of power tools next to it.

Antonio then took Joe into the office, where Joe also noticed two huge safes sitting against the back wall and motion sensors throughout the entire building.

Parked in the west bay of the shop, was a 2018 Ford F750 box truck, with the rear doors open.

Antonio called out for Gabriel who answered from inside the back of the box truck. Gabriel was just hopping down from the rear of the truck when Joe and Antonio reached it.

"Jose this is Gabriel Cardenas, and Gabriel this is Jose Mendez," Antonio continued. "Gabriel, would you please give Jose the tour, and fill him in on what we do here."

"It is good to meet you, Jose. Well, the short version is we pack and unpack items which are transported by commercial trucks, except these are items we do not want anyone to see, especially any of the border officials. To make sure nobody can find these certain items, we build false compartments, traps, false walls and ceilings, and just about anything that will hide what we need to be hidden for a trip south. We also unload items that are similarly shipped to us," Gabriel said.

"For example, this truck I am working on. For this job, I am building a false wall at the forward end of the box. Come, I will show you," Gabriel continued.

As Gabriel walked Joe to the forward portion of the truck, Joe noticed nothing had been done to the truck yet. The walls were all original and untouched. Joe stood looking at the front wall of the truck, trying to visualize how Gabriel was going to make a false wall.

The walls were covered in fiberglass reinforced plastic panels, which were riveted to what Joe supposed were small channel aluminum ribs, with the ninety-degree corners held in place with L shaped aluminum angle which was also riveted. As Joe looked closer he could see that on the aluminum angle, where the front panel met with the ceiling and side panels, was held in place with Phillips screws filling every fourth hole.

"As you can see, I haven't riveted these angles in place yet, so I can easily pull these off to show you what I built," Gabriel said.

With the use of an electric screwdriver, Gabriel removed the screws, all the way around the front panel. He then slid the forward panel out, revealing a compartment which was approximately seven feet tall, by three feet wide, by ten inches deep. The void had been filled with tightly wrapped packages, stacked from the bottom to the top.

"Holy shit," was all Joe could think to say. "How much is in there?"

"Six-hundred and thirty thousand dollars in cash," Gabriel said with a smile.

"This is incredible. This will not only be challenging but fun," Joe announced. "I have never seen that much cash ever."

"You are exactly right, it is challenging and fun to outsmart the people who are looking for our loads," Gabriel said.

"Is it always cash that you hide?" Joe asked.

Gabriel looked at Antonio before he answered, and after Antonio gave him the head-nod, Gabriel answered, "Mostly the goods coming north are narcotics, but the stuff going south is really interesting. We have smuggled cash, guns, ammunition, eggs, and even live animals. It seems that no two shipments are the same."

"I get the other stuff, but eggs. Who the hell smuggles eggs? Can't you buy eggs in Mexico anymore?" asked Joe.

Both Antonio and Gabriel busted out in laughter before Antonio explained.

"Think of us as a discreet, confidential, and more reliable, UPS. We will deliver anything for the right amount of money, and except for dealing with terrorist kinda shit, we will ship about anything anyone will pay us to ship, but we ain't cheap," Antonio continued. "The eggs he's talking about are very valuable, like from five to ten thousand dollars per egg. These eggs are from endangered birds and falcons, and sometimes we ship the live birds too."

"That's totally awesome. I think falcons are the coolest birds on earth. Did you know they can fly two-hundred miles an hour?" Joe said, "When do we get to see those?"

"Actually your timing is perfect because the birdman, which is what we call him, called a while back and said he will need to make a shipment in the next couple of weeks, but we don't have an exact date yet. Guess the birds haven't shit out their eggs yet," Antonio said.

"Well, do you want the job?" Antonio asked.

"Absolutely. I can't thank you enough. This is great. When do I start?" Joe asked.

"Monday morning at eight, but I want to make a couple of rules very clear to you," Antonio went on. "Never say one word to anyone about what we really do here, never bring anyone here, and of course never take anything, not one dime, from any of the loads. Violations of any of these rules will result in your death. Do you still want to work here?"

"Yep, those rules don't change a thing. I don't steal, I never break a promise, and I will never say a word of this to anyone," Joe said.

"That applies to Lucia too," said Antonio. "I understand you like her, and that is fine, but her business is her business and our business is our business. Clear?"

"Got it."

"At least for a while, you will not have access to the building, so either me or Gabriel will be your only way in," Antonio said. "Any questions?"

"I hate to ask, but when do we get paid? I need to find a new place to live, and I am a little short on cash," Joe asked, so as to stay in character.

Antonio reached in his pocket and pulled a money clip full of cash. Joe watched as he peeled off ten one-hundred-dollar bills which he handed to Joe.

"Will this help?" Antonio asked.

"Yes, thank you very much," as Antonio started for the door, Joe reached his hand out to Gabriel and thanked him for the tour.

"You are very welcome young man. I will see you on Monday. Don't forget the secret knock," Gabriel said.

"What secret knock?" Joe asked, which made both Gabriel and Antonio burst into laughter.

"Let's go, Jose," Antonio said.

On their way back to the restaurant, Antonio asked Joe, "Have you ever bought a gun through a licensed gun dealer?"

"Sure, a couple of them, why?"

"Just to get you back on your feet, there is another quick job you can do to make an easy grand," Antonio said.

"How's that?" asked Joe.

"I have all of your personal information now, so I can order a couple of guns in your name, then you just have to sign for them. That's it."

"What do I do with the guns?" asked Joe.

"You will just have Gabriel lock them in the safes when they arrive," answered Antonio.

"Sounds good to me. This morning I was broke, and now I have fourteen-hundred dollars in my pocket, and two jobs. Thank you, Antonio," Joe said.

"Just don't make me regret this," Antonio said as they pulled into the parking lot of his restaurant. "We have never hired anyone from outside of our organization before."

"I will do my best. I work hard," Joe said.

"Here you go," Antonio said as he pulled into the restaurant's parking lot.

"Well, I have to go find a new place to live. I will see you on Monday," Joe said.

"No, you will not," Antonio went on. "I run the restaurant, and Gabriel runs the shop. I am only in the shop about once a week."

With that, the UC contact was finally over, and Joe was back alone in his truck.

CHAPTER 27

Soon, Joe found himself sitting in the back of Captain Jacobsen's truck, reviewing the day for the captain and Lisa.

"First, I knocked on the door and Felipe came out to inspect the elk. It passed inspection and he paid me four-hundred dollars in cash, which is right here," Joe said as he handed the $1,400 cash over to the captain who secured it in an evidence bag. "I will explain the extra $1,000 in cash in a minute."

Joe continued, "Then Felipe told me he wouldn't buy any more elk meat because they had all they wanted. I asked if the other Buena Comida restaurant would want it, and he said he didn't know but he doubted it because it is highly illegal."

"Well, at least he knows the law," Lisa said.

"Then Felipe said his brother Antonio might have a permanent job for me and said he had told Antonio about me and he wanted to talk to me, so off to the Ely Street restaurant next," said Joe.

"Wait a minute. I think you are leaving something out. You were in the Buena Comida for over an hour. What the hell were you doing in there for so long?" asked the captain.

"One of the employees offered to make me lunch, so I stayed and ate lunch there," Joe answered.

"Let me guess. Lucia?" Lisa asked.

Joe said, "Well, yeah, who the employee was had nothing to do with it. I was just staying in character."

"Yeah right," Lisa said with a smile.

"Am I missing something here?" Jacobsen asked.

Lisa immediately spoke up, "Joe and Lucia have the hots for each other."

"We do not have the hots for each other. Now can I go on with the debrief?" Joe asked.

Lisa answered, "Sorry, go on."

Joe then spent the next thirty minutes providing details about the UC contact, including the two jobs he accepted, and the $1,000 Antonio had given him. Joe intentionally left out two details; his scheduled date with Lucia and the falcon eggs.

The captain sat quietly, contemplating what he had just heard. This case had just gone from a rather routine wildlife trafficking case, to an international gun and drug smuggling case, and it all hinged on an officer who had never worked UC before.

"Holy shit. This is unbelievable. I have way more questions than answers about all of this. With today's events, we are now entering into a world that is normally worked by DEA, ATF, FBI, or one of the other alphabet agencies. I'm not sure we have any business getting this deeply involved with people who have drug cartel partners. Also, for all practical purposes, our wildlife case is done. We already got everything we are going to get on this case, as far as wildlife crimes. I need to run this by the D.C. (deputy chief) because we are very quickly getting in over our heads here," said Captain Jacobsen. "Do you disagree Joe?"

"There is one other thing that was said, which might put this right back into our area of responsibility," Joe said with a smile.

"Oh yeah, what's that?" Jacobsen asked.

"They also smuggle falcons and falcon eggs," Joe explained.

"What the hell did you just say?" the captain asked, "Are you making this shit up?"

"No, as a matter of fact, Antonio said the Birdman will be making another shipment in the next couple of weeks," Joe answered.

"Did they say anything about him, who he is or where he is from?" asked Lisa.

"Nope, and I didn't ask any questions about him. I figured as I get to know Gabriel better, he will open up a bit more," Joe replied.

"That's a big if. If you get to continue this UC. This causes all kinds of logistics problems, not to mention the concerns for your safety," the captain explained.

"I have a proposal. Since we all need to drive right through Yakima on our way home, and since Yakima has both DEA and ATF offices, I propose we stop there on the way. I will need to call the deputy chief on the way there, and then contact ATF and DEA to try to set up a quick meeting," Jacobsen said. "Sound good?"

"Do you know anyone with DEA or ATF in Yakima?" Lisa asked.

"No, but one of my best buddies is an ATF agent out of Seattle. I will run it by him first," said the captain.

"Sounds good," said Joe.

"One thing bugs me about all of this," said Jacobsen.

"What's that?" asked Joe.

Captain Jacobsen answered, "I don't understand why they trust you so much so early. Showing you their operation like that, when they don't know you hardly at all, just doesn't make any sense. These guys are never careless, and this seems pretty damned careless."

"I know. I was pretty shocked by what they showed and told me too," Joe explained. "The only thing that explains it, is they apparently lost the two guys who assisted Gabriel, and they are falling way behind on their work."

"Well, grab your suitcases from my backseat, and let's head to Yakima. I have some calls to make along the way," said Jacobsen.

Joe and Lisa then followed the captain northwest on Hwy. 82 towards Yakima. As they followed behind him, Lisa and Joe laughed at all of his hand motions as he spoke into his hands-free phone system. Without hearing his voice, it was like watching a symphony conductor, as he swung his free arm all around the cab of his pickup.

Finally, just as they passed the exit to the town of Buena, the captain called Lisa, "We are all set to meet with ATF Agent Josh Tison, and hopefully his ASAC (Assistant Special Agent in Charge) at their office at 4:00 PM. Sounds like someone from DEA will also be there, so I guess we are going bigtime now."

"What did the D.C. say?" Lisa asked about newly promoted Deputy Chief Phil Silva.

Captain Jacobsen chuckled then said, "He said he will leave the decisions up to me, but to make sure we don't cause him any major problems or get anyone hurt."

"Guess the ball is in your court," Joe answered.

"Yep, that's why I'm paid the big bucks, right?"

At 3:47 PM the group arrived at the ATF office in Union Gap (just south of Yakima).

As soon as the three identified themselves to the receptionist, they were greeted in the lobby by Agent Josh Tison. Tison looked like he was barely old enough to shave but appeared to be in great shape. Using his electronic passcard, and a PIN, Tison opened the door for the state officers and walked them back to the conference room.

In the conference room, the state officers were greeted by ATF ASAC Brian Kinton and DEA Agent Grace Fenson.

ASAC Kinton kicked off the conversation, "Alright captain, Josh brought me up to speed a little, but I still have a ton of questions, but first, maybe we can hear the details from Officer Ramirez?"

For the next thirty minutes, Joe went into great detail about his undercover contacts, once again leaving Lucia out of the conversation.

As Joe spoke, Lisa noticed all three federal agents were taking detailed notes, which was encouraging as they at least were paying attention.

After Joe was done, ASAC Kinton said, "Before you guys got here, we ran those names through our system. It looks like we received an anonymous tip, almost a year ago, stating Antonio Vargas was, and I quote, "A very dangerous drug dealer, who needs to go to prison", but that was the extent of our information. We opened a file, but when I checked it today, it only had the cover sheet, the anonymous letter and the envelope it came in, looks like nobody had time to look into it. There was just not enough to act on."

"Well, I think you have enough to act on now," Joe said.

"Yes, it would certainly appear to be so," answered Kinton.

"Joe, you stated you used a covert camera to video-record the entire contact. Could we get you to burn us a copy of that video?" asked Agent Fenson.

At that moment, Joe realized how lucky he was that Washington state law does not allow audio recording in most cases, so his conversations with Lucia would remain private.

"Absolutely but remember there is no audio because Washington is a two-party consent state. If you give me a thumb drive, and if the captain will let me use his laptop, I will burn it off for you right here," answered Joe.

Agent Fenson replied, "Since these crimes are all federal, and since you will be working with us under a signed M.O.U., you will be audio recording from now on."

"Sure, as soon as you get me one, I will ship it to the chief and will have it signed within minutes," said Captain Jacobsen.

"Alright, now there is only one person who can answer the next question. Do you want to continue with this undercover, knowing the risks?" asked the ASAC to Joe.

Joe answered immediately, "Without a doubt. This certainly wasn't what we expected when we started this operation, but here we are in a position to take down a whole lot of really bad guys. So, yeah, I'm in."

"Then we will need to act pretty quickly. First, we need to come up with a detailed plan. Then we need to find you a place to live and wire the place up with covert cameras," ASAC Kinton said.

"One thing I am really concerned about is Joe doing these straw purchases for firearms which we would just have to let go south to Mexico. We sure as shit don't need a repeat of Operation Fast and Furious. None of us want to end up testifying in front of Congress," announced ASAC Kinton.

Joe had noticed that while Kinton was speaking, Agent Fenson was busy texting with someone.

"Operation Fast and Furious? What's that?" Lisa asked.

Kinton answered, "In 2010 and 2011 ATF conducted an operation targeting straw purchases of firearms being shipped to the Mexican drug cartels. The agency decided to let the firearms walk, with the intention of tracking them and busting the cartel members on both sides of the border. ATF allowed over 2,000 firearms to go through their hands, right into the hands of the cartels. It all came apart when Border Patrol Agent Brian Terry was murdered with one of the firearms which Fast and Furious had allowed to go south. In the end, only 710 of the 2,000 firearms were recovered, and at least 150 Mexican civilians were killed with Fast and Furious guns. That's something we don't want to repeat."

"So, what do we do? If we take them down as soon as Joe gets these firearms, then we lose everything else, the drugs, money, and the wildlife," asked Jacobsen.

The ASAC answered, "I am comfortable letting a few guns walk because we can justify it for the greater good, but we need to bring this whole operation down sooner rather than later. This one worries me for several reasons. A lot can go wrong here."

"And a lot can go right too. We can end up taking down some bad guys which apparently none of us knew were even involved in this stuff," said Jacobsen.

Agent Fenson spoke up next, "Brian, I'm on the same page with you here, and I'm not trying to get territorial here, but it does sound like with these guys the guns are secondary to the drug smuggling. I'm pretty sure my ASAC is going to want to call the shots on a lot of this. Just remember this has to be a true joint operation to succeed."

"Of course, I didn't mean to imply anything other than that, and ultimately it all centers around Joe Ramirez," Kinton responded.

Next Captain Jacobsen spoke up, "Earlier I heard something about getting Joe a place to live and wiring it up. Just how is all that going to happen by Monday?"

"If DEA doesn't object, it would likely go considerably faster if they take care of all that. DEA maintains safe houses all over the country, and those can double as undercover homes in these types of situations. Will that work for you Grace?" asked Kinton.

"Absolutely. Can you come back down here on Friday morning around 10:00 AM Joe?" asked Agent Fenson, "We will get you the keys and someone will meet you at the apartment in Pasco to show you how the covert video systems work."

"Wow, you think you can rent a place and get me the keys by Friday?" Joe asked.

A wide smile appeared across Agent Fenson's face as she answered, "As Brian said earlier, we maintain places all over, to use as safe houses for witnesses, or for just this purpose. We use them once, then move to the next one. I just now texted my ASAC, and he said we already have a two-bedroom furnished apartment in the Pinecrest Apartment complex in Pasco. The place is fully wired and has everything you will need, except food and your clothes. My ASAC said it's open for as long as we need it."

"Impressive," said Lisa.

"And Captain Jacobsen, my ASAC said we will need to have a signed MOU (Memorandum of Understanding) in place before we can officially get involved. He is burning one out now and will email it to you and your chief if you will please provide me with the email addresses," Agent Fenson said.

Captain Jacobsen immediately took a business card from his wallet, wrote on the back, and handed it to Agent Fenson.

Agent Fenton continued, "We need to include the US Fish and Wildlife Service too. Do you guys have a USFWS agent you like to work with?"

Lisa answered before anyone else could, "Yep, RAC Ryan Slader out of Spokane."

"Okay, I will give him a call after you all leave and see if he is available to come down on Friday," Agent Fenton continued. "I think I already know the answer to this one, but I am supposed to ask. Joe, do you see any way you could bring in another UC, one of ours, to work this with you?"

Joe gave it some thought before answering, "Boy, not at this point. I mean they barely know me, so I am sure they will be very suspicious at least for a while. Maybe after a week or two, I could try to work someone in, by saying a good friend of mine is looking for work, but right now, I don't see it happening."

"Just a few rules about your new home Joe. Obviously, you can't tell anyone about the place, other than the suspects you are working, and you don't bring your wife and kids down for a visit or anything like that, and no smoking in the apartment," Agent Fenson said.

"That no smoking thing only applies to tobacco, right?" Joe asked.

"Are you serious? You want to smoke weed while you are sitting in your undercover home, working undercover on a drug case? It's still illegal federally you know?" asked Agent Tison.

With that, everyone busted out laughing.

"Real funny," responded Tison.

Just then Fenson's cell phone buzzed with an incoming call, "It's my ASAC. I better take it," she said before stepping out of the room.

The group engaged in small talk while waiting for Fenson's return. Ten minutes later she came back into the room.

"Sorry about the interruption. Anyway, Friday, I will try to get our AUSA over here to go over this with us too," Agent Fenson said. "We will also have some documents for you to sign too, then we can get you on your way to your new Pasco home. Joe, make sure and bring some photos from home, and some other personal items to make it look like the place is your home."

"Which AUSA?" asked Lisa.

"Brock Shay. Have you met him?" asked Fenson.

"We all have, and he's awesome. It will be great working with him again," Lisa answered.

Fenson had one more question for Joe, "How well will your UC identification hold up under scrutiny?"

Joe replied, "I'm not sure what you are asking."

"Did you get a real social security card from the Social Security Administration?" Fenson asked.

"I don't know where it came from. I just got it in the mail from our headquarters office," Joe answered.

Captain Jacobsen stepped in, "He has an authentic driver's license, vehicle registration, social security card, and fishing license, all issued from the appropriate agencies, but we didn't set up a credit history, driving record, and all that, because we expected this to be more of a buy/bust kind of case."

Agent Fenson took some notes, then said, "Alright, we will take care of that too. We will give you the works, and the background to support it. I just need your UC phone number."

Without hesitation, Joe said, "509-555-8375".

"Joe, are you sure about this? You will need to live and breathe this operation twenty-four hours a day. You won't be able to see any of your family or friends until it's all done. Your whole life will revolve around a bunch of dirtbags, and you will always be in danger. This will be all you think about until everyone is in jail, and probably well after that. These people are serious and very dangerous. I just want you to know what you're getting into," warned ASAC Kinton.

"My only family are my parents, who are in Arizona. I'm not married and don't have a girlfriend. I don't even have a pet, so yeah, I'm good with this," Joe replied.

"As far as you two," Kinon said as he looked directly at Lisa and the captain. "You are both welcome to participate in any or all facets of the operation. This is a joint operation, three equal partner agencies, well four when USFWS joins us."

The captain answered, "I am going to head back to the westside today but will be available by phone any time of the day or night. Lisa can decide for herself, how she wants to proceed."

"Alright, now captain if you wouldn't mind getting that computer so we can get a download of Joe's video, and we are going to need a copy of Jose's driver's license and social security card for our records," said Agent Fenson.

For the second time in a day, Joe produced his UC identification so it could be copied.

"Any last questions from anyone?" asked the ASAC.

"Joe, on Friday I will have you come over to our office, so the ASAC can talk to you a bit. We will also conduct a thorough search of you UC truck, and everything in it to make damn sure there is nothing which would give away your true identity," said DEA Agent Fenson.

Everyone then arose, shook hands all the way around, and said their goodbyes, and with that Lisa and Joe were headed home.

"Holy shit Joe, you're sure in the middle of one wild-ass case. You just be very careful, I don't want to have to break in a new partner, plus I kind of like you. Just remember, nothing here is worth getting hurt or killed for, okay?" Lisa said, "Promise you will not take any unnecessary chances?"

"You've got it. I will keep my guard up, and I already know what worries you the most, and it won't be a problem?" Joe said.

"I'm confused, what do you think worries me the most?"

"My drinking. I see the looks you give me, and I hear the comments you have made, and I get it. I give you my word I will limit my on-duty drinking to only times that it's necessary to maintain my cover and very little at that," Joe said.

"Thanks, Joe, I only want what's best for you, and I hope you know that, but that's not what worries me the most right now," Lisa replied.

"Oh yeah, then what's your concern?"

"Lucia. For all we know she is in this up to her neck, and even if she isn't, I'm not sure it's smart to trust her. Those people are her family, and you're not. I'm not saying you shouldn't talk to her, just be careful of what you say to her and always stay in your role," Lisa answered.

Joe thought about arguing the point with Lisa but decided it wouldn't change her mind, "You've got it. I will play the role around the clock and will trust nobody."

As they continued toward Okanogan County, Lisa thought about the situation with Lucia. Although the concerns regarding Joe's growing interest in Lucia raised the risks for Joe, he deserved to have someone special in his life. Lisa smiled as she thought about the distant future, one in which Joe would explain to their children and friends just how he and Lucia had met.

Lisa could just hear it now, *Well. I was working undercover on a wildlife trafficking case when I first met Lucia. Lucia was related to several Mexican drug cartel members who we were investigating. The case took a strange turn and became a gun smuggling and narcotics trafficking case, which meant I had to move to Pasco to work the case long-term. During that time, we fell in love, and once everyone was arrested, we got married and fled the country for ten years going into witness protection.*

"This is all going to get very interesting soon. I never expected to run into anything like this working wildlife cases," Lisa said.

"Me either," answered Joe.

"Hey, I do have one question?" Joe said, "The captain said it's totally up to you on what you do from here on out, relating to the UC portion of this case. Have you thought about what you want to do?"

"I have. On one hand, I hate to sit up in Okanogan County wondering and worrying, but on the other hand, there's not a damned thing I could do if I stayed down there. DEA will handle the evidence and the recordings and will provide your backup. I probably can do more just working my regular uniformed duties at home, if you don't object."

"That's exactly what I was going to propose and remember you can call me anytime. If I say hi Anna, then you know I am with someone and can't talk," Joe said.

"Alright. Somehow it just doesn't seem right to leave my partner down in Tri-Cities working with a bunch of dangerous drug smugglers, while I'm at home relaxing," Lisa said.

"Hey, we all have our crosses to bear," Joe said with a laugh.

"Just don't let you guard down, even with Lucia, okay?" Lisa asked.

"You've got it, Mommy."

CHAPTER 28

At 9:10 AM, Frank Pierce received a call from Antonio, "I'm sending you the identification for a guy named Jose Mendez. He wants to buy a Glock model 21 .45 pistol, with four extra magazines for the same, and three Smith and Wesson AR-15s with twenty extra mags. He will probably want more later. Let me know if his background check goes through okay."

"I will put the order in now, and once I get the serial numbers, I will run his form through and see what we get. Are you expecting problems with this one?" Frank asked.

"No, just being careful," Antonio said before hanging up.

CHAPTER 29

It was just after noon when Adam Getty pulled into Ricky Williams' driveway. Adam smiled as Ricky's old black lab Tarball followed him up the driveway, wagging his tail the whole way. *Great guard dog* Adam thought to himself.

As Adam backed up to "his" mobile home, he noticed Ricky coming across the yard to greet him.

"Welcome, buddy. How was the trip?" Ricky said as he opened his arms to hug Adam.

"The same as always going from too much traffic to none. You live in paradise," Adam told Ricky.

"Let me help you," Ricky said as he helped Adam carry his gear, clothes, and food into the mobile home.

Adam grinned as he felt the warmth of the home's interior, indicating that once again Ricky had thought to turn the heat up for Adam's arrival.

After Adam's Ford Expedition had been emptied, Ricky told Adam to come over to his place once he had settled in.

Adam knew Ricky's only son, the one who had lived in this very same mobile home, had been killed by a drunk driver years ago, and Ricky hadn't touched a drop of alcohol since and would not tolerate drunk driving. Although Ricky didn't drink or use drugs of any kind, he didn't mind Adam bringing over a tumbler full of scotch. Adam enjoyed a touch of coke once in a while, but he respected Ricky too much to even discuss cocaine with him.

As Adam walked from his home to Ricky's, Tarball followed him the whole way bumping against his leg with a filthy slobbery tennis ball in his mouth. Finally, as Adam reached Ricky's front door, Tarball dropped the ball at his feet and took off running. Adam had just thrown the ball when Ricky opened the door. Ricky noticed his lab running back with a ball in his mouth, and said to Adam, "Now he will never quit bugging you."

As Adam reached down and threw the ball again, he said, "I don't mind at all. Tarball and me are buddies."

"Well, why don't both of you come in out of the rain," said Ricky.

As Adam sat back in one of the two overstuffed recliners, he asked, "So, how have you been?"

"Very well. My back is doing a lot better, and I'm healthy as far as I know, so no complaints. We are all getting older and slower, aren't we Tarball?" Tarball got up and wiggled his way to Ricky when he heard his name spoken. "How about you?"

"No complaints. I'm having a pretty good year, and I haven't fallen off a cliff yet, so all good," Adam said. "Are you seeing many birds?"

"That's my boy. Right to business huh?" Ricky said with a smile, "I took my spotting scope and a tripod out for a walk the day before yesterday, and hiked about two miles up the coastline. Hang on, let me get my glasses," Ricky said as he got up to find his reading glasses.

Once Ricky had located his reading glasses, he picked up a pocket notebook from the end table next to his chair, and read from it, "I saw a nesting pair of peregrines on Jagged Island and another pair on Dandayla Island. Then just north of Jagged Island, I found what I think was a nest on the mainland cliff, about thirty feet down from the top. I think it's still a little early, but they are starting to nest for sure now."

"Good. Very good. I read the marine forecast and tomorrow looks pretty good, so maybe we can start on Jagged Island tomorrow?" asked Adam.

"Sounds good to me. Are you ready to throw some dead cow on the grill? I have a couple of beautiful T-bones," asked Ricky.

"Absolutely, but I've told you a hundred times, you don't have to feed me," Adam said.

"Yeah, but even an old grumpy guy like you is still company. I will go start the grill."

Adam sat sipping his scotch as Ricky ignited the grill and began preparing the meal.

"What is your target number this time?" Ricky asked.

"I will need to pick up six adults, and thirty-four eggs or eyases (nestlings which have not yet fledged). I know I will have to get most of them in Eastern Washington, and I have some other orders coming too. If I grab two eggs per nest, then we need seventeen nests, and that's not gonna happen here. If I can come away with ten eggs and a couple of adults from here, I will be thrilled," Adam explained. "I also have a customer who wants a white gyrfalcon, which is kinda like ordering a two-headed cobra. We know they exist, but finding one on demand is nearly impossible."

"We will see what we can do to fill those peregrine orders, but I don't have a clue where you can find a white gyrfalcon," Ricky answered.

"Greenland," Adam answered.

"What? You mean you can find white gyrfalcons in Greenland?"

Adam replied, "Yep, that's where the largest population of them is, but getting a gyrfalcon out of Greenland is extremely difficult. One thing about Greenland is their customs officers are very serious, very thorough, and beyond malfeasance."

"So where do you come up with one then?"

"In the Arctic and Sub-Arctic regions of Canada. I have a ton of Canadian friends out looking for one now. I put a reward of $100,000 out for anyone who can get me one in excellent condition," answered Adam.

"Holy shit, I wish I knew where I could find one."

The steaks were done, and the conversation came to an end when the dining began.

"Thank you, that was excellent as always, but I think I will get the boat hooked up, then get ready for tomorrow. It gets light at seven, so you want to head out of here around then?" Adam asked.

"Seven it is. You need some help hooking the boat up?" asked Ricky.

"No, I've got it. Thanks. See you in the morning."

"Alright, see you tomorrow. Have a good night's sleep," said Ricky.

The next morning, Adam awakened well before daylight and started the day by brewing a cup of gourmet Costa Rican coffee, which he had brought from home. One look out the window confirmed what his ears had already told him, it was dumping rain. Although nobody liked working outdoors in a torrential downpour, at least the wind was dead calm, and that what was most important.

Once Adam had everything loaded in the boat, he went back in and made himself a plate of pancakes and bacon, which he scarfed down in a few short minutes. As he was putting the dishes in the sink, Adam looked out the kitchen window and saw Ricky loading his gear in the boat. A quick peek at his watch told him it was time to hit the road, so Adam donned his rain gear, and headed out to meet Ricky.

"Morning boss. How'd you sleep?" asked Ricky.

"Very well. Are you ready to get wet?"

"I live in LaPush, we are wet 360 days of the year here," Ricky answered with a chuckle.

It took only four minutes to get from Ricky's home to the boat launch, which was owned by the Quileute Nation. Before backing the boat into the water, Adam put the drain plugs back in and unhooked the tie-down straps. As always, Ricky had already aired up the boat's sponsons (the air chamber tubes which give the vessel flotation) and charged the battery, so when he turned the key the 70 hp Yamaha jumped to life, purring so quietly that Adam couldn't tell if Ricky had started it. Adam watched in his rearview mirror as Ricky gave him the thumbs up, right before he backed off the trailer. Once both men were onboard, Ricky took over the controls, and slowly navigated out of the marina, and past James Island, and into the Pacific Ocean.

Every time Adam went past James Island he shook his head. James Island always had several pairs of nesting peregrines, but was within two hundred yards of the boat launch, and was in full view of a 24-hour webcam set up by the Quileute Nation and the Forks Chamber of Commerce.

As the sun was coming up, the men made their way around James Island, then turned due north up the coast. The seas were about as calm as Adam had ever seen for this time of year, which would make the fourteen-mile run a great deal more pleasant.

Once the men arrived at Jagged Island Ricky pointed out the nest he had located with his spotting scope from shore. Adam confirmed the nest was a peregrine nest and was active. While the men made their way around the island, Adam noticed another nest, for a total of two nests on this one island.

As Ricky held the boat fifty yards off of the island, Adam began gearing up. First, his climbing harness, then he put on his heavy Carhart coat, followed by his helmet with the neck guards, a rolled-up towel, which he put over the back of his neck and then tucked into his coat, his gloves, and last was his pack. Fortunately, the northwest side of the island offered a very mellow gradient to the top, one which Adam could scramble up without the use of climbing gear. Once at the top, Adam walked along the edge until he heard Ricky say stop over their portable radios. Adam stopped, then asked Ricky how it looked.

"Take two steps to your left," Ricky said over the radio. "Perfect. Only about twenty to twenty-five feet below you now."

Adam looked around for a good spot to anchor his rappel and found a perfect spot to drive in a piton. Adam removed two pitons from his climbing sling and drove each piton into the crack in the rock until they could go no more. Adam then clipped a double carabiner quickdraw into each piton, threaded the rope through the quickdraws, tied the terminal ends of the rope together, and threw the rope off the cliff. Next, Adam fed the rope through his Petzl STOP assisted-braking descender and clipped the rope into a locking carabiner which was attached to his harness.

When rappelling and climbing solo, as he was doing here, Adam had two alternatives for getting back to the top, after he had taken the eggs. One alternative would be for Adam to continue his rappel to the bottom, where he would be picked up by the boat and taken back to the easy path to the top. The second choice would be to climb back up using a pair of Jumar ascenders (a device which allows the rope to slide freely through it on the way up, but instantly locks in place if the ascender tried to go down the rope). Climbing back up was faster if the climb wasn't very difficult.

Adam tested the piton anchors, then double-checked all of his gear, before walking backward off the cliff face. Adam had made it less than ten feet when a falcon began making passes at him, without actually hitting him, yet. Adam knew that was a sign the nest had eggs or eyas. When Adam reached the exact height of the nest, he locked his assisted-braking device in place, so both of his hands would be free. He had stopped just six feet to the west of the nest, close enough that he could simply "walk" sideways to it with no problem.

Next, Adam removed a yellow six-egg camping egg case. The case was the same as millions of others, used by campers to protect their breakfast eggs, except these, had a thin layer of foam weatherstripping in each egg space, and wrist strap (dropping $24,000 of eggs off of a fifty-foot cliff would make for a very bad day).

Adam's experience had been that peregrines have either three or four eggs per nest, rarely less and rarely more, which was why Adam was so pleased to see five eggs in this first nest. *I hope they all go like this*, Adam thought. Adam never took all of the eggs and preferred to leave at least one behind. As Adam began picking the eggs from the nest, the adult falcon continued to dive-bomb him, coming closer and closer each time. Adam quickly picked out three eggs, put them in the yellow egg container, which he returned to his pack.

In his pack, Adam also carried a rectangular section of mist netting (a netting made from very fine nylon webbing, which was almost impossible to see) with bungee cords attached to one end, and lead fishing weights on the other. When Adam was snatching eggs or eyas from nests, if the adult bird(s) were desirable to Adam, he would attach two anchors two feet above the nest, and four feet apart. He then simply hung the net in front of the nest, so when the adults returned, they would become entangled. Both male and female falcons will incubate the eggs, the female is larger and stronger and therefore is more desirable. Adam had decided not to take this adult, but to wait for a better bird.

After getting his work done on the nest, Adam looked up and down to determine which way he wanted to depart. After considering his options, and since Adam was only about twenty-five feet from the top, Adam decided to just climb up the same route as he had rappelled down. Ten minutes later he was back on top and was coiling his climbing rope, and recovering the pitons.

"Alright, three in the bag, now where's the next one from me?" Adam asked Ricky over the radio.

"About forty-five yards or so towards the ocean," Ricky said. "Start walking."

Adam walked along the edge, looking around. Even with the limited visibility, due to the heavy rain, Adam still thought this was one of the most beautiful areas he had ever seen.

"Five more yards. Stop, right there. These guys are probably about forty feet straight below you."

Adam anchored a rappel point, threw the rope over, clipped in, and was ready to go again. Since the nest wasn't visible from Adam's position, Ricky continued to guide him, "Stop. You are going to step right into the nest in about ten feet. Move to one side or the other before you come down any further. As Adam continued down, he was shocked when an adult falcon came screaming out of a three-foot-wide covered ledge, and right at him. As Adam instinctually ducked his head down, he heard and felt the falcon hit his helmet. A quick glance to the side and Adam could see the bird flying about twenty-five feet over his head. Adam worked his way over to the nest, removed the egg box from his pack, and quickly plucked two of the three eggs from the nest, while the falcon struck him again, this time in the back. Thankfully for Adam, the heavy Carhart coat kept the bird's talons from making it to his skin. With the eggs tucked away in his pack, he turned his attention to the adult.

The adult was most definitely a female and a beautiful bird at that. The more he watched the bird, the more certain he was. This bird was going home with him.

Adam climbed back up a few feet and placed a chock (a hexagonal block of aluminum with a looped cable running through it) in a small crack. Adam slid over about five feet and did the same thing on the opposite side of the nest, before removing the mist net from his pack. He spread the net out, fighting to keep it from snagging on the rock and becoming damaged, then hung it from the two chocks. The net now covered the entire entrance to the nest ledge. Since the drop from the top had been vertical or overhanging the whole way down, Adam opted to continue down. Six minutes later, Adam was sitting in the boat.

While Ricky took Adam back to the easier route up the rock, Adam transferred the five eggs to a Rubbermaid box. In the box, Adam had ten half-length socks and several packages of chemical hand warmers. He carefully wrapped each egg in a sock and placed them back in the box on top of the only two hand warmers Adam had activated. Once all five eggs were tucked away, Adam slid the box into a compartment under the captain's seat.

Since a bird caught in a mist net will thrash around so much as to cause severe damage to itself, once they reached the island again Adam hustled into position as quickly as he could. Adam stayed back from the cliff's edge, as Ricky sat back about fifty yards, watching the nest site from the boat. In less than two minutes after Adam got back into position, Ricky called to advise Adam he had a bird in the net.

Hurrying in rock climbing is never a good idea, but Adam had no choice. He once again clipped his assisted-braking descender to the rope and went over the side. Another minute, and he was at the nest site, and adjacent to the entangled bird. Quickly. Adam reached back into his backpack and removed a woman's nylon stocking, with the toe cut off. Adam carefully grabbed hold of the bird from its back, slid his hand back far enough to trap the bird's legs back, so the razor-sharp talons couldn't reach his fingers. Once Adam had slid the falcon's wings into their resting position, and had her legs back, he began untangling the falcon from the netting. Even though Adam took extra care not to damage the netting, untangling a live falcon from a mist net, while hanging seventy-five feet up a cliff was difficult and he couldn't help but break some of the delicate mesh.

Once the falcon was free of the net, Adam pinned the bird against his chest, while he slid the women's nylon over the bird's head and down the length of its body leaving the head protruding from the nylon on one end and the feet hanging out the other end. Once the falcon was snuggly wrapped in the nylon, he took the last egg from the nest, then packed the egg and the bird into his pack.

Adam had decided, on the way back to the top of the hill, that if he captured the female, he would not risk leaving the last egg behind for the crows to eat.

Adam rappelled back down to the boat, where he secured and secreted both the egg and the live bird.

"It's almost 1:00 PM now, how about we call it a day?" Adam asked.

"Works for me, bro. You buying again tonight?"

"No doubt about it. You earned your keep today," Adam told Ricky. "Now let's go home."

Years ago, when Ricky had volunteered to help spot falcons in advance of Adam's arrival, Adam made him a deal. Every successful day of falcon hunting would result in a thousand-dollar bonus and a dinner at the restaurant of Ricky's choice (not that there were very many choices).

On the way back to the house, Adam did the math in his head. At six-grand per egg, that was thirty-six thousand dollars. Add another fifty-thousand for the female peregrine, and it added up to a eighty-six thousand dollar day, more than most NFL quarterbacks make per game. Ricky certainly deserved his bonus.

Once back at Ricky's property, the first order of business was to take care of the eggs, then the adult bird. Adam took the eggs to the back bedroom of his mobile home, where he secured them in his HovaBator Advanced Egg Incubator. The incubator was the top of the line, fully automatic egg incubator. The unit was capable of holding up to forty-two eggs at once, keeping them at the ideal temperature (99.1 to 99.5 degrees Fahrenheit), and automatically turning them over every four hours.

Once the eggs were tucked into the incubator, it was time to deal with the adult bird. Adam opened the screened door of the mews, then carefully slid the nylon stocking down from the bird's neck down past the talons and off. Keeping the talons secured, so they didn't end up going through one of Adam's hands, he carefully examined the bird. Once he was satisfied the falcon was indeed in outstanding condition, he placed her in the mews and latched the door closed. The mews already contained fresh water, but to feed the raptors Adam removed a thawed, but previously frozen quail, from his cooler and dropped in in the cage.

Twice a year Adam would place large bulk orders for frozen rats and quail, from Rodentpro.com, a company that sold mice, rats, rabbits, hamsters, insects, quail, and more as feed for various carnivores. Falcons needed not only the nutrition provided by these small animals, but the roughage provided by bones, feathers, and fur.

Upon completion of his bird care duties, Adam jumped into a hot shower. Adam had worked outdoors most of his adult life and had experienced everything from the extreme cold of the Arctic to the stifling heat and humidity of the tropics, but nothing was as uncomfortable as a torrential downpour with thirty-five-degree temperatures. The cold and wet seemed to suck all of the warmth from

Adam's body, and he had found it took hours to get back to being comfortable again once back indoors.

Once Adam had warmed up a bit, and had dressed in several layers of clothing, he and Ricky headed to the River's Edge restaurant for a celebration dinner.

"According to the weather forecast, tomorrow will be our last nice day, before the wind and waves come up. Let's hit Dandayla Island first thing in the morning, then take a look further north," Adam told Ricky on the way to the restaurant.

"Sounds good. We will do great tomorrow too, we have to because I want you to buy me dinner at D &K Barbeque in Forks tomorrow."

"I hope like hell that I have to buy you another dinner," Adam said with a smile.

As they were walking into the restaurant, Adam reminded himself to give Mohammed Almaktoum a call and tell him to be ready for a trip to Mexico in ten days or so. Dubai is eleven hours ahead of the US Pacific time zone, so Adam would give him a call when he woke up in the morning.

CHAPTER 30

On the afternoon of Thursday, April 2nd, Antonio Vargas was busy working on the restaurant's books when he received a call from Frank Pierce the gun dealer, "Both your AR-15s and the Glock model 21 pistol came in today, so I ran the firearms transfer forms through ATF."

"And, what happened with Jose Mendez?" asked Antonio.

"Nothing. The sale was approved, and we are all done except for the signatures," Frank said.

"Alright, he is supposed to start work for me on Monday, so I will have him meet you to sign for the guns and pick them up for me. Thanks," said Antonio.

Frank responded, "Hey, no problem. Just give me a call and I will meet him anywhere you want."

At the same time, up in Oroville, Joe had just completed packing for his extended stay in Tri-Cities. Before anything went into his two duffle bags, Joe searched every piece of clothing for anything which might give him away to the suspects. Once he had everything packed, he went outside and searched the undercover truck from bumper to bumper but came up with nothing but some food wrappers. Joe had no desire to have one of the feds find anything when they were to search him tomorrow.

The last thing Joe did before turning in for the night, was to call his parents and check-in. Joe knew his mom would spin into a blind panic if she knew what he was really doing, so he told his parents he was going to be in training for two weeks at the academy and would have limited time to call, but would call at every opportunity.

Joe left home at 5:00 AM on Friday, so he would have plenty of time to get to Yakima for the 10:00 meeting. For the first time, Joe was getting nervous. Not nervous about the bad guys, but nervous that he would screw something up. For his entire career, he always had a safety net with Lisa there. Joe knew that if he were about to screw something up, Lisa would jump in and bail him out, as she had already done too many times to count. Now he was totally on his own, in a completely new environment.

Joe remembered back to when Captain Jacobsen had first told them about this UC assignment. There was no doubt, the captain thought this would be a straightforward simple case. Sell elk, get money, arrest bad guys, end of the story, but it turned out to be a completely different beast. Instead of making two or three quick sales with Lisa, he was now moving to Tri-Cities to work 24-hour a day undercover while all alone. He knew if he screwed this one up, it would be very public.

CHAPTER 31

US Fish and Wildlife Service RAC (Resident Agent in Charge) Slader and AUSA (Assistant US Attorney) Shay, who had carpooled down from Spokane, arrived at the DEA office on East Yakima Avenue about twenty minutes ahead of the meeting and immediately sat down with DEA ASAC (Assistant Special Agent in Charge) Denise Spomer and Captain Jacobsen in an empty office to strategize a bit before Joe arrived.

At 9:50 Joe arrived and was led back to a larger, fancier conference room than that at the ATF office. Joe took the seat of honor, at the head of the table directly across from DEA ASAC Denise Spomer and next to his captain. Also present were USFWS RAC Ryan Slader, AUSA Brock Shay, ATF ASAC Brian Kenton, and DEA Agent Grace Fenson.

"Before we do anything else, can I have the keys to your vehicle Officer Ramirez, and do we have your consent to install a covert GPS tracker?" asked Agent Fenson.

"Absolutely. Here you go," Joe said as he handed his keys to Agent Fenson, who immediately handed them off to two other agents, who had been standing in the hall.

Spomer began the meeting by asking everyone to introduce themselves. Spomer soon realized everyone at the table already knew Joe, except for her. She did find it strange a state fish and wildlife officer, so young, already knew so many federal law enforcement agents and the AUSA. Knowing absolutely nothing about game wardens or their duties, she had assumed game wardens were similar to state park rangers or something and were nothing more than a bunch of glorified security guards who were all wanna-be cops.

ASAC Spomer opened the meeting, "Officer Ramirez, we have all received your written report as well as those from Officer Lisa Bennington and Captain Cody Jacobsen, and hopefully, we have all had time to read them. Excellent reports by the way. I hate to ask this of you, but would you please run over all of this one more time for the group?"

For the next thirty minutes, Joe once again went over the details of the case, and what led them to the point they were at now.

"Thanks, Joe. At this point does anyone have any questions?" asked ASAC Spomer.

"I don't have a question, but I have a new detail we learned yesterday," said ATF ASAC Kinton. "Yesterday, Joe purchased a Glock 21 pistol and four AR-15s from Frank's firearms in Pasco. Joe, were you aware you, or actually, Jose Mendez, had just purchased this small arsenal?"

"No, but it doesn't surprise me," answered Joe.

Kinton continued, "This was the first time Frank's Firearms has ever come to our attention, and once we started looking into his firearms transactions for the last ten years, it became quite obvious he is a major player in providing firearms to the Mexican cartels by way of straw purchases. That alone made this case well worth anything we need to put into it. Great job Joe, and I want to thank you for handing us this case on a silver platter."

AUSA Shay spoke up next, "In reading Joe's report, the potential of this operation is beyond anything our office has handled in a very long time. After only three days of undercover work, we already have strong evidence of felony wildlife trafficking, bulk cash smuggling, drug smuggling, and straw purchases of firearms. Additionally, Joe has been hired to build, empty, and fill hidden compartments for cross-border smuggling assumedly for one of the cartels. Not a bad start Joe. Congratulations, you hit the big time."

Shay continued, "What blows me away is that WDFW entered into this operation to catch restaurants buying game meat. The next thing everyone knows the operation uncovers all of the drugs and guns, but then out of the blue, we are back into a wildlife case with these falcons. The odds of this drug and gun smuggling operation also involving smuggling wildlife has to be one in a million. This is certainly one for the books."

ASAC Spomer spoke next, "We received the signed multi-agency M.O.U. back from WDFW yesterday, so it is now officially a joint investigation with at least three federal agencies working in cooperation with WDFW. Joe, since you are the single most important person on this operation, it's up to you to name it."

Joe replied, "Funny you would say I get to name the operation since my partner Lisa and I came up with a whole bunch of potential operation names on our drive home, but we were just kidding around. My favorite was Operation Skyrocket, so I guess I will go with that."

ASAC Spomer asked, "Alright, I will bite, why Skyrocket?"

"Simple, the peregrine falcon is the fastest animal on earth and is capable of diving at speeds over 225 miles per hour. That makes them skyrockets to me," Joe answered.

"I like it," said Ryan Slader.

"Then Operation Skyrocket it is," announced ASAC Spomer.

"Now let's get down to the nuts and bolts of Operation Skyrocket. Please pipe up and let me know if any of you disagree with anything I say, or if you have something to add," said Spomer. "This will be a DEA/WDFW operation, run on the federal side by myself and AUSA Shay, and on the state's side by Captain Jacobsen. In your folders, you will find a contact list for everyone, except for Joe who will only deal directly with DEA Agent Grace Fenson. Grace will be the case agent and will pass any of your questions or suggestions on to Joe, and will do the same for any of Joe's questions or information for any of us."

"Since neither ATF nor USFWS maintains an office in the Tri-Cities, we will use the Kennewick DEA office for our base of operations. Backup and surveillance will be handled out of that same office with our local agents supplemented by anyone from your agencies. DEA will handle all evidence, including covert video downloads, and will store it in the DEA evidence facility in the Richland federal building."

Spomer looked around the room before continuing, "Now we all need to talk about operational duration, and goals. I would suggest a maximum operational duration of sixty days, with the possibility of extension if we all agree. Does that sound reasonable?"

"Sixty days is a long time to be under with guys like this, so I can't imagine Joe will want to stretch it out longer than that," said Captain Jacobsen.

"Then sixty days it is. Now, how about operational goals? When will we know we are the point we have everything we want to see out of this operation?" Spomer asked.

"From my perspective, we will be done when we can identify the person who is smuggling falcon eggs and birds, who he is sending them to, and where he is getting the birds from. Next, we will need to figure out who is smuggling what, to where, and to whom. We also need to know what role Angel Lopez has in this and what his culpability is. Finally, we need to determine who is involved in the straw purchases, besides the dealer and the documented purchasers, and we have enough good solid evidence on all of these to get convictions," said Captain Jacobsen.

"Who is Angel Lopez?" asked AUSA Shay.

"He is the man who owns the LITE trucking company, both Buena Comida restaurants and he a recently opened a winery next to his seventy-eight hundred square foot mansion outside of Richland, WA," answered Jacobsen.

"So, does everyone agree with Captain Jacobsen's optimistic goals?" asked Spomer.

"I'm not sure we will satisfy all of those goals, but yeah, I agree," said Brock Shay.

"To be clear, when we reach either the operational goals or the operational duration, we shut it down and take what we've got unless something earthshattering is just around the corner. Are we all in agreement?" asked Spomer.

Soon all of the other meeting participants agreed with the operational goals.

"I have something I need to say to Captain Jacobsen, to assure we are all on the same page," AUSA Shay continued. "This is not a problem we have ever had with either of you, but WDFW does have a history of prematurely releasing details of investigations to the media. The M.O.U. your chief signed details the media policy, which is all media releases will be handled by my office (The US Attorney's Office) and information will only be released with the consent of everyone in this room and myself. Can we all agree to these conditions?"

Everyone in the room agreed.

Captain Jacobsen spoke up, "You are correct about my agency's past practices, but I assure you those past practices are just that, past practices. You will never see us return to those practices under this current administration. I answer directly to our assistant chief, who was formerly a detective with SIU, so he fully understands the need for confidentiality. You have my word, no information about this operation will be released outside of my immediate chain-of-command."

Spomer continued, "Joe before we break, I want to thank you for your commitment and courage. There are not too many people I know who have had anywhere near the success you have had, especially on their very first UC, and even fewer who would have the courage to charge forward under these circumstances and alone at that. I only want to assure you that at any time you feel this is spinning out of control, get out immediately, and know none of us would fault you one bit. Thank you and be safe."

Soon the entire room spontaneously stood and applauded Joe. Joe, whose face had turned red, replied simply, "Thanks. I will do my best."

Spomer added, "Joe we have some paperwork for you and your captain to sign. After that, we will show you some of the covert camera set-ups we have to choose from, then you and Agent Fenson can head to your new home."

"Does anyone have any questions or anything to add?" Spomer asked, seeing everyone shaking their heads no, "Alright, thanks to everyone for attending."

Slowly one-by-one each person in the room shook hands with Joe, and wished him luck, until only Captain Jacobsen, Agent Grace Fenson, and Joe remained in the room.

Fenson reached in a folder she had in front of her and brought out a small stack of papers.

"If you two will read through these, sign them, and pass them back to me, I will go through Joe's wallet since it is the only thing we haven't searched yet."

Joe handed his UC wallet over to Fenson while he began reading and signing documents. Once both Jacobsen and Joe were done, Joe got his wallet back from Grace before asking, "Well, did I pass?"

"Yep, the only thing we found, which might have been hard for you to explain, was this," Grace Fenson said as she handed Joe one of those clear stickers the oil change places stick to the inside of car windshields. "This particular sticker came from a shop in Mill Creek, WA (a suburb of Seattle), two weeks ago."

Jacobsen saw the sticker and said, "That one is on me. I took it in for a lube, oil, filter service before I provided it to Joe and Lisa and didn't catch that. Thanks."

"Are you ready to go Joe?" Fenson asked.

"Yep, let's hit it, but I do need the address in-case I get separated from you on the drive," answered Joe.

"The address is in your truck's GPS under home," Fenson replied. "We wiped your GPS clean, and added a whole bunch of locations such as the two Buena Comida restaurants, the Dodge dealer, et cetera."

"That makes sense. Thanks," Joe said.

As Joe settled in for the hour and a half drive, he thought about how much had happened just in the last week. In a very short period, he had gone from working a simple game meat sale with his partner, to working a complex and high-risk international case alone. Joe thought about the fact that everyone around him seemed to be very concerned about his safety, but that was the furthest thing from Joe's mind. He was only concerned with screwing up the case and embarrassing himself and the agency. He had no concerns at all with his safety, and in-fact part of him wouldn't mind if he were to be killed. Joe thought if he were to be killed, at least his parents would benefit financially, and his nightmares would stop. He had given some real thought to ending his life himself and had even planned how he would do so, but maybe someone else would decide for him. He didn't care that much.

Before he knew it, Joe was pulling into the parking lot of the Pinecrest Apartment complex. The complex was clean and appeared to be well maintained but was right next to the busy Hwy. 395, which already had Joe concerned about road noise. All of the separate apartment buildings ran north/south, while the highway ran east/west, so as long as the apartment was on the south end of the apartment building, it shouldn't be too noisy.

Joe followed Grace Fenson to the far northern end of apartment building "B" and parked at the base of a set of stairs, which gave Joe another concern. Joe hated to have people stomping around above him, making the floor sound like a bass drum, add screaming kids to the mix and it was about enough to drive Joe over the edge.

As Joe exited his vehicle with one of his duffle bags thrown over his shoulder, he told Grace, "I hope it's at least on the top floor."

"Top floor just about mid-way down the building. Apartment B-12. Follow me," replied Grace.

Although it was not overly warm outside, the apartment furnace had kept the place at a comfortable sixty-eight degrees. As Joe walked around the apartment, he was pleasantly surprised to see the place was well furnished and was in pretty good shape. The furnishings were cheap, but at least they were new enough to still look good.

"Sheets and towels are in here, above the washer and dryer. Sorry but we do not provide maid service, so you will need to make the bed up yourself," Fenson said with a smile.

"As you will see, the kitchen is stocked with spices, cooking oil, and the essentials, but there isn't a thing to eat in here," Grace said, "So what do you think?"

"It's a hell of a lot nicer than I expected," Joe replied.

"Glad you like it. Now we only have two more things to talk about. First, your cover team. Someone will always be in apartment A-12, directly across the parking lot. We won't come over to visit, and you really should never even see any of us," Fenson went on. "Lastly, we need to go over the covert cameras in here. Take some time and see if you can spot either of them."

Joe slowly walked around the room, examining everything he suspected might hold a camera, but as expected struck out.

"Alright, I give up."

"One is in the TV remote on the coffee table. The remote is fully functional, but also includes a covert camera which is turned on and off simply by pushing the record button on the remote. One-click is on, two-clicks is off. The green light will blink once to show you are recording and a red light will blink twice when it's off. The second one is in the Xbox console on the TV stand. To activate this one, you have to turn it around, and flip the switch to on, which will start the motion-activated recording and will make the blue light next to the switch come on. The TV remote has a micro-USB slot in the battery compartment for downloading the video, and the same sized port is on the rear of the Xbox for downloading. I would strongly suggest playing with both, to make sure you have it right. The laptop on the table stays with the apartment and is loaded with a whole bunch of stuff anyone would have on their own laptop. The wi-fi code and laptop code are written on a sticker inside the door to the spice cabinet. Use the laptop to do the downloads onto a thumb drive, then once a week we will swap your thumb drive for a blank one."

"Wow, nice setup. This will do just fine. Thanks for taking the time to show me around, and to get me all lined up," Joe told Grace.

"Be very careful with these guys. You are into some serious badass dudes here, so if it feels wrong, trust your instincts and bail. Okay?" asked Grace.

"I will be very careful, don't worry," answered Joe.

"Looks like the weekend is yours, so get to know the area as well as you can. Take care Joe," Grace said as she headed out the door.

Once Grace had left, Joe sat in the recliner in the family room, and just took it all in. Joe was used to living alone, but that didn't mean he liked it. For some reason, the alone feeling at home was nothing compared to the alone he felt then and there. He knew nobody, other than the people associated with his undercover operation, in the entire area and didn't even know where he was in relation to everything around him. It was a good thing he had the weekend to acquaint himself with the area because right now he couldn't convince anyone that he had been living in Tri-cities for six months. There was one other huge benefit to having the weekend off, his date with Lucia.

The first order of business for Joe was to go grocery shopping. Joe smiled as he realized he didn't need a grocery list this time, since he had absolutely nothing, so he would just walk the aisles and throw in what looked good.

Joe got into his truck and entered "Grocery" into the GPS. Immediately Albertson's Groceries popped up under his favorites. Joe laughed as he thought, *they covered everything.*

Two-hundred and twenty-five dollars later, Joe found himself making four trips up and down the stairs, to get everything into his apartment.

After putting all of the food items away, Joe worked on unpacking his clothes and putting his personal touch to the place.

Joe had everything organized and looking sharp by 6 PM and was starting to make dinner when he received a text from Lucia, "8:00 PM tomorrow, we can go to Crave Eats & Drinks, it's a dance club. I will pick you up if you give me your new address if you have a new address yet."

"My new address is in the Pinecrest Apartments in Pasco at 2209 W Jay St., Apartment B-12. I will be glad to pick you up if you give me your address, but can we make it 7:00 instead of 8:00? I know a beautiful woman who I would like to take to dinner before we go dancing. I don't think we will have much opportunity to talk in a dance club."

"What a gentleman. I happen to know a woman who would love to go to dinner with a handsome man, as long as it's not Mexican food. My address is 7418 Jackrabbit Court, Pasco, but I will warn you, I live with my mom. I will see you at seven, and I'm looking forward to it. Gotta go."

Joe sat on the couch and picked through his dinner. Dating someone connected (even remotely) to the targets of a criminal investigation was probably a violation of some policy, but Joe saw absolutely no harm in it. Lucia certainly wasn't involved in drug smuggling, guns, or any of that crap, and had even warned him about her uncle. The only real concern Joe had about dating Lucia, would be her reaction when she found out who he really was. *Man, that's going to be a tough conversation which I'm not looking forward to.*

Joe had only met Lucia a couple of times and had really only talked to her that one time they ate lunch together, but he already felt a connection to her and he trusted her.

CHAPTER 32

It was 5:30 AM when Adam placed a call to Mohammed Almaktoum, "Good afternoon Mr. Almaktoum."

"Good afternoon Mr. Getty, but please call me Mohammed."

Adam then realized Mohammed was a personal assistant for whoever his boss was because men of nobility and wealth in the UAE would never allow someone of a lower class to call them by their first name.

"Alright Mohammed, I am calling you to let you know I have six eggs and one adult right now, and will work on picking up the remaining adults over the next week or so. I would suggest being prepared to fly to Mexico on the 10th, it may take another day or two, but at the latest the 12th. The eggs will come in an IncuView automatic egg incubator which runs off of a 12-volt car battery, so I would count on bringing a fully charged new car battery with you unless your aircraft has cigarette lighter plugs. The incubator has an automatic egg turner built-in, so you will only need to make sure the incubator stays on or your eggs will be dead by the time you get home with them. At the airport, you can test the eggs with a digital egg heart monitor which the courier will have with him, and any egg which is not alive will be deducted from your total, but once you leave with the eggs, there is no guarantee with them. The eggs have to be properly cared for and kept at just the right temperature. You will also get a sheet of instructions detailing everything I just told you. I will try to give you a full two days of advanced notice, but a lot depends on the duration of the trip from the US to Mexico, which is always quite variable," Adam explained. "The flight from Dubai to Chihuahua, Mexico is 7,400 nautical miles, so you will most likely need to refuel each way. I would recommend you fuel at the Cherif Al Idrissi International Airport in Al Hoceima, Morocco. I think you will find them to be very fast, helpful and discreet. Do you have any questions?"

"No, I understand. We will await your next call with excitement. Thank you and Ma'a salama (goodbye)," Mohammed said.

"Thank you. Ma'a salama," answered Adam.

CHAPTER 33

Joe had completed breakfast and was getting ready to head out the door to explore his new surroundings when his phone rang. Seeing the name Anna brought a smile to his face.

Joe answered the phone only to hear Lisa's standard greeting for him, "Morning sunshine. Are you up and at 'em yet?"

"You miss me already. That's sweet," Joe said with a grin.

"I do. I miss you bad enough that I signed up for your backup detail for all of next week. I'm gonna be your neighbor," Lisa replied.

For the first time, it finally dawned on Joe the backup team would probably see anyone who visited him at his apartment, including someone Joe did not want the backup team to see.

"Good deal, if I need a cup of sugar I will come by," Joe answered.

"Hey on a separate note, we both kinda screwed up. We promised to keep Logan (Sergeant Logan Howard) in the loop regarding how long this UC assignment was going to run, and he wanted us back in uniform once the snow was off and the lakes were thawing, which should be in the next couple of weeks. I called him last night, just to check-in, and when I told him you are into something which might take a substantial amount of time, he got pretty quiet," Lisa said. "I assured him he would fully understand and agree when we were able to tell him what we are doing, but I could tell he wasn't that excited to be down two officers again."

"Maybe you could ask Captain Jacobsen to give him a call. That might help him understand this is for the greater good," replied Joe.

"Good idea. We need to remember Sergeant Howard has been very supportive of us both, and he is our friend. We both need to do a bit better job of keeping up with him," added Lisa.

"You're right, and I promise to call him once in a while," Joe answered.

Lisa then asked, "So how's the new place?"

"It's far better than I expected. It was pretty quiet last night, the place is really comfortable. It's better than my real home."

"Since you don't start your new job until Monday, what are you doing this weekend?" asked Lisa.

For a brief period, Joe thought about lying to his partner but quickly dismissed that thought. Partners don't lie to each other, "I am driving all around the area today and tomorrow, to get the lay of the land, but tonight I'm going dancing with Lucia."

Lisa replied, "I know I shouldn't say a thing here. You are a big boy, but as your friend, I just have to say I think this is a mistake. You really don't know her and you are now essentially trusting her with your life, just be damned careful. You know this will probably come out in court, so keep that in mind with everything you say and do."

"Wow, for someone who shouldn't say a thing, you had an awful lot to say," Joe continued. "I know you are just looking out for me, and I appreciate that, but I've got this under control."

"Okay," was all Lisa answered.

"So, when are you coming down?" Joe asked.

"Sunday night. Ryan (USFWS RAC Ryan Slader) pointed out that the best person to pick up evidence from you is me because at least your new friends are aware I am hanging out with you sometimes," said Lisa.

"Makes sense and works for me. I guess we can even hang out together a bit," Joe added. "I would like that."

"You've got a date," Lisa said with a smile, "Actually, I guess you have two dates."

"Yeah, but only one is a smartass," Joe said.

"See you Sunday and do me a favor and name the baby after me," Lisa jabbed.

"I promise we will. See you Sunday," Joe said.

"Be careful partner. I kinda care about you," Lisa said.

"Thanks, partner, I kinda care about you too," Joe said as he hung up.

After tidying up a bit, Joe decided it was time to explore. Joe then spent the next six-hours touring the Tri-Cities area.

After taking a quick shower, a shave, and jumping into some better clothes, Joe headed out the door at 6:45.

Lucia's home was older, probably early '70s, but was well kept and attractive other than the ornate bars over all of the windows but was surrounded by dumpy houses and tagging (gang graffiti) everywhere. What once was a beautiful neighborhood, had just become a gang war zone, with good people trapped in the middle. It was the same story all over the US.

Joe's hands were sweaty, and his heart rate was accelerated when Joe knocked on the metal security door. After the sounds of multiple locks being disengaged, Lucia opened the door.

As Lucia spoke to Joe, he heard none of it, as he stood with his mouth gaping open like some fool mouth-breather. Joe had certainly known Lucia was beautiful but standing before him in her colorful dress she was simply stunning. As Joe took in her beauty, he silently asked himself *what the hell is she doing with me, she's way out of my league?*

As Joe began to gain his composure, he finally became aware of his surroundings and realized Lucia's mother was talking to him.

"I am sorry Mrs. Bailey, I haven't heard a word since Lucia opened the door. Truthfully, your daughter just took my breath away," Joe explained with a blushing face.

"She is beautiful, no?" Mrs. Bailey said.

"Let me put it this way, if Hollywood were to find Lucia, J.Lo would be looking for a new job," Joe said with a smile.

"J.Lo, who," asked Lucia's mother. "Who is J.Lo?"

"She is a celebrity who many people believe is the most beautiful woman in the world, but you and I certainly know better don't we?" Joe answered.

"Wow, should we just call it a night right now. I don't think the night could get any better than my fan club of two has already made it," Lucia said. "Thank you for your kind words, Jose, even if I don't believe you were accurate."

At that moment Joe just about corrected Lucia and said "Joe", but caught himself at the last second.

"Remember Momma, do not answer the door for anyone. I will try to be back around eleven, but don't wait up," Lucia told her mother. "I love you."

"I love you too. Have a great evening," said Mrs. Bailey. "Lucia, you don't let this one go."

"Momma!"

"Good night Mrs. Bailey," Joe said.

"Please call me Carmela," said Mrs. Bailey.

"Good night Carmela, I will take good care of your daughter," Joe said as they left the house.

Once in Joe's truck, Lucia asked, "Where are we going for dinner?"

"Have you ever had Brazilian grill?" Joe asked Lucia.

"No, I have never even heard of them, but it sounds very interesting. Where is it?" asked Lucia.

"It's called the Boiada Brazilian Grill, and it's over behind the Columbia Center Mall. Are you up for giving it a try?" Joe asked.

"Of course. I love trying new foods. Anything but Mexican. When I get a nursing job and can leave that restaurant, I never want to hear another trumpet and accordion song, or smell Mexican food again for the rest of my life," Lucia said as Joe began rolling in laughter.

"That must be the Bailey side of your DNA speaking," Joe said.

"Come on Jose, you're not trying to tell me you like that music are you?" Lucia asked.

"I grew up with it, so it doesn't bother me, but then again I don't hear it all day long as you do," Joe answered.

Soon Joe and Lucia were seated in a private booth, which had a single rose laying on one of the place settings.

"You did this for me?" Lucia asked.

"It is a very small gesture of my appreciation for you going out with me. You are way out of my league, and I can only hope your eyesight never clears," Joe answered.

For the second time that night, Joe could feel his face blush as Lucia bent towards him and kissed him on the cheek.

"Wow, I should have bought a dozen roses," Joe said.

"Why, what do you think that would buy you?" asked Lucia.

Joe stuttered over his response, "I didn't mean it that way. I was just. I don't know. I'm sorry."

Lucia burst out into laughter, "Relax Jose, I'm just giving you crap."

"I'm sorry. I am just really nervous. I don't date much, and never with anyone so beautiful. As we walked in here, every man in the restaurant stopped eating and watched your every step," Joe explained.

"Well Mr. Mendez, while you were keeping track of the men's reactions, I happened to notice you received more than your fair share of attention from the women. And from that little guy at the bar," Lucia said with a smile. "Let's just accept the fact that we are both perfect, and therefore the perfect couple. Now, what do we do here?"

Joe went on to explain how a Brazilian Grill works, "We don't select anything from the menu, other than drinks, the rest is brought to our tables one item at a time, and we pick what we want and how much we want."

"Would you mind taking care of the ordering, I will eat about anything?" Lucia asked.

"Anything but Mexican food," Joe corrected.

"Exactly"

When the server came to take their orders, Joe ordered two dinner plates and two Brazilian Caipirinha drinks.

"Alright, what's in a Brazilian Caipirinha?" asked Lucia.

"Well, let me think about that," Joe said as he opened the menu again and read from it. "If my memory is correct, it is a refreshing national treat perfect for any occasion. Made with Brazilian Cachaça, fresh Limes, sugar & an assortment of fruit."

"Wow, your memory is amazing, especially when you have the menu in front of you," Lucia said with a smile.

"I was only reading the menu to make sure they got it right."

Once the drinks were served, Joe asked, "I start my new job on Monday, and I keep coming back to your comments about your Uncle Antonio. What's the deal there?"

Suddenly Lucia's facial expression changed from joy to a look of gloom, and Joe instantly regretted asking the question.

After a few moments of thought, Lucia answered, "I don't want to ruin this night, so can we talk about this later?"

"Of course. I'm so sorry. I didn't mean to bring up anything that would upset you. Let's please forget I asked. I'm an idiot sometimes."

"What I will say is that he is a very very bad man. I don't know any of what he does now, but I know what he did to me when I was a little girl. That should give you a hint. Now, no more on that subject tonight, okay?" Lucia asked Joe.

Joe felt both rage and great sadness when he realized he had just dredged up memories which clearly Lucia didn't want to revisit.

"Lucia, please accept my apology. I am very sorry to bring up horrible memories," Joe said.

"Forget it, let's not let a piece of garbage like that interfere with our wonderful night. Now, what's in this drink again?" Lucia said as she hid the menu behind her back.

The remainder of their dinner went without a hitch, and Lucia seemed to have put the conversation about Antonio out of her mind.

After dinner, the two headed to the Crave dance club. The club was exactly what one might expect a dance club to look like on a Saturday night. It was packed wall to wall, and very loud. As they made their way through the club, in search of an open table, Lucia reached over and took hold of Joe's hand. That simple gesture made Joe feel happy in a way he hadn't felt in years. Once seated at a table, it wasn't ten minutes until a man came over and asked Lucia to dance.

"Thank you, but I would rather spend my evening with my boyfriend," Lucia told the man.

"I assume this happens all night long here? Men hitting on you?" Joe asked.

"I have no idea, I have never been here before," Lucia said. "Like you, I haven't danced since high school. I got the name of this place from a woman in my nursing class."

"Well, let's go try to figure this out," Joe said as he rose from the table and offered his hand to Lucia.

The two danced for a half an hour straight, before deciding to take a break, but just as they about reached their table, a slow dance song came on. Joe steered Lucia into a 180 degree turn back to the dance floor. Lucia and Joe were as close as two people could get, as they swayed to the music. At the end of the song and as people were leaving the dance floor, Joe leaned in and gave Lucia a kiss which was passionate enough to draw the attention and even some applause from a few of the other dancers.

By 9:30 Joe realized they didn't have much time until 11:00, the time Lucia had told her mother she would be home.

"Would you like to see where I am living for now?" Joe asked.

"I would love to see where you are living Mr. Mendez."

Twenty-five minutes later, Joe found himself, standing in his living room, with the most beautiful woman he had ever seen.

"Would you like a beer or some wine, I bought red and white because I don't know what you like," Joe said.

"Let's save the wine for another day. How about a beer?"

For the next hour, Lucia and Joe just sat and talked. It turned out they had a lot of similar interests and agreed on almost everything they discussed. Finally, it was time for Joe to take Lucia home.

As any gentleman would do, Joe walked Lucia to the door, "I can't remember ever having such a great night. I hope you enjoyed it as much as I did."

Lucia answered only, "Let me show you how much I liked it," as she held and kissed Joe even more passionately than they had on the dance floor.

"Time for me to run home and jump in an ice-cold shower," Joe said as he turned to leave. "We will have to do it again sometime very soon,"

"Agreed. Tomorrow you can make me dinner at your house if that is something you would like to do. I can be there by six if you would like," Lucia proposed. "I am done with my night classes, and just waiting for graduation so I will have all of my evenings free."

"It's a date, but don't expect too much with my cooking, but I will try," Joe said as he closed the door on his truck.

CHAPTER 34

After a day of strong winds and torrential downpours, Adam Getty was ready to hit Dandayla Island. The previous day, Adam and Ricky had collected three more eggs and a male adult bird, pushing their total egg count to nine and their adult count to two. On this day, Adam hoped to add at least one adult to the collection.

Ricky was certain of the one nest he had told Adam about on Dandayla Island but had also seen what he thought might be an active nest on a small unnamed rock located about 300 yards north of Dandayla Island.

As Ricky maneuvered the boat all the way around Dandayla Island, he pointed out the nest to Adam who fully agreed it was a viable nest. The only problem was that Dandayla Island was a formidable rock formation, with no easy route up.

"Would you mind giving me a belay on this one?" Adam asked Ricky.

"No problem, but it will have to be on the east (towards shore) side of the island so the waves won't bash the boat up on the rocks," Ricky replied.

Because Ricky needed to belay Adam, he too donned a climbing harness this time. Once Adam was outfitted and ready to go, Ricky and Adam began looking for the easiest route up the rock. Adam finally settled on the route, which had a rock shelf just above the tidal line where Ricky could position himself for the belay.

Ricky pulled the boat up to the small rock ledge, where Adam jumped out and began figuring out how he was going to do this particular climb.

"Since this ledge isn't big enough for both of us, I will climb up about ten feet, and wait for you," Adam told Ricky.

"Sounds good."

Once Adam was out of the way, Ricky stepped onto the ledge while holding the boat's anchor. Ricky looked around until he found a good place to wedge the boat's anchor, which was tied to the bow of the boat by a hundred-foot line. After making sure the boat wouldn't drift away and leave them on a rockpile in the Pacific Ocean, Ricky clipped the climbing rope into his belay device.

"I have you on belay," Ricky said.

Adam slowly and methodically worked his way up the rock face, clipping into anchors he had placed every ten to fifteen feet. To his surprise, the last twenty-five feet of the climb was just a scramble up the rocks, as it became much less vertical the closer to the top he got.

Finally, Adam stood on top and yelled down to Ricky, "Off belay".

Soon Adam saw Ricky pull the boat out far enough for him to direct Adam in. "Twenty-five yards to the west," Ricky said over their portable radios. Once Ricky had directed Adam to the exact spot he needed to rappel down from, Adam drove a piton into a crack at the very edge of the cliff. He then ran a loop of nylon webbing through it, fed the rope through the nylon loop, tied the ends of the rope together, and threw the rope off the cliff. Adam then clipped his Petzl STOP assisted-braking descender onto the rope and started his descent.

Adam was fifteen feet above the nest still when the dive-bombers started their attack. It wasn't all that unusual for both adult peregrines to remain in or near the nest, but both of them attacking at once to defend that nest was somewhat odd.

As the birds continued to attack Adam, he decided both birds were going home with him, if he could make it happen. The nest contained three eggs, but Adam decided to concentrate on catching the adult birds first. Fifteen minutes of work produced a perfect mist net set up, after which Adam simply scrambled back to the top to await the adult's return to the nest. This time it didn't even take five minutes before the radio came to life with Ricky announcing they had a catch.

Immediately, Adam went back over the edge and rappelled down to the nest, where he saw he had caught the female. Adam had already removed a women's nylon stocking and shoved it in a coat pocket. Adam went through the process of untangling the bird from the mist net, before sliding the nylon over the peregrine's body. Once the female was safely tucked away in his pack, Adam once again took up his place at the top of the island and waited. Adam and Ricky were one-hundred yards apart, one on land and one on the water, waiting for the male to return to the nest when he finally made his move to return home.

As soon as the male touched the net, Ricky told Adam to go. Adam then bailed over the side and slid down to the nest in quick order, grabbing the bird to keep it from becoming even more entangled. Twelve minutes later, Adam found himself rappelling down to the boat with three eggs and two adult birds in the bag.

As Adam sat in the boat and began the process of tucking the eggs into their protective and warm egg box, Adam mentally added up their total thus far. By Adam's count, they now had twelve eggs and four adults.

"This has probably been the best year we have ever had. We have never done so well in such a short time, and it's all thanks to your days of scouting and watching the birds. Thank you for all of your hard work," Adam told Ricky.

"It is my pleasure, but I won't lie, the money helps a lot too," Ricky said.

"Let's head back to your place, take care of the birds and eggs, then before long, it will be time for dinner. Where would you like to go tonight?" Adam asked.

"How about the Blakeslee Bar & Grill in Forks?" asked Ricky.

"Works for me. After I get everyone put away, my scotch and I will come over for a visit before dinner if that works," Adam said.

"Come on over. Tarball has been asking about you," Ricky said before he turned and walked across the driveway and into his house.

Once back in his trailer, Adam first unwrapped the adult birds and placed them in a mews. Next, Adam cleaned the eggs a bit before gently placing them in the incubator. Once that was done, and before he jumped in the shower, Adam decided he better start arranging for transportation for six eggs and four adults.

Adam opened the contact list on his phone, found Antonio, and pushed the dial button. As Adam listened to the phone ring, he looked at his watch and saw that it was Sunday. *He probably won't answer the phone* Adam thought.

On the fifth ring, Antonio answered, "Hola, long time no hear. And what can I do for you today?"

"I need to ship four of the big ones and six of the small fragile ones. When you have a chance over the next week or two, what do you have open?" Adam asked.

"Let me take a look at the calendar on my phone, but if I lose you, it's because I am not sure I can figure out how to read my calendar on this thing, without hanging up. Hang on," Antonio responded.

Two minutes later Antonio came back on the line, "Can we make it the ninth? The truck I need is down south, so I will need it to get back up here first."

"That will work just fine. Should I call Gabriel at the shop to arrange the time?" Adam asked.

"That will work. Diego is no longer there, so it will either be Gabriel or the new guy Jose answering the phone. If it's Jose, just ask for Gabriel. Jose's first day will be tomorrow, so he doesn't have a clue what to do yet," Antonio said.

"Still gonna cost me ten?" Adam asked.

"Yep, same great price for the same great service," Antonio answered.

"Alright, thanks," Adam said.

After the call, Adam thought about his shipping arrangement. If there was a reliable alternative, Adam would try it, because ten thousand per trip is a pretty good chunk of change, especially since he knew they were using the same truck for more than just his order. Adam knew this shipment would bring him $236,000, which makes the ten thousand seem like pocket change, but that was only because the order included four adult birds. Had the order been only for six eggs, for a total of thirty-six thousand, the shipping fee wouldn't leave him with much profit.

Up until about four years prior, Adam rarely received requests for eggs. In the old days, nearly all of his business was either for eyas (pre-fledgling juveniles) or adults. Adam theorized that the market hadn't changed that much, but rather he was getting orders from all of Lendrum's old customers who all wanted eggs. For a moment, Adam smiled as he wondered what impact his retirement would have on the world's raptor black-market.

After showering and dressing, Adam poured himself a generous glass of scotch, then reached in his suitcase and removed an Altoids tin and a sealed envelope. The tin contained a glass tooter (essentially just a short glass tube) and a glass vial containing pre-ground cocaine. Adam tapped out a small pile on the coffee table, before capping the vial. In one great snort, Adam consumed the entire pile. Once everything was put back away, Adam grabbed the envelope and walked over to Ricky's with a scotch in hand.

"Are they all tucked in for the day?" Ricky asked Adam.

"Yep, and all ready to meet their new parents," Adam said with a chuckle.

"We have had very good fortune this time," Ricky said. "And the number of dinners I won from you are starting to make my pants shrink."

"You know Ricky, the way you run that boat is utterly amazing. It seems the boat is just an extension of your body," Adam said as he handed Ricky the envelope.

"What's this?" Ricky asked as he held the envelope.

"Well I can't imagine you ever not having that boat, so in that envelope, you will find the titles for the boat and the trailer, signed over to you," Adam said. "As of now, that boat belongs to you."

Ricky opened the envelope as Adam sat sipping his drink.

"You do not need to do this. I am more than fairly compensated already, you do not need to do this. I can't accept this," Ricky said as he reached the envelope out towards Adam.

Adam, who had not taken the envelope back responded, "My understanding of your culture is it is rude to turn down a gift offered to you by another. So why do you think the same doesn't hold true to my culture. I want you to have this, as long as you will still drive me around one or two weeks a year."

Ricky then rose to his feet, walked to Adam, and extended his hand, "I accept your gift with my greatest gratitude. Thank you, and know you are always welcome here."

After dinner, and back in his trailer, Adam texted Mohammed, "Plan on being there on the twelfth. I will keep you updated."

Mohammed's reply said only, "Thank you, we will be ready."

CHAPTER 35

Joe awakened in the best mood he could remember. Here he was in a strange apartment, in a strange town, working undercover on what most likely was a bunch of drug cartel members, yet he was happier than he had been in years. The situation with Lucia certainly presented some unique challenges, and if he was wrong about her it might cost him his life, but right now he didn't care about any of that.

As Joe opened his refrigerator, he realized that even though he had just purchased a couple of hundred dollars' worth of groceries, he had nothing suitable to serve Lucia. Joe smiled as he thought about serving Lucia one of his Hungry-Man dinners or a beef pot pie. *Well time to go shopping again*, he thought as he put his shoes on.

When Joe was walking to the door, he received a call from Antonio, "Good morning Jose. I hope I didn't wake you."

"Not at all. I have been up for an hour," Joe replied. "What can I do for you?"

"Do you remember our conversation about firearm purchases?" asked Antonio.

"Of course."

"On your way into work tomorrow, I need you to swing into the gravel parking lot next to the Burger King by the King City Truck Stop, just down the road from the shop," Antonio explained "At 8:00 AM, you should see a white guy sitting in a dark green Chevy Tahoe.

The guy's name is Frank, and once he calls you by name, get in his truck, sign some papers, then take the guns to the shop with you."

"Got it. You can count on me," Joe answered.

"Here is the critical part. Do not bring Frank to the shop, do not show him the shop or refer to how close it is, and make sure he doesn't follow you," Antonio ordered.

"You've got it."

"Is everything good for you now. Did you find a place to live?" Antonio asked.

"Everything is great. I'm looking forward to starting the new job tomorrow, and I found a decent apartment, so all is good," Joe explained.

"Great. If you need anything or have any problems, just call," Antonio said before abruptly hanging up.

"Piece of shit!" Joe said aloud, "Your day will come asshole."

The call didn't do much to dampen his good mood, but it did remind Joe of what Lucia had said the night before, "I know what he did to me when I was a little girl." Joe knew exactly what Lucia meant, and he didn't need to hear any more to understand what had occurred.

Joe forced himself to put that behind for now and to focus on preparing a delicious dinner for a beautiful woman. Joe had very little skill in the kitchen and couldn't even think of a meal to attempt. His first thought was to call someone and ask for suggestions about what he should cook, but the only two he knew might ask more questions than he wanted to answer. He had told his mom he was at training, which might make it a little tough to explain the need for telephone cooking lessons. The other cook he could ask was Lisa, but again that would result in him being questioned about things he didn't want to answer. So he decided to just walk the aisles of Albertson's and see if anything called to him.

Before he left the apartment, Joe noticed the two bottles of wine he had on the counter, one red and one white. Both were sitting out because he couldn't remember which was supposed to be cold and which one was supposed to be room temperature. He decided to look it up on his phone and quickly threw the white wine in the frig.

Joe found walking up and down the aisles of Albertson's only made it harder to decide what to do, so he picked out an older female Albertson's employee and asked her, "I'm sorry to bother you, but I have a problem I hope you can help me with,"

"Oh, no problem at all young man, how can I help you?"

"Tonight, I am cooking dinner for a very special lady, but the problem is I don't know anything to cook. Is there any way you can steer me in the right direction?" Joe asked.

"Absolutely. Do you have internet on your phone?" the employee asked.

"I do."

"Then enter Albertson's recipes in your search engine and that will take you to our recipe page. You will see we have recipes for appetizers, salads, main courses, and deserts," she explained. "What is your cooking skill level?"

"Total novice."

"Then if you want my recommendation, I would suggest the Italian Vermicelli Skillet. It will take even a novice less than an hour, it's super easy, and delicious." The Albertson's employee said, "You will see all the required ingredients listed at the top of the menu, so there's your shopping list."

As the woman was talking Joe was checking out the recipes, "I would just go with a simple bagged Caesar salad, roasted asparagus, and an apple dump cake for dessert. All easy recipes that even a beginner can do successfully."

"Thank you very much. I appreciate you taking the time to help me," Joe said.

"You are welcome young man, and if you need any help finding the ingredients, just ask anyone," said the woman. "And your special lady is very lucky."

"So am I."

Two hours later, Joe was back in the apartment and started in on his recipes by first lining out the ingredients by which recipe they went with. The first item he decided to tackle was the dessert, then he planned on getting the asparagus ready to roast (when the time came), then the main dish.

Before long Joe noticed it was 5:15 PM, and he was almost as messy as the kitchen. For the next half-hour, Joe rushed to clean the counters, and the dishes, before running in and changing clothes. At 5:45 he was ready. The main course would take only fifteen minutes on the stove, and the asparagus would be in the oven for only ten minutes.

Ten minutes later, Lucia arrived right on time. Joe didn't quite know how he should greet Lucia at the door, but she decided for him when she gave him a quick kiss before stepping in.

Before Joe started the dinner, he poured Lucia a glass of white wine, which she said she preferred over red wine and grabbed a beer for himself.

"To us," Lucia said as she raised her glass.

"To us," Joe said as they clinked their drinks together.

Joe had just leaned in and had begun kissing Lucia when there was another knock on the door. Rather than responding or opening the door, Joe pulled the curtain back just enough to see Lisa standing at his door. *Crap, now what?* Joe thought to himself.

"It's Anna. Let me get rid of her, so we can get back to where we were," Joe said.

To assure Lisa knew Joe had company when he opened the door, he opened it all the way so she could easily see Lucia.

"Hey Anna, I didn't know you were going to stop by," Joe said loudly.

Lisa, who couldn't help but stand there in shock, finally replied, "Oh, I'm sorry, I didn't know you had company. I was just checking in on you and your progress on moving in."

Lucia stood and walked closer to the door, and Joe took the hint, "Lucia this is my friend Anna, and Anna this is Lucia."

"We met at my uncle's restaurant," Lucia said.

"I remember you. It is very good to meet you again. Well, I will get out of your way, and will catch up with you another time Jose," Lisa said as she turned to walk away.

"I'm sorry about the interruption, I just told her to come by and see my new place sometime, but I thought she would call first," Joe said.

"It's not a problem at all. I like meeting your friends," Lucia answered.

"Are you hungry?" Joe asked.

"Starving. I have been saving room for a special meal prepared by a special man."

"I hope it's edible. I am not much of a cook," said Joe.

As Joe started the stovetop and slid the asparagus into the preheated oven, Lucia walked into the kitchen and jumped up so she was sitting on one of the counters.

Joe and Lucia talked about Lucia's upcoming graduation, while Joe watched the Italian Vermicelli skillet as they talked.

Once everything was cooking away, Joe walked up and embraced Lucia and kissed her.

Finally, Lucia became quiet before she looked up at Joe and asked, "Jose, I need to ask you a personal question before we go any further in our relationship."

"Of course, anything. Ask away," Joe replied.

"It's very important for me to know the truth," said Lucia.

Joe was both nervous and puzzled by the direction the conversation was taking, "Yes, I will not lie to you."

"What's your real name?"

Joe's heart almost stopped, as he struggled with how to answer.

"What would make you ask such a question?" Joe asked.

"Because I really like you, and am starting to get attached, but I know you aren't who you say you are, and I really need to know the truth."

Joe released Lucia for a moment, while he turned around to turn off the stove and the oven, leaving the dishes right where they were. "I know I'm not answering your question yet, but can you tell me why you believe I am not who I told you I am."

"I knew from the first day you came to our backdoor with the elk. First Anna was your girlfriend, then she's just a friend and gay at that. You two don't fit together at all. Also, you fixed our dishwasher, then turned down $100 cash. Then all of the sudden you move into this place from wherever you came from. You are a cop of some kind, I just don't know exactly who you are," Lucia said.

"Do you realize this conversation could get me killed?" Joe said.

"I do understand that, so I guess this is my way of seeing if you trust me or if you are just working me," Lucia said.

Joe was scared of many different things at that point and felt like throwing up. What he said next could mean the end of the operation, the end of his relationship with Lucia, or even the end of his life.

Joe's eyes welled up as he slowly and methodically answered Lucia's question.

"My name is Joseph Ronald Ramirez and I am a Washington State Fish and Wildlife Officer, currently on an undercover assignment. I live alone in Oroville, WA. I'm really from Mesa, Arizona. Everything else I have told you is true. My dad runs a construction company, and my mom does all the office work and bids. I've never been married and have had only one serious girlfriend in the past. I did graduate from Arizona State and things hadn't been going very well for me until I met you. Anna, and that's not her real name either, is my partner and really is gay and married to a wonderful woman. I will probably lose my job because of my involvement with you, but it's worth it to me" Joe said, "And in case you are wondering, my feelings for you are genuine and I don't want to lose you, but clearly the ball is in your court now. There it is, I think I about covered it all."

Lucia showed a wide smile then answered, "Christ, it took you guys long enough."

"I'm sorry, what?" Joe asked.

"My mom and I turned this in over a year ago. First, we tried Pasco Police Department, they said they would keep an eye on things, but they did nothing. Then the Washington State Patrol, and the DEA, but nothing changed. Finally, my mother wrote a letter to the Washington Department of Fish and Wildlife. I still remember the letter mom sent in," Lucia said before reciting the same words Joe had read in the anonymous tip Captain Jacobsen had shown to them. "I told Mom she was wasting her time, but then along came my knight in shining armor," Lucia said.

Lucia then hopped off the counter, walked up to Joe and wrapped her arms around his neck, and said, "And as far as losing me Mr. Mendez/Ramirez, I'm afraid you're stuck with me. I am not going anywhere without you."

"Oh my God, thanks for understanding. I was scared to death I would lose you when the truth came out. So, we are good?" Joe asked.

"Haven't you been listening to me. I will be with you as long as you will have me," Lucia answered as she kissed him. "Now can we eat? I'm starving."

"This goes without saying, but you can't tell a soul about this, including your mother. Just leave me as Jose Mendez for now," Joe asked.

"You have my word," said Lucia.

Joe fired up the stove and oven again then poured Lucia another glass of wine.

"Your dinner was spectacular Chef Mendez, thank you," Lucia said.

"Mendez huh?" Joe asked.

"If it's okay with you, I am going to stick with Jose Mendez until this is all over, just so I don't screw up," Lucia said. "Plus it will be like having two boyfriends at once."

"Boyfriend?" Joe asked, "Is that what I am?"

"For now. You might even get promoted if you play your cards right."

"It's getting towards my bedtime, but I have had too much to drink and drive, especially with a cop right here," Lucia said. "So, I'm getting an Uber."

"You can always stay here. This place is a two-bedroom, with beds in each room," Joe said.

"I sat on the bed in the spare bedroom, and it felt like it would be awfully uncomfortable to sleep on. Come on," Lucia said as she took his hand and led him to the master bedroom.

CHAPTER 36

On the morning of April 6th, Joe awakened at 5:47 AM, and immediately checked to make sure Lucia was still beside him. As he watched her sleep, he felt like pinching himself to make sure he wasn't dreaming. Joe slipped out of bed as quietly as possible and made his way to the bathroom.

Joe had only been in the shower for a few seconds, when he heard the bathroom door open, followed by the shower door opening. The shower took longer than normal, but Joe smiled as he said, "That was, by far, the best shower of my life. I could get used to this."

"Me too," Lucia said smiling back.

Once they were both dressed and Joe was ready for the day, he told Lucia, "I hate to kick you out, but I need to talk to my partner before I head out for my first day at my new job."

"Not a problem. When will I see you again?" Lucia asked.

"I will call you tonight when I am done with work," Joe answered.

"Be careful Joe. I will talk to you later," Lucia said as she kissed him goodbye.

Once Lucia was out the door, Joe called Lisa, "You wanna come over and discuss the plan for today?"

"Yep, I think we need to talk. I will be right over," Lisa said.

A few minutes earlier she had heard someone coming down the metal stairs of Joe's complex and had looked out the window, just as Lucia was getting in her car.

"Shit Joe, are you sure you know what you're doing?" Lisa asked.

"Lisa, you know me better than anyone in my life, so you know I'm not going to lie to you," Joe said. "I didn't plan on any of this happening, it just did, and I'm awfully glad it did. I know you are concerned she will burn me somehow, but I'm telling you she won't."

"Joe, I love you like a brother, and I am only looking out for you. You know the rules, and you certainly deserve to be happy, so the decision is yours. I'm just worried this might blow up in your face," Lisa said. "I will do about anything in the world for you, except I won't lie for you, so please don't ask me to. I won't say anything to anyone about this, but I also won't lie if asked."

"I know exactly what you are saying, and I agree. This is on me, no matter how it works out, and I will take full responsibility. Maybe it will ease your mind to know that it was Lucia and her mother who wrote the anonymous tip the captain showed us. Last night Lucia recited it almost word for word to me. Trust me, she has a reason to want to see Antonio go away," Joe said.

"Alright, enough said on that subject, now let's talk about today," Lisa said.

Joe took the next ten minutes to tell Lisa about the guns, and the conversation with Antonio.

"I better hit the road. I don't want to be late for my first illegal gun purchase," Joe said as he headed out the door.

"Just be careful," Lisa said.

"I will be, and thanks partner," Joe replied. "I won't let you down."

At 7:50 Joe pulled into the gravel parking lot, next to the Burger King, where he had been told to meet Frank. Joe immediately noticed a dark green Chevy Tahoe with a huge white guy behind the wheel. As Joe approached the Tahoe, the man stepped out of the Tahoe and asked, "Are you, Jose Mendez?"

"Frank, I assume," Joe said as he put out his hand to shake. "Jose Mendez, glad to meet you."

Frank was a disgusting human being. He was at least three hundred and fifty pounds, looked like he hadn't shaved in two-months, and had food stains all over the shirt he was wearing which was too short to cover all of his substantial belly.

"Hop in, and I will grab a couple of signatures, then I will give you your guns, and let you get going. First, I will need your ID," Frank said.

Frank looked at the ID and immediately handed it back to Joe.

After Joe had signed the transfer of firearms documents, Frank handed him a cardboard box, and said, "Thanks. See you next time."

Once back in his truck, and after watching Frank disappear onto the highway, Joe quickly opened the larger box, which held a Glock model 21 .45 ACP pistol and the four AR-15s each in individual boxes. Each box had the serial number of the firearms contained in it, which Joe quickly verified before laying all four boxes on their sides. Next, Joe took a photo of the ends of all four boxes, thus capturing all four serial numbers at once, before opening the tops of all four boxes and taking a photo of the guns themselves. Once the guns were back to the way Frank had handed them to Joe, he texted the photos to Lisa with a message, "*Do not reply. Gotta go.*" Lastly, Joe deleted the photos, and the text message before heading to the shop.

Once he arrived at the LITE shop, Joe noticed the gate was shut, but Gabriel's 2020 Ford F-250 was parked next to the building. Joe got out and looked at the gate latch, noticing the gate was latched but not locked. He slid the gate open, pulled through it, then returned the lock which he snapped shut.

While carrying the box of firearms, Joe knocked on the man door of the shop, which opened almost immediately. "Jose, come in, come in," Gabriel said. "How are you this morning?"

"I'm fine Gabriel, how are you?"

"Good. What do you have there?" Gabriel asked while pointing at the box.

"Guns. I assume Antonio had told you about these?" Joe asked.

Gabriel went from a look of happiness to one of despair instantly, then said, "I was just hoping the box held something good, not more death for our people back home."

Gabriel took the box from Joe, walked it over to one of the safes, opened it, and placed the firearms and extra magazines in before closing and relocking the safe.

"Well, what should I do first?" Joe asked.

Gabriel leaned against a nearby workbench and stood silently for over a full minute before raising his head and saying, "Jose, you look like a nice young man. You ask me what you should do now, and the answer is run. Run as fast and far away from here as you can get. Once you are in this life, there are only two ways out and neither one of them is good."

Joe was stunned. On his first day at work, the man who was essentially his new immediate supervisor told him to run away and never come back.

"I don't understand. Do you not like the work you do?" Joe asked.

"I do enjoy the work. I have always been mechanical and coming up with different ways to hide things is challenging and rewarding, but lately, we are shipping more of these tools of death than ever before. My family has already lost too many people to this stupid turf war, and I hate that I have even a small role in this," said Gabriel. "The drugs only kill the people who pay to take them. Those people know what the risks of using these drugs are, and they choose to do them anyway. I have no problem with the drugs. God will decide if the drug users are to live or die, but I fear God will not want me in heaven because of what I have done here. The cash, I am fine with too, and the birds are a fun break from the regular cargo. I like the birds."

"I understand, and I agree with you. The guns are different, they are only shipped so they can kill people. It's sad really," Joe said.

"I'm sorry Jose, I should keep these things to myself. Speaking these things can get us big problems. Please forget I said these things."

"It is forgotten. Now, what would you like me to do?" Joe asked.

For the next five hours, Joe helped Gabriel remove the wooden bed of a flatbed truck. One by one the men removed the screws holding the 6" wooden boards which ran the length of the entire bed of the truck, all twelve feet of it. The boards, which appeared to be normal pressure-treated lumber, were actually made up of four separate boards all screwed together to create 4" wide channels for the length of the truck. On top (visible to anyone) laid a 1" x 6" x 12' board. On the underside (visible by crawling under the truck and looking up) was an identical 1" x 6" x 12' board. On each side of the 1" x 6," boards laid a 1" x 2" x 12' board so that the top board sat on top of these 1" x 2" boards, which sat on the 1" side, thus raising the top board 1 ¾" off of the bottom board and creating a 4" x 1 ¾" x 12' or 7 sq. ft void for each board. The truck bed was 7' wide, so Joe calculated the entire bed of the truck had 98 sq. ft. of space under the deck. As the men removed each top board, they would carefully remove the long skinny packages of meth, before laying the board back in place and moving to the next one. Joe soon learned how much meth would fit in 98 square feet of space, around 65 kilos.

Once all the meth had been removed, it was placed into 35-pound heavy plastic bags, and then all 4 bags were carried into the office on a handcart, where they were then transferred to the enormous safe on the right.

"Time for a lunch break," Gabriel told Joe.

"Works for me," Joe said as he followed Gabriel into the office.

"Did you bring something to eat Jose?" Gabriel asked.

"No, but do I have time to run down to Burger King to get something?"

"No, no, no. My wife Rosa asked me if I had told you to bring a lunch and I said I did not know, so she packed extra just for you," Gabriel said, "Come and eat."

"Are you sure," Joe asked.

"Of course. Just because I work for these people, doesn't make me an animal," Gabriel said.

"Then thank you very much," Joe said as Gabriel handed food to him. "Please thank your wife for me too."

As Joe and Gabriel ate, they made small talk about families, sports, and basically anything other than the work.

"Your English is very good, were you raised in America?"

"Yes, my parents came to America before I was born, so I was born in Fresno, California, where my family still lives," Joe replied.

"You sound as if you maybe have attended a university, true?"

Joe answered, "You are right again. I attended Fresno State and have a degree in chemistry."

"It would be best to keep that to yourself, or you might find yourself running a meth lab in the middle of the desert in Chihuahua."

"Chihuahua? Why Chihuahua?" Joe asked.

"You don't know who you work for now?" Gabriel asked.

"I thought I worked for Antonio."

"True, but Antonio and all of the rest of us work for the Juarez Cartel," Gabriel answered. "Do you still want to stay?"

"I need the money, and I didn't think I was working for the Boy Scouts here," Joe answered.

"Well, I warned you," Gabriel said.

"By the way, I am a graduate of the National Autonomous University of Mexico School of Engineering. I have a degree in mechanical engineering," Gabriel told Joe. "Right now you are wondering why someone with a degree in engineering is doing this work."

"Yes, that question did come to mind," Joe answered.

"This is what happens when you make a deal with the devil, you end up in hell," Gabriel said.

Just then Gabriel's phone gave a tone indicating the arrival of a text. After reading and replying to his text, he turned to Joe and said, "You get to meet my birds on Thursday."

"Oh, how's that?" Joe asked.

"That text was from a regular customer of ours, who uses us to ship his birds and eggs to Mexico, where rich Middle Eastern men come and get them," Gabriel said.

"What kind of birds are these?" Joe asked.

"Majestic birds. Falcons, hawks, and eagles. My favorite of all birds. They are fast, strong, and courageous, everything I am not. Maybe that's why I like them," Gabriel continued. "Mr. Getty is a very nice man, and very generous. He always leaves us sizeable tips, for taking good care of his birds, but I would do it for free, just don't tell him that."

"How many birds is he shipping?" Joe asked.

Gabriel took his phone back out to double-check the text message, "Six eggs, and four adults this time."

"I can't wait to see them," Joe answered.

"It's time to get back to work. You want to lose some money, Jose?" Gabriel asked.

"Not really, I don't have much to lose."

"It's better to lose other people's money," Gabriel said as he approached the left-hand safe. "Jose, would you please get the hand cart again?"

When Joe came back into the office with the handcart, Gabriel was wearing latex gloves and was standing in front of an open safe, which was at least half full of vacuum-sealed bags of cash.

"American currency bills are two and three-quarters of an inch wide, so we can only fit one column in each long void, but we should be able to fit all of this in easily. Let's start in the middle and work our way out from there."

Before starting, Gabriel reached in his back pocket and threw Joe a set of latex gloves, "You can never be too careful. Put those on."

Next Gabriel climbed back up on the bed of the truck and instructed Joe to toss the bundles of cash up to him. As Joe was pitching bundles of cash up to Gabriel, he asked, "How much cash is this?"

"Just over seven-hundred thousand dollars," Gabriel said. "It doesn't have to be done today, but we at least need to put the boards back in place before we leave, so if anyone broke in here they wouldn't be able to find the cash. Anything we don't get put in the truck will go back in the safe for the night."

By 5:30 PM, Joe and Gabriel had about half of the cash hidden in the truck's bed.

"Jose, if you will throw at least four screws back into each board, so they don't move, I will put the rest of this cash away, then we can go," said Gabriel.

By 6:15 Joe was done, and so was Gabriel.

"Let's call it a day Jose, I will see you in the morning. Do you have the code for the gate?" asked Gabriel.

"Not yet."

"You want to put it in your phone? It is 5102. Hasta mañana," Gabriel said.

"Hasta mañana."

Once Jose was out of sight, Gabriel called Antonio, "We just finished for the day."

Antonio asked, "And, what do you think?"

"I think Jose is honorable, trustworthy, very intelligent, and a hard worker. He is everything we had hoped for," Gabriel answered.

"Excellent, excellent. Keep me posted the rest of the week," Antonio said before hanging up as Gabriel started responding.

Gabriel spoke to his empty truck, "Estúpido (asshole)."

As Gabriel was talking to his boss, Joe was talking to Lisa, "It was far more successful than I ever could have imagined. I will be back in the apartment by 6:30. You want to come over and see if I got it all on my Dick Tracy watch?"

"Will you be alone this time?" Lisa said.

"You're a regular comedian, aren't you?"

"And you avoided answering the question," Lisa replied.

"Yes, I will be alone. At least for a while," Joe replied.

Once Joe was done talking to Lisa, he called Lucia, "I survived my first day at work. How was your day?"

"It was great. I met with my advisor to confirm I have completed all of my coursework and internship. I am done now, and will graduate in May," Lucia said. "Can I see you tonight?"

"As soon as I am done dealing with my people over here, I will give you a call. Can I pick you up and take you to dinner?" Joe asked.

"I would love that. Just be prepared for a scolding from my mother for keeping me out all night," Lucia said.

"Is she seriously mad?" Joe asked, "I hate getting my butt reamed, especially by a woman because I can't argue back."

"She was seriously mad at me. She probably won't say a word to you, but she said, and I quote, "this better be the one,"" Lucia said.

"What did you say?" Joe asked.

"I said I am pretty sure you are the one," Lucia said.

Joe didn't know how to respond other than to say, "I sure hope so. I will talk to you soon."

At 6:30 PM Joe pulled into the parking lot and walked up to his apartment. As he was putting the key in the door, he could already see Lisa and DEA Agent Jeff Lyles walking across the parking lot to his place. Joe left the door open, as he took his work boots off, and put them next to the front door.

Jeff and Lisa sat at the dining room table where Lisa pulled a laptop and a USB cord out of her backpack.

"Well, let's see the watch," Lisa said as she reached her hand towards Joe.

"Hi, how are you doing? Good, and how are you? Fine. Great to see you again," Joe said with a smile.

"Watch, now," Lisa replied with her hand held out to Joe.

As Lisa was downloading the watch camera, Jeff asked what the day produced.

"Well, first we unloaded one-hundred and forty pounds of meth, which we put in one safe, then we started the process of loading seven-hundred thousand dollars back into the truck we got the meth from," Joe told the two. "Then at lunch, Gabriel told me a guy named Mr. Getty will be bringing six falcon eggs, and four live adult falcons in this Thursday, for us to ship to Mexico. How's that for a first day."

"No way, bullshit! You are kidding, right? Seriously?" Jeff asked.

"Yep, and oh yeah, I was told I now officially work for the Juarez Cartel," Joe added.

"That's almost unbelievable. I have never heard of such a thing. It normally takes months to get into anything near this good. I'm impressed," Jeff said.

"Well it looks like we have seven files on here, so you definitely have something," Lisa said as she completed the downloads.

"The only problem I had with this thing, is there is no way to tell if it's recording or not. I sure as hell hope I got it right.

"Well, let's find out," Lisa said as she opened the first file.

The first video was of Joe meeting with Frank, and the entire gun transaction. The next video was of Joe walking into the shop, it got the truck and the office as well as Gabriel. The third video was of the truck bed, with several of the boards out, and the packages of meth sitting in the voids. Next was a video of Joe filling one of the thirty-five-pound bags with the smaller bags of meth.

Following the video of the larger bags of meth, was a video of Joe's leg. "This must be one of the times you didn't know it was recording."

"No, this one was intentional. This recorded the conversation between Gabriel and me about the cartel, the drugs, guns and cash, and the falcons. All in one."

The sixth video was a mistake, and the seventh video was of them loading the cash into the hidden compartments.

"Outstanding work Joe!" Agent Jeff Lyles said.

"Holy shit Joe, that is mind-blowing. I can't believe you got all of this in one day. If someone had told me about this, I would call bullshit. This just doesn't happen, and I mean never," Jeff said.

"You are the man Joe. This was amazing," Lisa added.

"Any idea when the cash is going out, and to where?" Jeff asked.

"I don't know the schedule, but I believe it all goes to Chihuahua, Mexico," Joe answered.

"Any physical evidence for us?" Lisa asked.

"No, and I doubt I ever will have any. The last thing I need is to be caught carrying anything out of there," Joe said.

"Understood. Well, we better get out of here and let you go. I know you are probably pretty anxious to get to bed," Lisa said with a wide smile.

"Way to go. Keep it up, and be safe," Jeff said as they walked out the door. "The way this is going, we may be serving search warrants by the weekend."

Once Jeff and Lisa were gone, Joe called Lucia back, "You still want me to come and grab you to go to dinner?"

"I'm counting on it. I'm ready when you are," answered Lucia.

"I need to jump in the shower quickly, then I will head right over," Joe said.

"See you soon," Lucia said.

Thirty-five minutes later, Joe was knocking on the steel security door of Lucia's home.

Lucia opened the door, then called back inside, "I'm going now, Mom. Love you."

"Have a good time honey. I love you too," answered Lucia's mother.

Once Lucia was outside, she kissed Joe, then held his hand to walk to Joe's truck, but Joe lagged behind.

"What's wrong?" Lucia asked.

Joe turned Lucia back so she was facing him, and said, "I have never been one to run from problems, and it feels like that's just what I am doing here. If you and I are going to have a future together, then your mother is going to be a part of it right?"

"Sure, why?" answered Lucia.

"Because tonight the one I should be taking out to dinner is her. Would you mind if we asked her to join us?" Joe asked.

"Oh my God. I think you are positively perfect," Lucia said as she embraced Joe. "That is the kindest thing I have ever heard. I will go ask her."

"No, please just unlock the door for me. This is for me to do."

Lucia then unlocked the multiple door locks and kissed Joe on the cheek as he knocked then walked in. Lucia's mother was sitting in an older stuffed chair reading a book when Joe stepped in.

"Mrs. Bailey, I would be honored if you would please join us for dinner tonight," Joe stated.

"Why would you want an old woman to mess up your night?" said Lucia's mother.

"First, you will not mess up anything. Secondly, the only thing better than going to dinner with one beautiful woman is going to dinner with two beautiful women, and if Lucia is going to be a part of my life, then you are too." Joe answered.

"Thank you, Jose, I would love to accompany you, and if Lucia doesn't want to marry you, I will," Lucia's mother said with a smile and a wink.

This evening Joe took his ladies to Sterling's Steak and Seafood in Richland, where the three had a relaxing meal, shared a lot of stories, and learned more about each other. After dinner, Joe drove the women back home, saying goodnight to Mrs. Bailey at the front door.

"Thank you for a wonderful evening. You are a very nice young man, and you need to be careful with that brother of mine, Antonio is not a good man," said Lucia's mother.

"Thank you, Mrs. Bailey. It was great to get to know you better, and now I can see why Lucia is so kind. Have a good evening," Joe said before receiving a big hug from the five-foot-tall woman.

"That was sweet of you Joe. You know what my mom said when you were bringing the car around at the restaurant?" Lucia asked.

"No, what?"

"She leaned over to me and said, if you don't marry him, I will," Lucia said. "She loves you, and I can sure see why."

After a long goodnight kiss, Lucia said, "Please be careful Joe, and call me every day when you get out of there, so I know you are safe."

"I will be fine. I will call you tomorrow. I promise." Joe said as he walked to his truck.

CHAPTER 37

Joe awoke at 6:42 on Tuesday morning. After checking to confirm his "Dick Tracy watch/camera" was fully charged, he made a cup of coffee and turned on the news. After the lead story, which was about a residential fire, where a seventy-eight-year-old man was killed, a story came on about a local jail murder. The reporter said that the previous evening, a forty-eight-year-old man named Diego Martinez was stabbed to death in the Franklin County Jail. Police were working to identify everyone involved, but so far there had been no arrests.

Joe waited until 7:00 AM, before calling his partner.

"What, did you already piss her off? I saw you came home early and alone last night," Lisa said with a chuckle.

"No, I didn't piss her off, we went to dinner away from the stalker pervert watching me from across the parking lot," Joe replied.

"I'm just making sure all of your practices are safe," Lisa said with a laugh.

"Wow Lisa, did you write this material last night or did you come up with this comedy act this early in the morning?" asked Joe.

"What can I say, it's a gift," Lisa answered.

"Well, gifted one, anything you need to pass on before I get back to drug running?" Joe asked.

"Not really. Captain Jacobsen said to tell you great job. Ryan (USFWS RAC Ryan Slader) and DEA ASAC Spomer are in a pissing match about when to do takedowns and warrants. Spomer wants to wait, to see if you can link the drugs and guns to anyone higher up the chain, but Ryan realizes this might be our only chance at those falcons. I will pass on your recommendation, so what do you think?" Lisa asked.

"I agree with Ryan. You and I went into this with the goal of making a good wildlife case, and now we have an even better case than we had ever hoped for. I say, let's be ready to go by Thursday, but keep our options open until I see if I can get more information over the next couple of days," Joe answered.

"Sound good. I will pass it on," Lisa said.

"Thanks, partner, now I better get to work," Joe answered.

"Be careful, and know Lucia and I both have something in common, we both care about you an awful lot. So, don't take any unnecessary chances," Lisa said.

"You've got it," Joe said as he hung up.

It was 7:45 AM when Joe pulled up behind Gabriel's truck, parked in front of the gate.

"I'll close it, Gabriel," Joe shouted to Gabriel as he pulled through the gate.

After shutting and locking the gate, Joe followed Gabriel to the door, where Gabriel entered his PIN and then placed his right thumb on the print pad, opening the lock.

"Good morning Gabriel. How are you doing this morning?" asked Joe.

"Not so good," Gabriel answered.

"Why, what's wrong?"

"Did you see the news this morning?" Gabriel asked.

"Some of it, why?" answered Joe.

"There was a story about a man named Diego Martinez being stabbed to death in the Franklin County Jail. Did you see that?"

"Yeah, I did, what about it?" asked Joe.

"You took Diego Martinez's job after he got arrested for beating his stepson to death and almost beating his wife to death too. Diego was killed to keep him from saying anything about all of this," Gabriel said as he opened his arms to show the shop.

"Are you saying Antonio killed him?" Joe asked.

"I have already said too much. Let's get to work," Gabriel added. "Jose, all of my friends call me Gabe, and you are my friend."

"Alright Gabe, are we going to start back on that flatbed this morning?" Joe.

"Yes, that should take us until around noon, and by then we should have another truck to work on," said Gabe.

"What's the deal on the next truck?" asked Joe.

"It has a load on the roof of the truck, and some in the reefer unit. I had my cousin send it up because that's the one we use for the birds," Gabe explained.

"Your cousin? He works for the same people?" Joe asked.

"Yes, but back home in Chihuahua. He has never been to America," Gabe answered.

For the next four hours, Gabriel and Joe worked away at stuffing all of the cash into the deck boards of the flatbed. They were just about done, when Joe heard a diesel truck pulling in, followed by a loud horn honk.

"They are here, come on," Gabe said as he pushed the button which controlled the west truck bay door.

Joe watched as two Mexican men backed the reefer truck into the bay before Gabe closed it. As the driver got out, he shouted, "Gabriel, Es bueno verte amigo (It's good to see you my friend)," then gave Gabe a bear hug.

"How have you been Hugo?" Gabe asked.

"Well my wife told me I drink too much, so I finally decided to do something about it," Hugo answered.

"So, you quit drinking?" asked Gabe.

"Hell no. I divorced her," Hugo said before the group burst into laughter.

"How was your trip?" Gabe asked, just as the passenger from the truck came around to join the conversation.

"How good can spending thirty hours in that thing be. The seats suck, probably because you and Jorge keep stuffing the seats with dope. Maybe you forgot to take some of it out," Hugo said with a smile.

"Gabe, this is Juaquin. He has been with us about a year now," Hugo said as he pointed at the passenger from the truck.

Gabe signaled Joe to come over then said, "This is Jose, the best assistant I have ever had."

Both Hugo and Juaquin shook hands with Joe. Hugo then asked, "What happened to Diego?"

"He was stabbed to death in jail last night," Gabe answered.

"Was he fucking with the wrong guy in jail or was this business?" Hugo asked.

"I don't know, but if I had to guess, I would say it was business," Gabe answered.

"Too bad, I liked him," said Hugo. "Did he get caught with sticky fingers?"

"No, but he was in jail for beating his stepson to death and nearly killing his wife," Gabe said.

"I see, so he might have been tempted to give information in exchange for a deal. As they say, a loose cannon," Hugo said.

"Perhaps," answered Gabe.

"How long until this one is ready to go?" Hugo asked as he pointed at the flatbed.

"I promise it will be done in another two hours. Go have lunch, and it will probably be done by the time you get back," Gabriel answered.

"You want me to drive one of these trucks to lunch or are you gonna give me the keys to that fancy pickup of yours?" asked Hugo.

Gabe tossed his keys to Hugo, and asked, "Where are you going?"

"We are going to Felipe's restaurant. That hot little piece of ass waitress in there has made it pretty clear she wants me, so I might give her a try today, or at least let her give me head. She's been begging for it," Hugo said with a smile.

"Why don't you shut the fuck up before someone shuts you up?" Joe yelled into Hugo's face.

Hugo closed the distance between himself and Joe and said, "Who's going to shut me up little bitch, you?"

Just then Gabriel wedged himself between the two men and looked right at Hugo when he said, "That girl you are talking about is Antonio's niece. I agree with Jose, even if he could have worded it a little better, none of us want to be caught talking like that about Antonio's family."

"Yeah, well your puppy there better learn to watch his mouth or you will be looking for another replacement," Hugo said.

"Go eat, and your truck should be ready when you return," Gabe said to Hugo.

Hugo said nothing as he and Juaquin walked out of the man door.

After they had left, and locked the gate behind them, Gabriel leaned against the flatbed and said to Joe, "Jose, that was a big mistake, saying those things to Hugo."

"I'm not scared of that loud-mouth," Joe answered.

"Well you should be, and now he knows your weak point," Gabe said.

"What do you mean?" Joe asked.

"Jose when you responded as you did, everyone in the room instantly knew you care a great deal about Antonio's niece, and they can use that against you. Hugo takes people out. He murders them when he is ordered to, and I believe he enjoys doing so. He is not someone you want to anger, especially if he knows your vulnerabilities," Gabe said. "Jose, I like you and I do not want to see anything bad happen to you, but there are many dangers in this business and you need to think of the consequences of everything you say and do. Do you understand?" Gabe asked.

Joe answered, "Yes I do, and thank you for helping me. I will keep my opinions to myself from now on. I sure don't want to cause problems for anyone."

"I don't suppose I can get you to apologize to Hugo can I?" Gabe asked.

"Let me think about that one," Joe answered.

"Let's get going on the flatbed. The faster we can finish, the faster we can get Hugo out of here," Gabe said.

An hour and fifteen minutes later, Gabe put the last screw in place and stood back to look at the work.

"It looks perfect. There is no way anyone could tell," Joe said.

"There are two ways they can know, a dog or an x-ray, but if we can make it obvious the truck bed is empty, it should fly through as it always has," said Gabriel. "Now I need you to take this shovel and broom, drive the truck behind the shop, shovel a bunch of dirt and gravel on the truck's bed, then sweep most of it back off."

"Good idea, so the deck screws we used don't look all shiny new?" Joe asked.

"Yeah, you always want your work to look just like the rest of the truck. If the truck is new, make the alterations look new, but if the truck is old and beat up, then new bolts, screws, silicone, or welds are dead giveaways," answered Gabriel.

As Joe was sweeping off the truck's bed, he saw Hugo and Juaquin pull back into the yard, then walk inside. Instead of pulling the truck back into the shop, Joe left it parked in front, to ease Hugo's departure.

"How was lunch, Hugo?" Gabe asked.

"Informative," Hugo answered with a smile.

"And what did you learn?" asked Gabe.

"I learned your puppy here is dating the boss's niece," Hugo said. "No wonder why he got the job."

"Your truck is ready to go, and the keys are in it. Have a safe trip back," Joe said as he walked into the office, took a chair, and began eating his lunch.

As Gabe walked Hugo out to the flatbed truck, he said to Hugo, "I consider you a friend Hugo, and I hate to see something happen to you, but I strongly advise you to not to anger Antonio. The boss loves his niece, and is happy she is dating Jose, so be careful."

"What? Do you think your puppy will run to his future uncle-in-law and tell on me like a little schoolgirl?" Hugo asked.

"I know for a fact he will not. Jose is a good honorable man, which is why he stood up for the girl just like you or I would. Give him a chance Hugo," Gabriel said.

"For now, I will let him live, just for you," Hugo said as he shook Gabe's hand before climbing in the truck.

Gabriel walked into the office and asked Joe, "Why didn't you tell me you are dating Antonio's niece?"

"Simple, it's nobody's business. I didn't think Antonio even knew," Joe answered. "And I don't think I need anyone's permission to date who I want to."

"You are right. I was just trying to help. I implied to Hugo that you were protected by Antonio. He will not harm you or Antonio's niece. He is not stupid," Gabe said.

After both men had finished their lunches, Gabriel walked Joe out into the shop and told Joe, "Find the dope. I already told you where it is, so I want to see if you can figure it out."

First Joe opened the back doors of the reefer, climbed inside, and began knocking on the ceiling. After that, he went to the inside vents of the reefer unit and using a flashlight, looked it over too. Next, Joe used a ladder to climb onto the roof of the truck, where he walked up and down the length of the reefer knocking and pushing. Finally, Joe worked his way over to the reefer unit. The reefer unit had two large doors for access and was made of a diesel engine, surrounded by a mass of tubes and wires, all looking perfectly normal.

"I can feel some give when I walk on the roof, so the roof-top might be false, but I don't see anything weird on the reefer unit. If there is dope in there, it can't be very much," Joe said.

Gabe looked at his cell phone, then said, "There are thirty-four kilos, about seventy-five pounds, under the roof. You are correct, that is a false roof, but there are ten more kilos in the reefer unit."

"Where? I didn't see anything that looks out of place," Joe said.

"The whole unit is out of place," Gabe answered. "The plastic housing which encloses and protects the unit is from a Carrier Vector 8600MT reefer, but the reefer unit is actually a much smaller Carrier X4 7500 reefer unit, which left us enough extra room under the unit to make an aluminum box which measures 67" x 48" x 10", or 18.5 cubic feet."

"Absolutely brilliant. How do you come up with these things?" Joe asked.

"My cousin Jorge came up with the roof idea, and I did the reefer unit," Gabe answered. "For the roof, we lay the product down in bags, spread out over the entire roof of the reefer. We then cover the bags with a layer of visqueen, followed by a layer of fiberglass reinforced plastic panels like the pile of them over in the corner. Next, we walk all over it to make sure we squish it down as flat as we can get it, hopefully no thicker than a half an inch. Last, we use paint rollers and cans of white Flex Seal liquid, and coat it until we can feather the Flex Seal into the roof seams all the way around the roof of the trailer."

"How do we get to the compartment in the reefer?" Joe asked.

"First we remove the plastic housing, then when we look at the reefer unit from the passenger side, you will notice the reefer unit is sitting on a ten-inch tall aluminum frame to keep it in place. With the housing off, the passenger side of that frame will slide forward and out, giving you easy access to the compartment. This is the compartment we use for the birds, at least when the truck passes through the border," Gabe said.

"Wow, impressive," Joe replied.

"Let's get to work. This can take a full day, and we have those birds coming on Thursday. We will start on the roof first since that will take the most time." Gabe said.

Joe sat perched on the edge of the trailer roof, while Gabe handed tools up to him. When done, Joe sat looking down at two utility knives, a pair of electric HardiPlank shears, and two things which Gabe called margin trowels (used for bricklaying).

"There is no easy way to take this roof off because we can't afford to accidentally cut through the bags of the product. This will take a lot of time," Gabe said.

Gabe showed Joe how to run the utility knife down the edge of the roof, cutting through the Flex Seal at the very outside edge of the fiberglass reinforced plastic panels. Next, Gabe showed Joe how to carefully slide the margin trowel between the plastic panels and the layer of visqueen, until he could get his fingers under the plastic panels. While one man pulled up the reinforced plastic panels and held them in place, the other man cut through them with the electric shears. This process was slow and tedious but made the load almost undetectable.

It was 5:30 when Gabriel said, "Jose, let's clean up, then call it a day. I'm tired."

Joe began picking up the pieces of reinforced plastic panel and chunks of Flex Seal, which they had removed from the truck's roof, while Gabe ran the broom.

"The boss is coming in tomorrow, and he insists on a clean and organized shop, and that's fine with me," Gabe said.

"What's Antonio coming in for?" Joe asked.

"About once a week he comes in and takes some stuff out of the incoming safe, and puts other stuff in the outgoing safe," Gabe said.

When the men completed the clean-up, Gabe asked, "Jose, are you a man of God?"

"Yes, of course, why?" Joe asked.

"Are you Catholic?" asked, Gabe.

"Yes, I am," Joe said, becoming curious where this conversation was going.

"I know you have never met him, but would you pray for Diego Martinez and his family?" Gabe went on, "He was a man who did terrible unspeakable things to his family, and he is not a man of faith. That is why we need to pray for him and his family because nobody else will."

Joe replied, "Gabe, you are my friend, so I will pray for his family, but I don't think I can pray for a man who did the horrible things he did."

"I understand. I will see you in the morning. Thank you," Gabe said before locking up the shop.

"Thank you, Gabe, and I have changed my mind. I will pray for Diego," Joe said.

On the way home, Joe called Lisa, "I think it's time to put our heads together to figure out what we are going to do and when we are going to do it."

"We are way ahead of you. Instead of driving home, we need you to drive to the Columbia Center Mall and park in front of the Barnes and Noble bookstore, and we will pick you up there in fifteen minutes. We are heading to the DEA office for a meeting," Lisa told Joe.

"Sounds good. See you soon." Joe replied.

Next, Joe called Lucia to update her, "I'm done at one job, but have to go meet with my partner on the other job. Sounds like we are having a little meeting, so I will give you a call when I'm done there."

"Jose, I would love to see you tonight, but I have kept you to myself lately, and that's not fair, so if you want to hang out with your colleagues tonight, I understand. I know your partner means a lot to you, and you need to keep up with your friends too. I can always study, so don't worry about me," Lucia said.

"That's one of the things I love about you, you are so kind and understanding, and you're right, my partner is more than a partner to me. Until I met you, she was my only real friend. She has been the only one I could talk to about anything, and I trust her completely. She has helped me through some pretty tough times, and without her, I doubt I would have kept going this long. Thank you for understanding. I will call you after the meeting," Joe explained. "Before I hang up, aren't you done with school now?"

"Yep, I am done with classes forever and will graduate in May. It's finally over." Lucia said, "Thank you for calling, and Momma says for me to tell her boyfriend hi. I think at some point I'm going to have to fight my mom over you, but I am pretty sure I can take her" Lucia said with a laugh. "Jose, when this is all over I would like to get to know your partner, so maybe she and her wife can go do something together with us?"

"I would like that. Thanks," Joe said.

A few minutes later, Joe slid into the backseat of newer Lexus driven by DEA Agent Grace Fenson, and with Lisa on the passenger side.

"I never thought I would say these words, but I'm awfully happy to see you, partner," Lisa said with a smile. "This worrying about you all day, without knowing what's going on drives me nuts."

"Aw-shucks, you care," Joe said. "Well if you are going to get all soft and mushy, I missed you too."

"I didn't say I missed you, I said I was worried about you. There's a big difference you know," Lisa said with a smile.

"How was your day?" Lisa asked.

"Very productive, how about yours?" Joe asked.

"We are making some real progress here too. Now it's time for the bosses to decide when we call off the UC part and start kicking down doors," Lisa said.

Fifteen minutes later, the car pulled into a parking lot next to a nondescript building, which had no signs indicating what the building housed.

"Welcome to DEA Kennewick Station," Agent Fenson said.

In the conference room sat Captain Jacobsen, DEA ASAC Denise Spomer, USFWS RAC Ryan Slader, and ATF ASAC Brian Kenton.

As soon as Joe and Lisa entered the room, Captain Jacobsen stood and offered his hand to Joe, "Congratulations on an outstanding case. You far exceeded our expectations."

"But to be fair, that's only because he had really low expectations for you," Lisa said resulting in a room full of loud laughter.

Ryan Slader added, "You have done an outstanding job, Joe."

"Thanks," was Joe's only response.

Captain Jacobsen spoke next, "Maybe while Lisa downloads the video from today, you can give us a rundown on what you have so far."

"This morning Gabriel and I first finished stuffing the hollow deck boards of a flatbed truck with seven-hundred thousand dollars in cash. We were almost done with that when a guy named Hugo, who Gabe told me kills people when he is asked to do so, and his assistant Juaquin arrived. They brought us a reefer box-truck with drugs built into the roof of the truck's box and more in the reefer unit. In total, the truck is supposed to have forty-four kilos of dope hidden in it. I don't know what kind of narcotic it is yet. There are thirty-four kilos in the roof, and ten more in the reefer unit. We started the process of removing the dope today, but have a full day ahead of us to finish. This truck is the one they use to smuggle the birds and eggs," Joe explained.

Joe went on, "The birds are supposed to get here Thursday, and will probably leave out of the shop that same day. The birds are driven to Chihuahua, Mexico, where they will be picked up by a wealthy Middle Eastern man. Tomorrow Antonio is supposed to come by to put some things in the safes, and to take some things out of the safe. Also, I guess the guy who I replaced, was a guy named Diego Martinez. Diego was arrested in Pasco for murdering his stepson and nearly killing his wife, then yesterday he was stabbed to death in the Franklin County Jail. Gabriel thinks the murder of Diego was a business murder, to keep him from even considering providing information to the police in exchange for some leniency. It sounds like Antonio might have ordered the hit, but it was nothing but speculation as far as I could tell."

"That's it? That's all you came up with today? What a waste of time," Ryan Slader said, making everyone in the room break into laughter.

Captain Jacobsen spoke next, "I have always said one of the most obvious differences between UC cases and traditional investigations is with traditional investigations we know what happened but we need to find out who-done-it, but in undercover cases, we already know who done it but we have to prove it."

"This case is totally different. We started out like every other UC, going to the person we thought was buying game meat, and selling it to him, but holy shit did this expand amazingly fast. I can't imagine where we would be if we kept Joe under for another month, but my first obligation as a supervisor is the safety of my people, and this one makes me very nervous. These are serious guys," the captain said. "I am in no way saying Joe can't handle it, but I'm not sure I can. I want what we all want, the best and biggest cases we can get, but not at the risk of getting one of my guys killed."

DEA ASAC Spomer spoke next, "Captain, what do you consider to be the greatest cause of risk for Joe on this case?"

"That's easy. These guys have a photocopy of Joe's driver's license. How long do you think it would take them to find that nobody matching the name Jose R. Mendez has never lived in the house listed on his driver's license and there is nothing to confirm he is who he says he is. His cover wasn't built for this kind of operation, it won't stand up under close scrutiny, and we know these guys could buy the best private investigators known to man, or just threaten people into telling them what they want to hear," said the captain. "What happens when Joe runs into someone while working UC, who knows him, or someone he arrested before? So, if we are voting now, I vote we pull him out on Thursday."

Ryan then added, "I agree with the captain, I vote to pull him out on Thursday."

ASAC Spomer asked ASAC Brian Kinton, "Brian, what do you think?"

"From an ATF perspective, Joe has probably gotten all he is going to get out of this. We have the dirty gun dealer under electronic surveillance right now, and just by his records, we can come up with all of the suspects who did straw purchases. I say, shut it down Thursday," Kinton said.

"Lisa, what are your thoughts," Spomer asked.

"When it comes to my partner's well-being, I would say end it today, but I also have faith in Joe, so I will defer my vote to Joe. Joe, you now have two votes," Lisa answered.

Spomer then asked Joe what he thought.

"I know for certain that with more time, I could come up with more cases on more suspects, but this Thursday we will have everything all in one location. We will have the falcons, lots of dope, hundreds of thousands of dollars in cash, and a lot of guns all in one place at one time. I have mixed emotions, but I also have to trust the experts, and it sounds like everyone thinks we should shut down on Thursday, so I agree," Joe answered.

Spomer spoke again, "Joe will you have time to write a detailed report, so we can use your information for our search warrant affidavits?"

"Sure, I can take care of that tonight, if Lisa will let me borrow her laptop," Joe answered.

"We will certainly have PC (Probable Cause) to search the shop, vehicles, Frank's home gun shop, but what do we have on the restaurants and Antonio's home?" Spomer asked.

"If nothing else, we can get a warrant to search Antonio's restaurant because of the state crime of trafficking wildlife, as for Antonio's home, I would suggest we put a tracker on his truck, and/or conduct rolling surveillance on him all day tomorrow to see where he goes to pick stuff up and where he takes it from there," Lisa suggested.

"Brilliant idea Lisa. We will take care of the surveillance. We can easily follow him, especially with the helicopter. We've got this," DEA ASAC Spomer said.

Spomer then said, "Now let's talk about how many bodies we will need and where those people will come from. From what we know at this point we will be able to search both restaurants, the shop out by King City Truck Stop and all of the vehicles on that property hopefully including Getty's vehicle, probably Antonio's home, and Frank's Gun Shop. That's five separate search locations. I don't think we need representatives from each agency at each search location. I would suggest DEA and one USFWS Agent handle the shop, ATF handles Frank's, Washington Fish and Wildlife and one DEA agent handle the restaurants, and DEA handles Antonio's house too. Will that work for everyone?"

Agent Spomer continued, "We will need at least five people per search location, so that's at least twenty-five people. Since we don't know what time this mysterious Mr. Getty will arrive on Thursday, we will need to be ready to go from 8:00 AM on. On Thursday we will all be ready to go by 8:00, but none of us will move until Joe gives us the signal."

Lisa spoke up, "I do see one potential problem. We know the falcon guy is shipping his birds out on Thursday, but we don't know where he is from or what time he will arrive correct?"

Everyone in the room nodded their head yes.

Lisa continued, "So, if he had to drive from a long distance, he may be staying in a motel, so we need to proceed as if he is potentially staying in the same motel all of our people are staying in. If we park eight black Chevy Suburbans in the motel parking lot and have a whole bunch of guys carrying black rifle cases up to their rooms, and he sees it, I assume we will never get to meet him."

"Damn good point Lisa, and a good catch. You may have just saved the operation with that thought. Alright everyone, pass the word to everyone to be very conscientious about how they look, what they drive, what they carry, and what they say. We do not want to blow this because our guys are sitting in the bar talking about the search warrants," Spomer said. "Tell them to assume they are staying in the same motel with one of the suspects, and let's spread the wealth and stay in multiple different motels instead of all of us staying at the same place."

Spomer had one other agenda item to cover, "Everyone in this room, except for Joe, will meet back here at noon tomorrow, then all agents and officers involved, including Joe, will meet here tomorrow at 7 PM for the takedown briefing."

"Alright, it sounds like we all have our assignments, so unless anyone has any questions or suggestions, I guess we should all get busy," Jacobsen said.

After looking around the room Spomer said, "Well that's it for today. Thanks, everyone for coming in, and all of us except for Joe will meet up here again tomorrow at noon."

"As the meeting broke up, Joe made his way to the captain, and asked, "Can I talk to you in private?"

"Sure Joe, let's just sit in my truck."

Joe turned to Lisa and said, "I will be with you in a minute. I need to talk to the captain."

Once they were in the captain's truck, he asked Joe, "What's up Joe?"

"I need to tell you something about the case, and you are probably going to be furious with me," Joe said.

"Alright, let's hear it."

"Antonio and Felipe Vargas have a niece named Lucia, who works part-time at Felipe's restaurant. Somehow Lucia figured out I was in law enforcement from the time Lisa and I first went into the restaurant. Anyway, she told me she and her mother were the ones who sent you the letter reporting the game meat sales. She said they also sent letters to Pasco PD, the DEA, and the Washington State Patrol, but those agencies didn't do anything, which we know is true because we ran this through the deconfliction program and came up with no active investigations of the Vargas' brothers." Joe said.

"Okay, and?" the captain asked.

"Well, anyway, Lucia and I have been seeing each other after work," Joe said.

"I already knew that, is there anything you need to tell me that I don't already know?", asked Jacobsen.

"How did you know?" Joe asked.

"Give me some credit Joe. As a normal part of this investigation I ran the license numbers you video-recorded of the cars at the Clearwater Buena Comida then ran checks of all of the car's owners. I ordered driver's license photos of all of the registered owners of all the cars parked there, and when I saw the photo of Lucia Bailey and saw she was about the same age as you, I figured you might find her tough to stay away from. Then, perhaps you forgot, but you have a GPS tracker on your truck. I noticed you went to one particular house, a couple of times after hours, so I looked up the owner of the house and found it belonged to Carmela Bailey. As they say, the rest is history," Captain Jacobsen said.

"I'm sorry captain, I didn't plan on this happening, it just did. I know it's probably a policy violation and I will take whatever discipline is coming my way," Joe said.

"I looked up the policy and ironically you are not breaking the policy unless you had sexual contact during work hours, because the policy only relates to sexual relationships with suspects. I don't know if you have had a sexual relationship with Lucia, nor do I want to know, but either way you were not breaking the policy since she is not a suspect. However, it was very stupid to trust someone as much as you have, when you didn't know her very well at all. That could have cost you your life. Remember the cartel knows how to work undercover too, but I do respect you for being man enough to look me in the eyes and tell me the truth," Jacobsen said. "My biggest concern is the danger you just put Lucia and her mother in. Did you even think of the fact that when we arrest Antonio, it won't take him long to realize you were the one working undercover, and since you and Lucia are hot and heavy, it's reasonable to assume she may have had something to do with your showing up here. You just put a target on her back."

"Oh shit, I never thought of that at all. Oh my God, what have I done?" Joe asked, "How can we protect them?"

"I will talk to the feds, and even if they can't do anything, we can at least put them up in a motel for a while but we sure aren't built to run a fish and wildlife witness protection problem. Don't worry, we won't leave them hanging," Jacobsen said.

"Thanks, captain, but I think I will offer them my house at least for the time being," Joe said.

"Works for me. Alright, now you better get back and start in on your report," said the captain as Joe was exiting his truck. "I hope you know you have a pretty damned good partner in Lisa."

"I know that, but what made you say so?" Joe asked.

"Because this afternoon I asked Lisa if she knew anything about any relationship between you and Lucia Bailey, and while she didn't lie to me, she sure ran the question around in circles without ever answering it, which of course told me I was on the right path, but she tried like hell to cover your butt. Looks like you have two great women in your life now," said the captain.

"Actually, four great women when you add my mom and Lucia's mother. Thanks, captain," Joe said as he walked over to the Lexus Lisa had arrived in to pick him up at the mall.

When Lisa saw him coming to the car, she came up and asked Joe, "Is everything alright Joe?"

In response, Joe wrapped his arms around Lisa and gave her a big hug and held on while he spoke in a quiet voice, "No, but it will be. Thanks, partner, you will always be one of my best and most trusted friends on earth. I believe you are the only reason I'm still living. Without you, I was lost. I can never thank you enough."

Joe noticed tears gathering in the corners of Lisa's eyes as she said, "I will always have your back, as I know you will always have mine. But one thing you better promise me."

"What's that?" Joe asked.

"I better get an invitation to your wedding," Lisa said with a smile.

"I would want you to be my best woman if there is such a thing," Joe said.

"It's your wedding, you can have whatever you want. Now let's get going," said Lisa.

Once he was back in his truck, Lisa handed Joe her laptop and asked him to bring it back when he was done with his report, so she could print it and get Joe's signature on it.

At 7:22 PM, on his drive back to the apartment, Joe called Lucia, "I'm on my way back to my apartment, and I have homework tonight. I need to write a report, and I won't be done until around nine or ten."

"That means the only time I can see you is between 10:00 PM and 6:00 AM, so I better bring my toothbrush, if that will work for you," Lucia said.

"Only an idiot would turn down an offer like that, and I'm not an idiot. Why don't you plan on coming over around nine-thirty, and if I'm not done, you can watch TV until I finish," Joe said.

"I will see you at nine-thirty. Is there anything you want me to bring?" Lucia asked.

"Just yourself. I will see you soon." Joe answered.

Back at the apartment, Joe threw a Hungry Man dinner in the microwave and sat down to start on his report. Joe would type for a couple of pages, then scarf down his dinner while he proofread what he had just written, before doing the cycle again.

When Joe had finished the report, he looked at the time and saw it was 9:15 PM and realized he could get the report printed and get back to the apartment by 9:30 if he hustled, but before he left he sent Lucia a text stating that if he wasn't there when she got there, he would be back in a couple of minutes.

Joe walked across the parking lot and knocked on Lisa's door. He noticed the curtains move, as someone looked out at him. Lisa then opened up the door and asked, "All done?"

"Yep, and proofread, so it should be perfect. If you will print it, I will sign it so I can get out of your hair," Joe answered.

As Lisa handed the printed report to Joe for his signature she said, "You seem like you are awfully anxious to get to bed. Are you sure you can't stay and have a beer with us?"

"No, but thanks for asking. I am looking forward to climbing into bed tonight. I will talk to you in the morning," Joe said as he hustled out.

While Lisa watched Joe go out the door, directly across the parking lot she saw Lucia going up the stairs to Joe's apartment. *Have a great evening Joe. You deserve it,* Lisa thought to herself.

Joe asked Lucia to have a seat on the couch, as he had something important to tell her.

"What's going on, you look very upset?" Lucia said.

"I am sick to my stomach because today I came to realize by dating you, I have put you and your mother in grave danger," Joe said.

"Yes, because my uncles will think I am the reason you are here, and I have been helping you all along. Is that why you are so upset?" asked Lucia.

"How did you know that?" Joe asked.

"My mom and I knew this would happen when we sent the letters, but this crap my uncles are doing has to stop. In Mexico, you can't go to the police with information, because the police are under the power of the cartels, but here it's different. Here you can tell the police and they will do their best to arrest the bad guys if you can get their attention. We knew the risks when we sent the letters, but we can't let our home in America become just like Mexico, people need to grow a spine and make these murders and drugs stop. You did not endanger us, we endangered you by bringing you here in the first place. You must also remember had we not brought you here, you and I would have never met, and for me, that would have been a real tragedy," Lucia asked.

Joe took out a notepad, wrote out an address, a name and a phone number on a sheet of notebook paper, which he handed to Lucia before saying, "You and your mom need to leave town tomorrow. It won't be safe for you to be here on Thursday. This my home address. It will take you about four hours to get there. You can't miss my house since it is the only house in town with a marked Fish and Wildlife patrol truck in the driveway. I leave a spare key on top of the back porch light. Once you are in the house, my truck keys are in a bowl on the counter. Pull my personal truck out of the garage and put your car in there and don't drive it again for a while, only use my truck. There is plenty of food, so you won't need to go out unless you want something I don't have. When you get there, I want you to call Clay Newberry at the number on that paper, and tell him you are there. Clay will take care of you and protect you until I can get there," Joe explained. "Obviously, I can't make either one of you go, but I am asking you to please leave tomorrow anytime during the day, so I can finish this case without worrying about the two of you. I will be in touch as often as I can, and I should be there by Friday at the latest."

"I will do as you ask, and I think I can get my mother to go too since her boyfriend is asking," said Lucia.

"I am essentially done with school, so that won't be a problem, but I really want to come back for graduation on May 23rd, will that work?" Lucia asked.

"We will make it back for your graduation no matter what. I wouldn't miss that for anything. You have my word," Joe said.

"Who is Clay Newberry?" Lucia asked.

"Clay is a retired game warden who lives down the street from me. I will call him next to make sure he will be around. Also, my partner's wife is a detective with the sheriff's office there, and I will talk to her too," Joe explained.

"How long until we can come back to our home?" Lucia asked.

"Plan on it being a week, and after that, I have a plan I'm working on," Joe said. "My number one goal is keeping you and your mother safe."

"Speaking of my mother, can I finally tell her who you really are now, so I can explain why we need to go?" Lucia asked.

"Absolutely. I forgot she doesn't know. I have just been extra careful because of you two," Joe said.

"Joe, we will be fine, and if we are going to do what you ask, then I want you to do one thing for me. I want you to focus on the case and on staying safe so you can come home to me. You will come back to me safe and sound. Is that clear?"

"Crystal clear. I love you," Joe's heart almost stopped when those words came from his mouth. He had only said those words to one other girlfriend in his life, and he had only known Lucia for a week. *Oh, that's going to freak her out* Joe thought *I shouldn't have said that.*

Lucia wrapped her arms and Joe and said, "I love you too Joseph Ronald Ramirez."

CHAPTER 38

Once Adam was able to focus enough to read, he noticed the alarm clock said 7:18 AM. Today he had to pack for yet another trip, this time to eastern Washington. Adam knew from experience the trip to Tri-Cities would take about three and a half hours, and since he wanted to arrive at the Kennewick Red Lion by 7:00 PM he would need to leave around 3:30.

When he had returned home from LaPush, Adam hung all of his gear in the garage to dry. Once Adam was in the garage, he began the process of packing. First, Adam needed to flake (coil) his climbing rope, followed by collecting the remainder of his climbing gear, which he then systematically stored in his climbing pack, along with his mist net, egg containers, and nylon stockings.

Next, he collected his climbing clothing including the protective gear, and boots, which all was shoved into a large duffel bag.

On one of the garage shelves were forty-something PVC "bird tubes". These tubes were made by cutting a length of PVC pipe a little larger in diameter than the diameter of the bird, with dozens of large air holes all up and down the side of the tube, on the terminal ends of the tubes were screw-on PVC caps, with plenty of holes in them too. One simply had to pick the right size tube, unscrew one of the end caps, slide the bird in headfirst, then return the cap. Adam picked ten of his falcon-sized tubes and put them in his Expedition along with two folding cages and two incubators.

Adam then packed his clothing, scotch, and a quarter ounce of cocaine. After Adam got these birds and eggs going south, he was heading to Northeast Washington and Idaho, to capture more falcons and might be gone for up to three weeks.

The last thing Adam did before hitting the road, was to call the Kennewick Red Lion to make a reservation for the night. He would get rid of these eggs and birds, then head north.

CHAPTER 39

It was Wednesday morning, the day before it was all going to hit the fan. Joe awakened to find an empty bed. He could see the bathroom was empty too. Lucia was gone, and he had no idea where she had gone. Joe noticed the bedroom door was shut, and he never had closed it. Joe was instantly consumed with fear. Joe grabbed his cell phone off the dresser and ran into the living room so he could look out the window for her car, a blue Toyota Corolla. As soon as he rounded the corner of the hallway he saw her.

"Good morning Joe. I thought you were going to sleep all day. How do you like your eggs?" Lucia asked as she was busy cooking breakfast.

Joe was trying to calm himself as he answered in a shaky voice, "Over easy."

"It seems like I have known you for years, but that proves I still have a lot to learn about you. Now I can add over-easy eggs to the things I know about you," Lucia said with a grin as she finally looked directly at Joe.

While Lucia gave Joe a hug and a kiss she asked, "What's wrong Joe? You are shaking."

"Nothing, just me being stupid," Joe answered.

"Come on, what's going on?" Lucia asked.

"I woke up and you weren't next to me, and the bathroom was empty too. I didn't hear you out here and I was scared I had lost you," Joe said.

"Trust me, Joe, if anyone ever tried to take me, you wouldn't be able to sleep through it. Now quit worrying about me. We agreed to that, remember?"

"I know, it's just that I am constantly worried I will lose you or you will get sick of me or something," Joe said. "I am so scared you will just disappear."

"I won't disappear. Nobody just disappears, so relax," Lucia said.

"I'm sorry for worrying so much, but you are wrong on one thing. Sometimes people do just disappear. I know," Joe said.

As Lucia and Joe sat at the table eating breakfast, Lucia wondered where that last comment Joe had made about people just disappearing had come from, but she decided this was not the time to ask.

After breakfast and a shower, Joe looked at his watch and realized it was time for him to go. "Lucia, it's time for me to get going. Stay as long as you want, and I will talk to you when I can."

"Be safe today, and remember that I love you," Lucia said.

"I love you too," Joe said as he left the apartment.

After doing the dishes, Lucia decided she should head home to talk to her mother and pack before they both headed north that afternoon.

Lucia was just coming down the exterior stairs to the apartment parking lot when she noticed "Anna" throwing garbage in the dumpster at the end of the parking area. After giving it some thought, Lucia decided it was time they met in their real roles.

"Excuse me," Lucia said as she approached Lisa by the dumpster.

Lisa turned, and smiled, "Lucia. How are you this morning?"

"I am well, but I thought it was time we met in a non-undercover kind of way," Lucia reached her hand out to Lisa and said, "and you already know my name, and probably a lot about me."

Instead of a handshake, Lisa took Lucia's right hand into her left hand, then reached for Lucia's left hand. While holding both of Lucia's hands Lisa said, "My name is Lisa Bennington, and I am so very glad Joe has met you. He deserves some good in his life, for a change, and I haven't seen him so happy in years."

"That goes both ways. I have never been so happy before. I was beginning to think I would never meet the right guy. Joe is an incredible man," Lucia said. "One thing I am clear about is that you mean an awful lot to him, so if I am going to be a part of Joe's life, then you will be a part of mine. You two have a special relationship, and I never want to get in the way of that," answered Lucia.

Lisa went from holding Lucia's hands to hugging her tightly. As Lisa held Lucia, she whispered, "I am so glad you have come into Joe's life, but I want you to know if you hurt him in any way, I will make your life a living hell, and I will never let up."

Instead of pulling away, Lucia continued to hug Lisa as she replied, "I would sure hope you would. That's how best friends look out for each other. Thank you so much, Lisa, for being there for Joe these last years. I don't know what Joe has gone through, but I do know you were there for him, and he credits you for saving his life. I will always be indebted to you for that. Please be safe."

"I will be, and when this is all done, Joe tells me we are all going somewhere for a mini-vacation," Lisa said.

"I very much look forward to it," Lucia said as she walked to her car.

Joe arrived at the shop's gate at 7:50 AM, to find Gabriel's truck was already there.

After a couple of knocks on the door, Gabriel opened it up, "Good morning Jose. Did you have a good night?"

"I did, how about you Gabe?" Joe asked.

"I slept like a baby, which is a dumb saying, since babies wake up ten times a night screaming their lungs out, so let's just say I slept well," Gabriel said with a laugh.

"I guess you are right, that is a dumb saying," Joe said.

"Well, back to the roof it is for us," Gabe said. "I want to be done getting the product out by 1:00, so we have time to put the roof back on by 6:00."

"Are we using the roof for an outbound haul?" Joe asked.

"Yep, but we are only sending two-hundred and seventy-thousand dollars this time," Gabe said.

While state and federal officers were working on securing search warrants for the various target locations, Joe and Gabe were stripping the false roof off so they could recover the thirty-four kilos hidden beneath it.

"What is this shit?" Joe asked, "It looks different from that last load."

"Cocaine, almost pure Columbian cocaine," Gabe answered.

"Have you ever used drugs, Jose?" Gabe asked as they continued pulling the panels off the roof.

"Just weed, but not since high school," Joe answered.

"You are more daring than me, I have never even tried marijuana, and I quit drinking over twenty years ago," Gabriel said.

"Congratulations, twenty years is a long time," Joe replied. "So how did you get into this business?"

"My idiot cousin is how I got into this business," Gabe said. "He told his boss in Chihuahua I was a mechanical engineer, so the next thing I know, there is a knock on my door from some cartel goon. He explained how I was needed to help them construct a tunnel under the border. I refused, so they grabbed my wife Rosa by the hair, put a gun in her mouth, and said now will you work for us?"

"Holy shit Gabe, that's horrible," Joe said.

"Once the tunnel was completed, including a train and hydraulic elevator lifts on both ends, the boss told all of the workers to show up at a warehouse for their pay," Gabe said. "Over forty men who labored on that tunnel showed up to be paid, but instead of being paid, they were all cut down by machine guns, then buried in a mass grave. The boss said the workers created a threat of the word getting out on the tunnel, so they just murdered them instead."

"I was then offered this position in Pasco, Washington and I took it just to get out of Chihuahua. I am still not free to go, but at least nobody has held a gun to my wife's head since I have been here," Gabe finished.

"That's horrible Gabe, I'm sorry you went through that. Maybe someday you will find an opportunity to be free of this," Joe said.

"Only when I am in prison or the grave."

By 11:30 AM, Gabe and Joe were almost done removing all of the panels, the visqueen, and the drugs, when Antonio walked in.

"Good morning boss," Joe said from the truck's roof.

"Oh, there you are guys," Antonio said. "Come on down."

"How's the kid working out Gabriel?" Antonio asked.

"Far better than I had even hoped, he is hard-working, smart, and a genuinely nice guy," Gabriel answered.

"Better than Diego?" Antonio asked.

"Yes, better than Diego," Gabriel answered.

"Too bad about that wife-beater Diego huh?" Antonio said.

"Was that you?" Gabriel said.

"I told you I had no use for a man who does these things to his own family," Antonio said. "I didn't hold the knife, but I made the call that took that piece of shit out. So yes, it was me."

"So how do you like working here Jose?" Antonio asked.

"I love it. The work is challenging, interesting, and never the same thing twice," Joe said.

"Good, good. Jose, can you help me carry in some firearms from my truck?" Antonio asked.

"Sure boss," Joe said as he followed Antonio out.

"What hell is this thing?" Joe asked as he held up a Barrett M107A1 .50 caliber sniper rifle.

"That is a gun which will cut a man in half a mile away," answered Antonio, as they carried in three AR-15s with the Barrett.

As they walked past Gabe, who was already back on the roof of the truck, Antonio said, "These will need to go out next week on the cattle truck."

"Got it," was Gabriel's only response.

Once in the office, Antonio asked Joe to step out while he entered the combinations to the safes.

"Alright," was Antonio's signal to Joe that he could come back in.

Before him, Joe stared into two huge open safes. The safe on the right was full of cash and guns, with four more new guns added to the mix by Antonio. The safe on the left, held bags of various narcotics nearly filling the safe. Antonio dug around in the left-hand safe, before taking out two of the four thirty-five pounds bags of meth, which Gabe and Joe had removed from the flatbed trailer.

After locking up the safes, Antonio picked up a bag in each hand and walked toward the man door. As he walked past the box truck, Antonio called up to Gabriel, "Birdman said he will be here by 9:00 AM tomorrow. Bembe and Gerardo will be here by 10:00 AM to drive the truck south. Make sure and have everything ready to go for them and walk them through how to take care of the birds and eggs."

"You've got it, boss," Gabriel said to Antonio as Antonio headed out the door.

"Thank God," Joe yelled up to Gabe, I'm about ready to explode, I gotta go," Joe said as he ran for the bathroom, locking the door behind him.

Joe sat on the toilet and composed a quick text to Lisa, "Antonio just left with two black garbage, each with 35 lbs. of meth. Birdman will be here by 9:00 AM tomorrow. The load will head south no later than 10:00 AM. Do not reply."

Joe pressed send as he flushed the toilet.

"If you can hold it long enough, get up here and let's finish this roof," said Gabe.

The remainder of the day was taken up by removing the cocaine, replacing it with cash, then resealing the roof. The last thing the men had to do for the day, was to remove the other ten kilos from the reefer unit.

After cleaning and sweeping out the shop it was still only 5:25 PM, but Gabriel called it a day, "I will see you in the morning, and tomorrow you get to see the birds you wanted to see. They are very beautiful."

"See you in the morning, Gabe," Joe said.

Once back in the truck, Joe's first call was to Lisa, "I'm done for the day. I should be back at the apartment by 5:45. What's the plan?"

"I will come and get you at 5:45, then back to the conference room over here," Lisa said.

"See you soon," Joe answered.

Next, Joe called Lucia and immediately recognized she was in a car, "Where are you?"

"We just went through Moses Lake. Mom wasn't upset about leaving but was bummed that this was the first time she has called in sick in over twenty years and this broke her perfect record."

"Tell her she has a perfect record as a Mom, and that's way more important," Joe answered.

"She heard that and is grinning from ear to ear. How are you doing Joe?" Lucia asked.

"I'm doing fine, but I have to go. I have an important meeting to attend. Please send me a text when you arrive at my house," Joe asked.

"I will, and please be careful Joe," Lucia said.

Fifteen minutes later, Joe was sitting back in the same conference room, but this time there were a lot more people there even though the briefing wasn't supposed to start until seven. Joe made his way around the room, meeting and greeting all of the WDFW officers and federal agents, most of whom Joe had never met.

Joe sat down with Lisa, Jacobsen, and Agent Spomer for a pre-briefing debrief, filling all of them in on the day, while Lisa downloaded his watch camera video.

Soon it was seven and time for the briefing. The briefing was run by Captain Jacobsen and ASAC Denise Spomer and included a PowerPoint presentation showing all of the suspects and the places to be searched, and the team assignments. Once they got to the portion of the briefing dealing with Antonio Vargas, Denise Spomer said, "Today Officer Ramirez sent us a text indicating Antonio had just left the King City shop with seventy pounds of meth. Surveillance picked him up, with the aid of our chopper, and followed him to a storage facility, where agents observed Antonio carry two large black plastic garbage bags into a storage locker and lock it up tight. We now have a live video feed on that storage unit, and two agents have the unit under active surveillance. We will keep the surveillance of that locker until we cut the lock off and enter it ourselves."

"Is there anyone in here who doesn't know what search team they are on, or have any questions at all?" Jacobsen asked.

"Alright then, for those of you spending the night in a motel, please leave your black guns here, so you can pick them up in the morning. As we showed you in the PowerPoint, we all have to assume one of the suspects is staying in the same motel you are, so please keep that in mind," Jacobsen added. "One more thing. In each of your folders, you will find the search warrant for the location your team is searching, and you will also find the inventory and return of search warrant, and the search warrant affidavit. We put the affidavit in your package so you will know what our probable cause is, but under no condition should that affidavit ever leave your hands unless it's into a shredder. Remember the affidavit has confidential information which might endanger people's lives, so it has no business being in the locations we search."

Both Joe and Lisa knew why their Captain had given that warning, as several months back a WDFW officer had left the affidavit with the search warrant, and inventory/return of service at the suspect's home, which allowed the suspect to know who had turned him in and what other suspects were being investigated, resulting in the loss of a great deal of physical evidence at the other locations.

"Remember people, Angel Lopez is either the kingpin of this whole operation or the dumbest business owner on earth, so look for anything that connects him to our other targets. If in doubt, seize it," ASAC Spomer said.

"We will see everyone here at 7 AM sharp," Spomer said.

After the briefing, several agents approached Joe and congratulated him on his outstanding work.

Once Joe and Lisa were back in the truck, Lisa asked Joe, "Have they made it to your house yet?"

"No, I talked to them around six and they were in Moses Lake, so they still have almost three hours to go," Joe said. "I figured they will get there about nine."

"Good deal. I told Emily to check in on them once in a while, and I'm sure between her and Clay, they will have all the help they need," Lisa said. You are a good man Joe, and she is very lucky to have you."

"Don't go and get all mushy on me now," Joe said with a smile. "But thanks, partner."

Once they pulled into the apartment parking lot, Joe said, "Hey Lisa, I'm going to try to get some sleep. I will talk to you tomorrow."

"Get some sleep partner, tomorrow's a big day," Lisa replied.

Once back in his apartment, Joe nuked another Hungry Man dinner, while he anxiously waited to hear from Lucia.

Finally, at 9:07 PM, Lucia called, "What is wrong with you?"

"What? What's wrong?" Joe asked.

"No bachelor ever leaves a house this clean and organized. Just another thing to love you for," Lucia answered.

"Is everything okay there for you guys?" Joe asked.

"Absolutely perfect, except it's a little strange having a deputy sitting in a patrol car across the street, watching the house," Lucia said.

"They won't be there all the time, but when they are waiting for calls or catching up on reports, they were told to sit there as much as they can," Joe replied.

"Well, your home is beautiful, especially for a single man. I can hardly wait to see you," Lucia told Joe.

"It will be soon, just relax and feel free to check out the big city of Oroville if you want something to do for ten minutes. I am going to hit the sack now, so I am well rested for tomorrow," Joe said.

"You know you have never told me what happens tomorrow, but I am guessing it will be a bad day for Uncle Antonio," Lucia said.

"I hope so," answered Joe.

"Good night, and I love you," Lucia said.

"I love you too. We will talk in the morning," Joe said as he hung up and headed for the bed.

CHAPTER 40

On Thursday morning, at about 6:40 AM, Adam Getty walked into the motel's continental breakfast room, only to pass two very large men and a small woman who were getting ready to leave the room. As Captain Jacobsen and two of his detectives passed Getty, the captain said, "Good morning. I don't think we ate it all."

Getty said, "Thanks for leaving some and have a good day."

"We will, and you too," answered the captain.

Once again Gabe had beat Joe to the shop. Upon entering the shop Joe noticed Gabe was back up on the roof.

"I thought we were done with that?" Joe asked Gabe.

"I always like to check it to make sure there aren't any bubbles or gaps in the Flex Seal. Today, it all looks good," Gabe said. "Well, it looks like we sit on our asses until the Birdman gets here. But the good news is, he is almost always early."

"That's good, will he stay long?" Joe asked.

"No, the boss won't let anyone enter the shop, so he backs up to the man door and we meet him out there,"

Sure enough, at 8:37 there was a knock on the door. Gabe looked at the video feed for the front door, and said, "Birdman is here", as he went to open the door, Joe sent a text to Lisa which said, "NOW"

Joe then went out to talk to the birdman and to see his birds, with the goal of keeping him there until the calvary arrived.

As Joe walked out, he could see four hooded adult falcons sitting in a cage, with an egg incubator full of falcon eggs next to it, "These are beautiful birds," Joe said. "What are they?"

"These are Peale 's Peregrine Falcons from the Olympic Peninsula. They are worth fifty-thousand apiece. You guys take them to Mexico, where their new owners will then take them on to the United Arab Emirates. Do you want to hold one?" Getty asked.

"I would love to," Joe said. "Why do they have those leather hoods on?"

"It simply calms them for travel or handling," Getty answered. "Here, put this on," Getty said as he handed Joe a glove with protection up the wrist.

Undercover game warden Joe Ramirez was holding a peregrine falcon on his arm when three vehicles pulled in with their blue lights on.

"Shit," was all Adam had time to say before he was being ordered to the ground.

"Take out those cameras," Agent Kinton yelled as he pointed up at the security cameras.

After three quick shotgun blasts, all of the front cameras were taken off-line.

The officers had their guns trained on Gabe as they ordered Gabe and Joe to the ground. Joe first gently placed the falcon back in its cage before laying prone on the ground with the other two suspects.

"Open this door," one of the officers demanded of Gabe.

"I can't. I don't have the code," Gabe answered.

"No problem, I have a key," ATF Agent Brian Kinton said, as he stepped up to the door with a battering ram.

As other officers were telling the three proned out suspects about their Miranda rights and reading the search warrant to them, Agent Kinton started swinging the battering ram as hard as he could at the door lock. It took six full swings to break the door open, two more swings than Kinton had ever had to use before. Once the door flew open, the shop was flooded with heavily armed agents and officers.

After clearing the entire shop, the agents began searching for evidence and found there wasn't a single shred of evidence, of any crime ever having been committed, in the open areas of the shop. It was critical they got into those safes.

"Get the safe combinations from Gabriel," ATF ASAC Brian Kinton told ATF Agent Laura Frei.

"Yes sir, I will work on it," Agent Frei responded.

By the time Agent Frei got back out of the shop, she saw Gabriel Cardenas sitting in the back of one of the police cars.

"Mr. Cardenas, my name is Agent Laura Frei, with Alcohol, Tobacco, and Firearms. Have had the search warrant been read to you?"

Gabe answered, "Yes."

"Then you know the warrant covers those two safes in the office, so one way or the other we are getting into them. It's just a matter of time, and if you care about the safes being destroyed or not." Agent Frei said, "I won't lie to you Mr. Cardenas, you are looking at serious prison time here. I think you are a good man who got in with the wrong people and couldn't get out. Your only chance is to start cooperating with us, so will you give us the combinations to those safes?"

After taking a minute to mull it over, Gabe gave up the combinations to the safes. Three ATF agents and Captain Jacobsen were in the office when the first safe was opened. In the safe was an arsenal of firearms and hundreds of thousands of dollars in cash, all vacuum sealed.

"Holy shit. It's the motherload. There must be close to a million dollars in here," said one of the agents. "Let's see what's behind door number two."

When the agent opened the second safe, everyone stood in silence. Under the two garbage bags, each containing thirty-five pounds of meth were row after row of kilo bricks of narcotics.

"That's gotta be a hundred kilos at least," said an agent.

"You boys will be busy logging and tagging evidence, that's for sure," Jacobsen said.

As Jacobsen walked back into the shop, he saw two agents on the roof of the box truck, throwing down bundles of cash to the agents below.

Once outside, Jacobsen saw Joe standing by his truck.

"Where's Ryan? I thought he was going to be at this search," Joe asked about Fish and Wildlife Service RAC Ryan Slader.

"He took Mr. Getty to go have a little chat," Jacobsen. "How are you doing buddy?"

"Nervous. I don't know why, but I am nervous as hell," Joe said.

"I get that all the time with big cases. You bring in a ton of other people, all on your word that this is going to be a big case, and the search warrant turns up nothing at all. Big goose egg and that's total humiliation," Jacobsen said. "But if you have any doubt this case is big time, go into the shop and take a look around."

"Have you heard from any of the other teams? Is everyone okay?" Joe asked the captain.

"Both Vargas brothers are in custody with no resistance from either of them, except for Antonio who kept yelling "Mendez is a dead man". Both restaurants have been shut down. Frank Pierce is in custody and Frank's Gun Shop is getting torn apart as we speak. Antonio's home is being searched, and all without any violence." Jacobsen said, "And your ladies are all safe and tucked into the middle of nowhere."

"Is anyone talking?" Joe asked.

"It's too early to know, but I know Antonio isn't going to talk, he's already demanded his attorney. Even if this is all we get, this is still big-time national news kinda stuff you did here. You should be proud Joe," Jacobsen said as he patted Joe on the back.

"Thanks," Joe said. "Hey captain, Gabe is a good man who was forced into doing bad things. Can you ask the feds to go easy on him?"

"It will depend on if he accepts our offer, but he will have to cooperate. I will do my best," the captain answered.

"Thanks."

"What do you want to do now Joe. We can't use you for interviews, it always pisses off a suspect really bad when they see the UC who got them. We can't involve you in the searches either, so why don't you head home. You deserve a break," said Captain Jacobsen.

"I will, right after I see my partner. Thanks, captain, it has been an honor to work with you, but I don't think this UC stuff is something I want to do again," Joe said. "Where is Lisa anyway?"

"No problem buddy, it's not for everyone, plus you could never top this case in a million years. Take care Joe," Jacobsen said as he shook Joe's hand. "Lisa is at Antonio's restaurant."

"Thanks. Hey, I may never see you again, so thanks for everything. You're alright for a captain."

The captain replied, "You're wrong. I will see you at least two more times, once when you bring my undercover truck back, and second at your wedding, and I damn well better get an invite."

"Count on it boss," Joe said.

As Joe pulled up to the restaurant, he saw the building was surrounded by a dozen reporters among a sea of looky-loo citizens.

Joe opened his cell phone and keyed out a text, "Hey partner, I'm heading home. Drive carefully and don't forget to call me when you get back."

"Will do. Take good care of that woman. She's got guts and I respect that," Lisa texted back.

Next, Joe called Lucia, "Everyone is in jail, nobody was injured at all and I'm on my way home. I should be there by three at the latest. It's over."

"I hope you are right about it being over. I, no actually, we are looking forward to having you here with us. Drive carefully," Lucia replied.

"Thanks. See you soon." Joe answered.

As Joe drove north he began thinking of the possible aftermath of this operation. Clearly, Antonio had figured out "Jose" was an undercover cop, which instantly increased the risk to Lucia and her mother Carmela. Even from the inside of the jail, Antonio was still a threat to Lucia, Carmela, and Joe.

Joe thought he had a solution to their mutual problem, but he would need some help, and a little luck to pull it off, but first, he had to call his parents and bring them up to speed.

At 2:43 PM, Joe passed the sheriff's patrol car in front of his home and pulled in the driveway. Before heading to the door, Joe walked over the patrol car, and thanked the deputy for keeping the women safe, and told him he had it from then on.

To avoid being shot entering his own home, Joe knocked on the door and shouted his name, rather than using his key and just walking in.

When the door opened, two women wrapped Joe up in a group hug, with tears flowing all the way around.

Carmilla asked Joe, "Please fill us in. We have been watching all about it on the news, but the police only say no comment on every question they are asked. Tell us how it went."

For the next hour, Joe sat on the couch holding Lucia's hand while he explained everything from start to finish.

"When can we go back to our own home?" Carmilla asked.

"I don't know the answer to that right now, but I am working on a plan to keep us all safe," Joe replied.

Carmilla asked, "Joe, can you please tell me all about yourself and your family. I seem to be a little bit behind in that department."

For the next two hours, Joe, Lucia, and Carmilla told stories of their backgrounds, laughed, and learned more about each other.

At 7:40 PM, Joe received a call from Lisa, "All done for today at least. We came up with thirty-seven assault rifles, twelve pistols, tens of thousands of rounds of ammunition, live grenades, hundreds of pounds of narcotics, elk meat, falcons, falcon eggs, close to a million dollars in cash, thousands of pages of documents, computers, and cell phones. SIU and the feds will have their hands full for months, but I'm coming home tonight. Jacobsen gave me the option of staying or coming back home and to uniform. You made one hell of a big case Joe. This case was bigger than anything in WDFW history. Congratulations!"

Joe replied, "We made one hell of a case partner. Drive carefully, say hi to Emily and Mayhem, and I will call you tomorrow."

"Hey Joe, I think I know what you are thinking, and anything you need, you come to me first alright?" Lisa said.

"You've got it," Joe answered. "Talk to you tomorrow."

After Joe got off the phone, he asked Lucia to come with him to the master bedroom so they could talk.

"What's wrong Joe?" Lucia asked.

"I don't know what to do about the sleeping arrangements. I only have two bedrooms with one bed in each. Of course I want you to sleep with me, but I also don't want to do anything to offend your mother, so should I take the couch or what?" Joe asked.

"I've got this, come with me," Lucia said as she turned around and walked back towards the family room.

"Mom, as you know there are only the two bedrooms and the two beds, so the question is would you rather share a bed with me, or should I share a bed with Joe?" Lucia asked.

Joe and Lucia broke into laugher over Carmilla's one-word response, "Duh".

The three of them stayed up talking until well after midnight when they all called it a night. Before heading to bed, Joe told Lucia he would be a few minutes as he had to look something up on the computer first.

Joe was still asleep when his cell phone rang at 7:20 AM waking both Joe and Lucia. Joe rolled over and saw the call was from Captain Jacobsen and decided to take the call in bed, rather than waking Carmilla by taking it in the family room.

"What's up captain?"

"At around 2 AM this morning, multiple men opened fire with automatic rifles at the Bailey's house. From the looks of it, I would say around two-hundred rounds were fired into the house. If anyone had been in the house, they would certainly be dead. Good call on getting them out of there Joe," said the captain.

"Yeah, but having Carmilla call in sick for the first time in history, on the day of the arrests probably raised a red flag," Joe said. "Was anyone hurt?"

"Nope, and of course, nobody saw anything," said the captain.

"We will secure the house, and will see to it that it is repaired one way or the other," the captain said.

"Captain, are you still in Tri-Cities?" Joe asked.

"Yep, and I probably will be here, with all of my detectives, for at least a week. What's up?"

"Would you please see if I can get a conference call with you and ASAC Spomer today when it's convenient for you both?" Joe asked. "And if she isn't aware of Lucia and Carmilla's role in this, please make her aware of everything related to them."

"Sure. I will find her and set it up. I will be back in touch," said Jacobsen.

Once off the phone, Lucia asked, "What's wrong. You look concerned?"

"At 2 AM, multiple men fired somewhere around two-hundred rounds into your house. If anyone had been home, they would certainly be dead," Joe said.

"What do we do now Joe? How long will it take them to figure out who really you are, then coming here looking for us?" Lucia asked.

"Lucia, trust me, I am working on this, and I will make sure you are both safe," Joe said.

"Me being safe without you is not an alternative. We are all safe, or none of us are, okay?" Lucia said.

"I do have one question. When you and Carmilla sent out the anonymous letters, did you wear gloves?" Joe asked.

"No, we never thought of wearing gloves, was that a big mistake?"

"Not this time. This time it might help tremendously," Joe answered.

"Give me a day to work on this. I think I have a way out," Joe said.

"I trust you completely Joe," Lucia said as she kissed Joe. "Now go save us."

As Joe was getting dressed, he received a text from Jacobsen, "We are ready for the call if you are?"

"Yep, call when ready," Joe answered.

"Joe, before we begin I am speaking on behalf of everyone here, and we appreciate the hard work you put into this case, and the dangers you, and the Bailey's are in because of it. You are all heroes in my book," Denise Spomer said. "Now, what's on your mind?"

"The US Department of State Narcotics Reward Program which was established by Congress in 1986," Joe answered.

"I see someone has been doing their homework, and I know where you are going with this, but I am not sure the Baileys would be eligible for the reward," answered Spomer.

"Why not, the law says the program offers rewards up to five million dollars for information leading to the arrest or conviction of major international narcotics traffickers who send drugs into the United States," Joe explained. "Antonio alone checks that box."

"It's not that. It's the fact the information received was anonymous so we can't verify who wrote the letter. We rarely pay when someone comes forward, after the fact, and says they were the author of an anonymous tip," Spomer explained.

"How about if Carmilla or Lucia were to tell you word for word what was in the anonymous tip letter?" Joe asked.

"Someone could have told them what to say. That doesn't prove anything," Spomer answered.

"You still have the letter right?" Joe asked.

"Of course. We started a file on the Vargas brothers, but it never got any traction, but yes we always save the letters and the envelopes they come in, why?" Spomer asked.

"Which way do you want to prove they wrote the letter and sent it in, by the DNA on the envelope, or by their fingerprints on the letter?" Joe asked, "I can have the sheriff's office here take prints or DNA from Lucia and Carmilla, and send it wherever you want for comparison."

"Take their prints on an AFIS (the Automated Fingerprint Identification System), and we will do the same here with the letter, and I will have an answer for you by this afternoon, but I still can't guarantee anything," said Spomer.

"Agent Spomer, you have been helpful and professional all along, and I appreciate it, but this needs to happen. I will not allow harm to come to either of these women because of red-tape and bureaucracy, so I want to remind you Pasco PD, the Washington State Patrol, and the DEA all received the same tips from the Baileys, and none of you did anything. This huge case, as everyone calls it, wouldn't have happened if it weren't for a bunch of state game wardens and these two heroic women. That would give the press a heyday," Joe said.

"Joe, I normally don't respond well to threats, but you have a valid point. If we can confirm Lucia and/or Carmilla authored those tip letters, I will recommend reward payment," Spomer said. "Is there anything else?"

"Yes, as a matter of fact, Lucia, Carmilla, and I will all need new identities. Not interested in witness protection, but we need new names and identifications. And last, we need someone very high ranking to talk to the Board President of the Arizona State Board of Nursing about honoring Lucia's Nurse Practitioner License in Arizona under her new name. That's all," Joe said.

"The new identities are a piece of cake, you can count on that," said Spomer. "We can certainly have someone talk to the state's head of nursing."

"Joe, does this mean you plan on leaving the department?" the captain asked.

"As long as Lucia and Carmilla are in any danger, I am not leaving them, so yes I guess this does mean I am leaving if we can get this all put together," Joe said.

"We will make it happen, Joe," Captain Jacobsen said. "We owe you three that much. We will get to work on this immediately. I will be back in touch."

Next, Joe called Lisa, "Lisa. I need to get Lucia and Carmilla fingerprinted on AFIS as soon as possible. Can Emily do it for us, so it is kept in confidence?"

"She is working now, so I will call her, but you can count on it. I will see you at the sheriff's office," Lisa said.

Joe walked out into the family room and asked, "How would you ladies like to go see the Okanogan County Sheriff's Office?"

"Why?" Lucia asked.

"I will explain on the way," Joe said as he led them out the door to his truck.

After both women had been fingerprinted, Joe sent a text to Captain Jacobsen, "Done on our end, their fingerprints are now in AFIS. It's the feds turn. Thanks."

CHAPTER 41

Upon arriving home again, Joe excused himself and walked to his bedroom, "I need to call my parents and check in."

Joe spent the next thirty minutes on the phone with his parents and came out of the bedroom to find a full plate of juevos rancheros. As Joe scarfed down his brunch Lucia asked him, "You are up to something, so are you going to let us in on it?"

"Okay, but I want to warn you this is just a plan at this point. A lot of other things have to fall into place for it to work," Joe said. "If I understand correctly, you have no living relatives in Tri-Cities, other than Antonio and Felipe correct?"

"So far so good," Lucia answered.

Joe then asked, "So what would you think of moving to Arizona?"

"What would we do? Where would we live?" Carmilla asked.

"Here is what I propose, but it's entirely up to you. If you don't like this idea, we will find another way," Joe explained. "I propose we all three move to Arizona. Very soon, we will all three receive new identities, and identification to match. I have spoken to my parents about it, and they are behind this one-hundred percent."

Joe went on, "I told my dad I would accept his offer to run the family business if he could find us a place to stay. As I told you, he owns a construction company and instantly offered me a free 2,200 square foot spec home for as long as we need it, forever if we want.

We all three can live together, or if you would like more privacy, I can stay with my parents."

"By now, federal agents are checking out the fingerprints on the letter you sent in, and if they find your prints, I think both of you will be on your way to a significant cash reward," Joe continued. "Federal agents are also contacting the President of the Arizona State Board of Nursing, to discuss honoring your Nurse Practitioner's license, under a new name."

"I like Mesa. Let's move, and if anyone needs privacy it's you and my daughter. I heard you last night," Carmilla said with a smile.

"Mom, you're a troublemaker. The only thing you heard from us last night was snoring," Lucia said. "Joe, I will go anywhere you want to go, so count me in too."

"Great, we will see what comes together over the next couple of days," Joe said. "Lucia, can I talk to you in private?"

"What is on your mind, Joe?" Lucia asked.

"Two things; first I want you to know we have a lot of friends working to keep us safe, so don't worry," Joe explained. "Secondly, I want you to live with me in our day to day lives, to make sure this is what you really want. After at least six months if you have not thrown me out, left me, or killed me, I would like you to marry me."

Joe continued, "I am officially proposing to you, with a mandatory six-month engagement with options for extensions if necessary. I don't have a ring or anything, but Lucia, will you marry me?"

"Your proposal sounded a little like a contract proposal. We can work on your presentation later, but Joe Mendez, I would love to be your wife," Lucia said. "Now do I have to sign something?"

"Can we tell Momma now?" Lucia asked.

"Yep, the secrets are over," Joe said. "Let's go talk to my mother-in-law."

After a long and happy conversation, Joe suggested they leave for Arizona sooner rather than later, so they decided to leave in two days.

"We will have someone else pack the belongings in your house, and get it to us, so all we need for now is what we have here," Joe said. "I will need to come back to take care of this house, and get all of our stuff, and probably go over the case details and possibly for court, but there is no reason you two will ever have to return."

"Now I need to create a very detailed document on my computer, so excuse me for a while," Joe said.

Joe worked on the document for over two hours, making certain it was perfect. When completed, Joe printed the document, donned gloves, then scanned and copied the document (shredding the original) before sliding it into an unused manila letter-sized envelope. Before Joe put the letter in his truck, he addressed it simply by writing a single name "Angel".

At 5:15 PM he received a call from a number which he did not recognize. "Joe, this is ASAC Spomer. You will be happy to know we verified both Lucia's and Carmilla's fingerprints were on both the letter and the envelope, so I already submitted the request for a reward payment. My SAC assures me it will go through, but it might take up to three months."

"That's great news," Joe answered. "Any idea what dollar amount they might be looking at?"

"You are kinda putting the cart before the horse since it hasn't been approved yet, but I would expect they are looking at a range between one and two million dollars," Spomer said. "Also, I need to know who in your group of three should have the same last names?"

"Just Lucia and her mother," Joe answered.

"You will receive drivers licenses for Arizona, but with a fictitious address, so you will need to update your address at some point," she continued. "AUSA Brock Shay must really like you because he put in an expedited request for an AUSA in Phoenix to talk to the president of the nursing board, and that will happen in-person tomorrow. It looks like all of you are on the way to becoming new people. I will need the name and contact information for one person who will always know how to get in touch with you, so when you get time let me know that too."

"Officer Lisa Bennington will be my contact, and thanks for all you have done," Joe said. "And sorry about the threat."

"Don't apologize, I passed it on to get these things done. Worked great for me too. Take care Joe," Spomer said.

Over dinner, Joe updated Lucia and her mother on the progress which had been made but left out the dollar amount of the reward so as not to get their expectations too high.

After dinner, Joe told Lucia and Carmilla that he needed to leave around midnight, and wouldn't be home until 8:00 AM. "I promise you will be safe, and I am not doing anything dangerous," Joe said. "But this is something I must do to make sure we are all safe."

Once in bed for the night, Lucia asked Joe what he was going to do, and if it was legal or not.

"Lucia, I promise it will be safe for me, but you are safer not knowing what I am doing," Joe said. "Do you trust me?"

"With my life," Lucia said.

"Then trust me on this," Joe said.

At midnight, Joe put on a baseball cap and a hooded sweatshirt and headed out in his personal pickup truck for Richland, WA.

It was 3:42 AM when Joe saw the sign for the Angel's Touch Winery. Joe pulled over about 200 yards short of the vineyard and parked behind a concrete pump station. After pulling down his baseball cap, donning his gloves, and slipping the sweatshirt's hood up to further hide his face, Joe took off on a jog. After running past the winery entrance, Joe noticed a separate paved and gated driveway with LOPEZ on the brick gate support, right under the address. Below the address and the brass LOPEZ tag, Joe found what he was looking for; the Lopez mailbox. Joe kept his face down to avoid any security cameras as he slipped the envelope into the mailbox.

Joe was back home by 7:30 AM, just in time to sit and have coffee with two of his favorite women.

"Was your trip productive Joe?" Carmilla asked.

"We will know soon," Joe replied.

CHAPTER 42

Jaime Ruiz was sitting comfortably in his security office when his cell phone rang. Jaime looked down and saw the call was from the boss, Angel Lopez.

"Jaime, come up to the house right away," said Angel.

"Yes sir, right away," Jaime replied.

Jaime took his security golf cart from the security office, through the winery, and to the front door of Mr. Lopez's mansion.

"Do we have people in the Franklin County Jail right now?" Lopez asked.

"Yes sir. The same two men who took care of that Diego guy for Antonio," Ruiz answered.

"A million dollars for Antonio Vargas, and an extra million if it's done before midnight tonight," Lopez said. "Make it happen now!"

At 8:15 PM, Antonio Vargas walked into the jail restroom to get ready for the 9:00 PM lights out. As he stepped up to one of the sinks, he heard the door open and turned to see ten Hispanic men walk in together. When Antonio saw four of the men were holding shanks in their hands, he knew he was dead. Left with no other options, Antonio charged the closest attacker, only to be met with a knife coming up through his diaphragm from under his ribcage. Vargas only felt the first three stabs.

Angel Lopez received a call at 10:23 PM confirming Antonio's death.

As Angel fed the document into his shredder, he took a moment to silently thank whoever had saved him from arrest, by providing him a copy of the plea agreement between the United States District Court, Eastern District of Washington, and Antonio Vargas. In the plea agreement, Vargas had agreed to receive a one-year minimum security sentence in exchange for "testimonial and documentary evidence leading to the arrest and conviction of Angel Lopez".

I can't believe that coward turned on me to save his own ass. If I knew who provided this document to me, I would give him a million dollars too. I only wish I knew how the mystery man got a copy of the plea agreement, Lopez thought to himself.

EPILOGUE

On May 18th, Joe received a large padded envelope in the mail with Lisa's return address. The package contained birth certificates, passports, driver's licenses, social security cards, and dozens of other documents in the names of Luna M. Salinas, Teresa R. Salinas, and Felix R. Vasquez.

On Saturday, May 23rd, Luna Salinas and Felix Vasquez attended the graduation of Lucia M. Bailey. It was the last time Lucia Bailey was ever heard from.

On Tuesday, July 14th Adam Getty pleaded guilty to four felony counts of unlawful trafficking in wildlife and one count of possession of a controlled substance- cocaine, in the Franklin County Superior Court, and was given a sentence of four years in prison. Additionally, the US Attorney charged Getty with seventeen counts of violation of the Lacey Act, for which he received an additional ten years in federal prison, to be served before the state prison time.

Getty "couldn't remember" any of his clients other than the most recent: Mohammed Almaktoum. Getty provided investigators with information regarding Mohammed's travel schedule, as well as his cell phone number. The US Fish and Wildlife Service agents were required to transfer the case to the United Arab Emirates Special Police, who after a thorough investigation, determined Mohammed Almaktoum acted alone. Mohammed was sentenced to twenty-five years of hard labor.

On August 9th, Frank Pierce pleaded guilty to thirty-five counts of unlawful sales of firearms and was sentenced to a minimum of twenty years in federal prison. Pierce refused to cooperate, but his documentation let to the arrest of over forty others who had conducted illegal straw purchases of firearms.

Gabriel Cardenas and his wife Rosa entered the witness protection program after Gabe had provided over seventy-five hours of testimony, leading to the arrest of Angel Lopez, along with six other cartel members.

On September 1st, Angel Lopez was found guilty of money laundering, murder, racketeering, and narcotics smuggling, and was sentenced to life in prison.

Yakama Tribal Members Wade and Fred Shereford were charged with wildlife trafficking in tribal court and were sentenced to thirty days of probation.

On September 7th, Teresa R. Salinas was awarded her Arizona Nurse Practitioner's License.

On Saturday, November 1st, Luna Salinas gave away her daughter Teresa in marriage to Felix Ronald Vasquez, at a private ceremony in the Ramirez backyard. The maid of honor Lisa Bennington was accompanied down the aisle by Sergeant Logan Howard, while Captain Cody Jacobsen presided over the ceremony.

Felix Vasquez now owns and operates Mesa Paradise Custom Homes, along with his office manager Luna Salinas. Teresa Vasquez is a practicing DNP Family Nurse Practitioner at Banner Desert Medical Center in Mesa.

On Monday, December 14th, Teresa, and Felix noticed another letter from Lisa. In the envelope, they found a folded piece of paper with MERRY CHRISTMAS hand-written in red ink. On the opposite side of the paper was a letter from the US Treasury to Teresa Vasquez, and Luna Salinas stating a direct deposit would be made to the women's checking accounts on December 21st, in the amount of seven hundred and fifty thousand dollars each.

On December 23rd, Lisa and Emily received an envelope with no return address. The envelope contained two round trip tickets to Kauai, Hawaii for January 9th through January 19th with directions to the Grand Hyatt Kauai Resort & Spa. A note said, "Merry Christmas. Let the annual vacation trips begin! See you on the beach."

Nine months after the Hawaii vacation, Teresa and Felix Vasquez gave birth to their first child, a baby girl named Lisa Maria Vasquez.

ABOUT THE AUTHOR

Todd Vandivert grew up in the Washington D.C. suburbs of northern Virginia until his love of the outdoors led him to the northwest. He attended Washington State University, and in 1978 graduated with a Bachelor of Science degree in Forest Management, hoping to start a career working in the outdoors. While in college he met Judy whom he married just after graduation. A few years later, Todd and Judy had their daughter- Beth.

Todd began his career with the Washington Department of Game in 1979 and has been stationed in three of the six regions of the state. During his career, he started the agency's FTO (Field Training Officer) program and has trained approximately fifty new officers. Todd was the first game warden in the world to design and build a radio-controlled (robotic) deer decoy, now being used in almost every state in the country. He was a Defense Tactics Instructor, as well as a Critical Incident Peer Support Counselor. He has taught classes on ballistic forensics, recognizing false identification, clandestine methamphetamine labs, and wildlife criminal investigations.

Todd served as the editor of the Washington Game Warden Association magazine, the editor of International Game Warden Magazine, and is the author of OPERATION CODY, POACHING SPREE, TO PROTECT A PREDATOR, and A FALCON'S TALE.

He is one of only two officers who have received the WDFW Statewide Officer of the Year award twice. His other awards include; the NWTF Officer of the Year award, the WDFW Case of the Year award, WDFW Detective of the Year award, the Shikar-Safari Club Officer of the Year award, the American Police Hall of Fame award, the Legion of Honor Award, the US Forest Service Award of Merit- Outstanding case, and the NAWEOA (North American Wildlife Enforcement Officers Association)- Outstanding officer award.

Amazon also offers these other books by Detective Todd Vandivert (rt.)

Made in the USA
Middletown, DE
13 June 2020